A LIGHT IN THE DARK

DARK STARS TRILOGY: BOOK 2

A K DUBOFF

www.akduboff.com

Published by BDL Press

ISBN-10: 1643650203
ISBN-13: 978-1643650203
Copyright Registration Number: TXu002110161

0 9 8 7 6 5 4 3 2 1

Produced in the United States of America

TABLE OF CONTENTS

KEY TERMS, CAST & LOCATIONS

Key Terms

Crystalline network – A series of special crystals scattered across the known worlds; unique properties allow the crystals to record the physical state of reality at set moments in time, enabling "resets" to past configurations

Darkness – An alien weapon spread throughout the crystalline network, which transforms and shrouds the infected worlds in shadow

Hegemony – The collection of settled worlds in known civilization

Master Archive – A central repository of all backup data from the crystalline network; seems to exist outside of normal space and time, accessed on the planet Crystallis

Reset – A roll back to a previous physical state of reality from a past moment in time; resets can be on a local scale within a specific crystal's zone or on a universal scale

Dark Sentinel Team

Elle – Point-of-view character, wields the Valor sword artifact (strength focus); also exhibits traits from Spirit and Protector (magic and defense) focus areas

Kaiden – Spirit caster (magic focus) with Spirit circlet artifact, agriculture background; Elle's romantic interest

Toran – Protector (defense focus) with Protector gauntlets artifact, engineering background

Maris – Spirit caster (magic focus) with restorative and defensive spell specialization

Ship Crew

Commander Alastair Colren – Captain of the *Evangiel* and Hegemony representative

Chief Taminoret (Tami) – Head engineer and maintenance tech

Locations

Evangiel – Hegemony ship that serves as a mobile base

Capital – Seat of the Hegemony government and records repository

Crystallis – Planet containing the Master Archive, the backup for all reset crystals

Erusan – Elle's homeworld

Dunlore – Toran's homeworld

Falstan II – Kaiden's last world of residence

Yantu – Maris' homeworld

THE STORY SO FAR...

CRYSTALLINE SPACE: BOOK 1 RECAP

The unique crystalline network spanning the Hegemony's worlds records physical states at set moments in time, allowing reality to be reset.

Elle Hartmut was a regular teenager living on the backwater world of Erusan, getting ready to attend college in the coming months. She had dreams of going to Tactical School and becoming a Space Ranger for the Hegemony, but a childhood injury derailed those aspirations.

One afternoon, while enjoying her last summer break, Elle and her friends discover a dark cloud in one of the crystals outside their hometown. Before they can investigate, the mayor calls a town meeting and initiates what should be a routine planet-scale reset.

Instead of returning to the reset point, Elle awakens on a spaceship. Her consciousness has been extracted and synced with a new, enhanced body. She also has new abilities, granting her amazing fighting skills and the ability to cast magic, though she's not sure to what extent. Most crucially, she's told that she holds the fate of known civilization in her hands.

An alien Darkness is corrupting the crystalline network, threatening to destroy the Hegemony as it transforms the infected worlds into twisted wastelands. The only hope of saving the Hegemony's worlds is to seal the Master Archive, the backup record for the reset points of all known worlds.

Elle joins a team with Kaiden (a magic caster) and Toran (a fighter built like a tank). They begin searching for ancient artifacts that will allow access to the Master Archive so they can seal it. After retrieving the Protection artifact for Toran (a set of gauntlets), the team get a new member, Maris—another magic caster specializing in haste, protective, and restorative magic. The quartet then retrieves the Spirit artifact (a magic circlet) for Kaiden, and then the Valor artifact (a sword with magical blue flames along its blade) for Elle. Finally, they are ready to take on the last trials to seal the Master Archive.

The team enters the Archive and defeats a series of foes, using the skills they have mastered in their respective disciplines. Elle discovers that she has capabilities in all three disciplines, including the ability to cast magic. In the process, they each receive visions related to the Darkness: an invasion force is coming.

Upon passing the tests, the team is greeted by an ethereal voice who confirms that their visions will guide them in the fight to come. The team is then given a small shard of a Master Crystal. With the Archive sealed, it will enable them to control a universal-scale reset. They now have a means to fight back against the Darkness.

THE STORY CONTINUES IN *A LIGHT IN THE DARK…*

1

LIMBO WAS MY least favorite state of being.

I drummed my fingers on the touchscreen surface of the conference table, not sure if I could sit idle in our lounge aboard the *Evangiel* for a moment longer.

The other members of my team seated around the table looked as anxious as I felt, their brows furrowed and lips drawn into scowls. In the week since we'd sealed the Master Archive, we'd hit dead end after dead end with our investigation into the Darkness' origin. If we didn't have a breakthrough soon, there wouldn't be any worlds left to save.

"We can't just sit around here doing nothing," I insisted.

"We've been training and preparing," Toran replied.

I shook my head. "But practicing isn't *action.*"

Kaiden sighed in his seat next to me. "Elle, we've already been over this."

I raised an eyebrow. "We agreed to give it a week, and it's been a week."

"As I recall, *you* set that timeframe, not the rest of us," Toran countered. He crossed his muscular arms and fixed me in a level gaze.

"Yeah, it's a terrible plan," Maris agreed, flipping her dark hair behind her shoulder. "I say we keep waiting."

"Look, if our visions in the Archive were even remotely accurate, then an alien invasion force could be coming any moment," I continued. "Do we really want to sit around and wait for them to come to us, or are we going to *do something*?"

I turned to Kaiden for backup. I wasn't sure if our budding romance was enough to buy me favor for my crazy idea, but if I could convince one of my three companions to go along with it, it'd be him.

He shifted in his seat. "I don't like the 'wait and see' approach, either, but intentionally exposing ourselves to the Darkness is reckless."

It wasn't an outright 'no'. I could work with that.

I smiled disarmingly. "We've already faced it once. This is what we were called to do."

"No, we were brought together to seal the Master Archive—which we've done," Maris said.

"You don't need to come," I told her. "But this is something *I* want to do, because I think it's the right move. If there are any clues to be found about the Darkness and how to stop it, we'll find them on the first world that was consumed."

Kaiden sunk deeper into his seat. "It's been more than three months since the Darkness appeared. There's no telling what that world might be like by now, considering the transformations that have happened on other worlds in *hours*."

"All the more reason for us to investigate," I replied.

He examined me. "You won't let this go, will you?"

I shook my head. "I'll go alone, if that's what it takes."

Toran sighed. "I can't endorse this plan, but I also dislike the idea of any one of us going off on our own."

"So, you'll come with me?" I asked.

The huge man nodded. "Very well."

Kaiden threw up his arms. "All right."

I looked to Maris. "What about you?"

She frowned. "This is a terrible idea."

"So you've said." I started to stand up. "All right, we'll see you when we get back."

"I didn't say I wouldn't go." She folded her hands on the tabletop. "You'd all probably die without me."

I smiled. "Let's talk to the commander."

The lines of reporting and leadership had been somewhat blurred since our arrival on the Hegemony's ship, the *Evangiel*, two weeks prior. We were civilians, yet we'd been tasked to serve the government and military in an attempt to stop the Darkness slowly consuming our worlds. With the leadership having nowhere else to turn, we'd been given a degree of autonomy far outside standard operating procedures, and I knew it would ruin me for life.

We made our way to the top deck and proceeded to the nose of the vessel, where we were buzzed into Central Command through the main door.

Commander Alastair Colren rose from the lone seat at the center of the bridge when we entered. "Do you have news?" he asked.

The dynamic threw me off every time I talked with him. A hardened military commander in his fifties, and yet he was looking to me—a teenager from a backwater world—for a plan of action. My universe had been turned upside down in more ways than one when my consciousness was extracted and downloaded into my new, enhanced body bioprinted to my personal specifications.

"Not news, exactly, but a proposed plan," I replied.

He motioned us toward the conference room adjacent to the bridge on the port side of the ship.

When we were seated around the table, I took a deep breath and spread my hands on the tabletop. "I know this is going to sound crazy, but I think we should go to the world that was first consumed by the Darkness."

Colren's eyes widened. "Why?"

"Well, we've only been to one world that was tainted, and that was when the Darkness was still in the process of spreading across the planet. With what we learned on Crystallis in the Archive, we now know the Darkness is some sort of alien invasion—transforming each planet to suit them. But we've never seen the finished product. If we go to one of the first worlds, we can see the result of the transformation, and maybe we can learn more about the enemy we're facing."

"While I don't disagree with the reasoning, it's a huge risk to go into that unknown environment," the commander replied after a slight pause.

"You brought us here to help. Shouldn't we be doing everything we can?" I pressed.

The commander shook his head. "Yes, but there are other factors."

It didn't take much to read between the lines. The Hegemony needed representatives from all three disciplines— Valor, Spirit, and Protection—to un-seal the Master Archive once the Darkness was defeated. Losing all of us would mean starting over. I hated to think of myself as replaceable, but the fact was that we were resources, not just people.

"What if two of us went to scout it?" Kaiden suggested, clearly thinking along the same lines as me.

"But the team—" Maris started to protest in a surprising turn from her earlier objections.

"I can't in good conscience send all four of you into a dangerous, unknown environment on a whim," Colren cut her off, firm.

I understood the commander's reasoning, but I didn't like it. We were stronger together, but I was desperate to have *any* forward progress, even if it meant only half of us got to go. "That might be a good compromise."

"Magic casting would be a good complement to Elle's skills," Kaiden continued. "Plus, we already have two Spirit casters, so that minimizes the risks."

Maris eyed the two of us. "Yeah, I'm sure that's the *only* reason the two of you want to go alone together."

My cheeks flushed in spite of myself. "This is about what's best for the mission."

"Sure," she muttered.

I couldn't tell if her reaction was coming from a place of envy about our relationship or just her incessant need to be contrary. Either way, I figured it was better to ignore her.

Colren steepled his fingers while he sat in thought. "Very well. That's a reasonable course of action," he agreed.

"Where is the first world, anyway?" Kaiden asked.

"The first planet touched by the Darkness was Windau," the commander replied, seemingly unfazed by the other comments. "It's one of the outer colony worlds—fewer than ten thousand residents."

I straightened in my seat. "How long did it take before the Hegemony realized what had happened to the world?"

"That was before my involvement in the matter," Colren stated. "As I understand it, several days passed. There was a report of a cloud in one of the crystals, and then it wasn't until a supply freighter arrived three days later that anyone outside realized the seriousness of the issue. The world was already fully shrouded in the Darkness."

"I guess it's time we find out what's happened on the surface in the three months since then," I said.

He inclined his head. "I was hesitant to suggest it myself, given the dangers, but an investigation does seem like the best course of action at present."

"And what about the alien ships?" Toran asked. "Can we help prepare?"

The commander folded his hands on the tabletop. "The accounts of your visions are everything we need at this time. The admiralty has already begun planning."

"The aliens are close. I know it," Toran murmured.

I shared his concerns about a potential invasion. However, as much as I wanted to prepare, we had no idea what timeline may have been attached to our visions. Beyond that, we didn't have a way to fight the aliens unless we got more information related to the Darkness. Our new recon mission was the best bet for both countering the Darkness and fighting whoever was behind it.

"We'll be ready," I tried to assure Toran, despite my own doubts.

His eyes revealed that he didn't believe the assertion, either, but he nodded.

"I'll make the jump arrangements to Windau," the commander said, rising from the table. "As always, thank you for the proactive attitude. I hate that all of our moves are now acts of last-resort, but I'm willing to try anything."

"We're committed to the cause," I replied.

He nodded absently then departed the conference room.

Kaiden sighed. "I already regret this."

Toran sat in silence for several moments. "It still unnerves me every time to see someone in Colren's position unsure about what to do."

"Can you imagine what it was like for him before we got here?" I asked. "He was in a command of a group who were sent down to planets and killed without warning. I don't blame him for wanting people to volunteer rather than order anyone to go into a dangerous situation."

"That's the job of a commander—to make those tough calls," Kaiden said.

"But we're not soldiers; we're private citizens. The most he can do is request we do something, unless it's an order related to him captaining this ship. I think we'll need to keep driving the investigation forward ourselves."

"It'd be great if some of that involved worlds *not* already overtaken by the Darkness," Maris interjected.

"Don't count on it. If Kaiden's and my upcoming field trip doesn't kill us, that means we'll have a lot more worlds we can explore," I replied.

Toran paled. "That means we could visit our homeworlds."

I nodded. "Not sure if I'm looking forward to that prospect or not."

"Let's not get ahead of ourselves," Kaiden cut in.

"Yeah, we have to survive our visit to the first planet." I rose from my seat.

Kaiden crossed his arms. "That's not what I meant."

"I know, I know. One planet at a time—systematic investigation and all that."

"The scientific method has been drilled into me, what can I say?" He cracked a smile, but it didn't touch his eyes.

"We'll get to the bottom of this. Soon." I took a deep breath. "Should we get out of here?"

Maris jumped to her feet. "Yes, please. The sooner you go do your thing, the better."

We headed for the exit.

"I wish we'd done this a week ago," I said.

"A week ago, I would have called you a crazy person," Kaiden replied.

I frowned. "Actually, I think you did when I first mentioned it—in those exact words, no less."

"That sounds about right."

We walked through the bridge and out to the main corridor.

"There's something I don't get," Maris said when we were in the empty hallway.

I looked over my shoulder at her. "What's that?"

"We got that shard of the Master Crystal… so, why haven't we done a universal reset?" she asked.

Kaiden and I exchanged glances.

"It would be pointless right now," Kaiden stated.

Maris placed her hands on her curvy hips. "But why?"

"Yes, the crystal gives us a control point," I replied. "That does no good, though, when we don't know where the Darkness is coming from. It would just spread again as soon as the reset is complete."

"But we know where it's going and what it will do," she insisted. "We can reset, evacuate the affected worlds, and then deal with the problem without everyone's bodies getting turned to black soot while their consciousness is who-knows-where."

I shook my head. "I don't think a universal-scale reset would be *nearly* that straightforward."

"Agreed," Toran broke his long silence. "Having worked on the interface stations for local crystals, I have a decent understanding of what it takes to get to an exact reset point. We have a crystal, but we *don't* have an interface console for it.

If we attempt a reset, we won't have much control over where it resets *to*. Unless Colren knows something he hasn't shared with us."

"Can you make an interface?" I asked.

He released a long breath. "I could try. Unfortunately, the only way to test out if it works would be to use it."

I frowned. "And if it's wrong…"

"People could find themselves a decade too young, or it might be after the Darkness has already arrived," he continued. "That kind of reset would place enormous demand on the crystalline network—I'm not sure how it would respond. I also have no clear idea of what will happen to *us* at the epicenter. We could be unchanged, or we might end up back in our old bodies, too. This wouldn't be the kind of reset we're used to."

"Maris does have a point, though," Kaiden countered. "Wouldn't it be better to save people now if we can?"

"I'd think Colren would have jumped all over that idea if it was reasonable," I said.

"Agreed, and it's not just about the risks," Toran added. "There's also a large logistical component. If we were to reset with the intent of evacuating the affected worlds, where would all of those people go to?"

"And which worlds will the Darkness spread to next?" Kaiden added.

"Wasn't there information about that in the Archive?" Maris asked.

I nodded, thinking back on what we had been told regarding the information the Hegemony had been able to extract using their mysterious 'viewing' device. As far as I knew, they had been able to use the remote hyperdimensional link with the Archive to anticipate which worlds would be infected by the Darkness, but the information was too vague to draw conclusions about specific timing. "Not enough details," I replied. "We don't know how long it will take to stop this invasion, so if we were to start evacuating people, how long would we be able to keep moving them around to avoid the spreading Darkness?"

"Not to mention, is the crystal shard a one-time use thing, or do we get multiple shots to get it right?" asked Kaiden.

"Good question." I pursed my lips.

Toran took a deep breath. "Given that, I'd say we should wait to use the crystal shard as a last resort. If we *do* only get one shot, we would need to make it count."

"Yeah." I looked to him. "Maybe you should start working on a potential reset interface for the shard, just in case."

He inclined his head. "I suppose that would give me something to do while you and Kaiden go exploring."

"What about me?" Maris asked.

"I guess you get to go back to lounging around and doing whatever you do when we're not planetside," I replied flippantly.

Maris bristled. "I could use the time to test out my healing magic in the infirmary."

I wanted to ask her why she hadn't been doing that for the last week rather than repeatedly going over the same skills with us in an empty cargo hold, but I kept the comment and eye-roll to myself. "Sounds good," I replied instead.

"Jump in T-minus ten minutes," a female voice stated over the central intercom.

"The commander moved fast," Kaiden said.

"We should get to the jump pods." I picked up my pace down the corridor.

Toran took a deep breath and shook his head. "No turning back now."

I smiled. "Hey, you'll have it easy."

"Being the one left behind isn't always easier—too much time to think and worry," the large man replied.

Despite his tough exterior, it warmed my heart that Toran was such a caring guy on the inside. I really couldn't imagine having a better companion to watch my back. "We'll be in comm contact," I assured him.

"So we can learn in real-time if something goes horribly wrong. Great." Maris quipped.

I smirked. "Guess we'll just have to avoid it getting to that point, won't we?"

We descended the lift two decks to the level with our living quarters, lounge room, and jump pods. Several crew members were jogging down the hall toward their own pod rooms in preparation for the upcoming jump.

When we reached the pod room, we stripped off our outer clothes and weapons, storing the items in cubbies behind each pod. Hyperspace jumps were by far the most disorienting experience I'd had since leaving home. The first several jumps, I'd loathed getting into the pod. This time, however, I was excited—though nervous—to finally be taking proactive steps to stop the Darkness. Everything up to this point had been efforts to safeguard worlds so they could be restored after the menace was defeated, but I felt like we hadn't done anything to fight back. As risky as it was to visit an infected world, I hoped it would take us one step closer to defeating our faceless foe.

"See you on the other side." I reclined on the ergonomic couch in my pod.

"Can't wait." Kaiden smiled at me from the next pod over while he got settled in.

I secured my harness, then placed my arms at my sides and breathed steadily in preparation for the jump. Hyperspace was uncomfortable and disconcerting no matter how much I mentally prepared myself, but I'd found that being calm and centered did help minimize the bizarre synesthesia side effects.

The announcer gave a final countdown through the speaker in my pod as the translucent hatch extended to seal me inside. Moments later, I was pressed against the floor of the pod as we transitioned into hyperspace. My heart felt like it dropped into my feet and my vision blurred. I kept my breathing as slow and steady as I could throughout the jump, entering an almost dream-like state as we traveled without a clear sense of time passing.

When we finally arrived, the pod hatch retracted and I unbuckled my harness. Shaking slightly, I propped myself up on my elbows until my head stopped spinning, and then I sat up the rest of the way.

Kaiden had also roused. "Hey," he greeted.

"Hey yourself," I replied, climbing out of my pod.

"Ugh, I hate jumps," Maris groaned while sitting up in her pod across from me.

I steadied myself on my feet. "They really need a better jump system."

"The fact that FTL travel is possible at all is amazing," Toran interjected. He shimmed his broad shoulders through his pod's open top.

"Yeah, yeah." I stepped behind my pod to retrieve my clothing and weapons. I slipped the black pants over my white base layer and then donned the black, belted overcoat. Knee-high boots with purple accents and my Valor artifact—a sword—completed my ensemble.

I pulled my long, fuchsia hair outside the coat's collar when I'd finished dressing. "I hope Tami doesn't freak out when she learns we're taking another shuttle down to an infected world."

"Oh, I'm sure she'll be having a fit on the inside while never letting it show." Kaiden grinned.

"I don't envy her maintenance crew having to deal with the mess," Toran murmured.

"Hey, *we're* the ones who've been down on the frontlines," I pointed out.

He shook his head. "Elle, everything we've done up to this point is just a prelude. The real engagement is about to begin."

"Yeah, I guess it is."

Kaiden finished fastening his cloak. "You ready to do this?" he asked.

I placed my hand on my sword hilt. "I was literally made for this mission."

Kaiden raised an eyebrow. "Really, you went there?"

I shrugged. "Hey, who said you can't try to have some fun while saving the universe?"

THE FOUR OF us descended a lift to the hangar deck in the belly of the ship.

"You don't need to see us off," I said to Maris and Toran, whose mouths were contorted into scowls as we walked down the corridor.

"I still don't like the idea of breaking the team apart," Toran replied.

I shrugged. "This will just be a quick scouting mission."

Maris scoffed. "Yeah, on a planet where everything wants to kill you."

"If something goes wrong, we'll need people who are able to un-seal the Archive after this thing is defeated," Kaiden said.

"The likelihood of something *going* wrong increases exponentially if we don't stick together," the other man insisted.

I stopped and looked him over. "You know... we don't *have* to listen to the commander."

Toran raised an eyebrow. "Disobey orders and have the four of us go anyway?"

"They weren't 'orders' exactly," Kaiden mused.

"You two are going to get a hero complex if we don't keep you in line," Maris said while eyeing me and Kaiden.

"I have no objections," I said. While I'd been trying my best to act like a responsible adult, given the challenging circumstances we were facing, I was still the youngest on our team. If my older, wiser counterparts were okay bending the rules…

Kaiden nodded. "I'm all for keeping the team together."

We continued down the corridor until we reached the double doors leading into the hangar.

Technicians were in the process of completing a pre-flight check on our typical shuttle while the chief engineer, Tami, consulted a tablet nearby.

"Long time no see," I greeted when we were within earshot.

Tami looked up, her eyes bright. "Hey there. Do I want to know why we're prepping for a full decontamination protocol when you return?"

I smiled. "Probably not."

The engineer sighed. "You're going down to another infected world, aren't you?"

"The first one, in fact," I replied.

Her eyes widened. "We're at Windau?"

I raised an eyebrow. "That infamous, huh?"

"Probably not to others. I had family here," she revealed.

"Oh, I'm sorry."

She forced a smile. "Hey, each of us have family and friends at risk. All the more reason for us to work together to beat this thing."

"Do you ever get ruffled, Tami?" I asked. "When we've trashed a ship you've stayed calm, and even now you seem so collected."

The engineer laughed. "Oh, Elle, when you've seen as much crazy shit as I have over the years, you learn to keep things in perspective."

I cocked my head. "And what perspective is that?"

"If you're not going to die in the next five seconds, things could always be worse."

"Can't argue with that," Kaiden agreed.

She nodded. "So, the commander said just two of you are heading down, right?"

"Change of plans," I lied. "All four of us are going after all."

"Stronger together," Toran added.

Tami looked us over. "This is probably something else I shouldn't ask about, huh?"

"We're just striving to give ourselves the best possible chance to succeed," I replied.

"Complementary skillsets, and all that," Maris chimed in.

"Well, your four packs are already in the common area of the shuttle, in addition to pressurized hazsuits for each of you," Tami said.

"Maybe just wait to report our departure to the commander until we've left," I advised.

She rolled her eyes. "Yeah, I figured that was coming."

"You're the best, Tami." I grinned.

"Better make this trip worthwhile." She backed away from the shuttle. "Safe travels. I'll give you a five-minute head start."

Kaiden ascended the ramp. "Plenty of time."

"Not like anyone else would be able to follow us, anyway." I followed him on board.

We passed through the compact common area where our supply backpacks had been arranged near the built-in dining table, and then continued down a short corridor on the starboard side to the bridge. I took my typical seat in the front right while Kaiden took the pilot's seat on the left, with Maris behind him and Toran behind me. The shuttle's automated systems would normally do most of the work, but the unique properties of the Darkness had a bad tendency to interfere with the navigation and stabilizer systems. If this planet was anything like the others, Kaiden would likely have to take manual control.

"What's the plan?" I asked. "Risk landing the shuttle or set it to drop us off and come back later?"

"I maintain that landing it would be bad," Toran stated.

"But if we need to make a quick escape, we'd be trapped," Kaiden countered.

I nodded. "That's what I was thinking, too. Except, what if we *do* land the shuttle and need to make a quick escape, but the vessel has been compromised and we can't use it anyway?"

"That's assuming we need to land at all," Maris pointed out. "We can learn a lot just by flying around."

"True," I admitted. "I guess we can play it by ear."

"Because things never go poorly when we do that." Kaiden buckled his flight harness.

"You have another idea?" I asked.

"Nope, just laying the foundation for a future 'I told you so'."

I rolled my eyes. "This relationship is off to a great start."

Maris raised an eyebrow. "Trouble in paradise already?"

"*Nothing* about this is paradise," I shot back.

"Wow, thanks." Kaiden started up the engines.

"I don't mean you, just the situation." I reached over to pat his knee. "*You're* great."

"None of this is relevant," Maris huffed.

I glanced at her over my shoulder. "Sorry, but I can't promise new relationship-y stuff won't creep in now and again."

"Oh, well aware of that." Maris crossed her arms.

I couldn't tell if her exasperation stemmed from this exchange directly or if it was a more general frustration with the position we had been placed in with the Hegemony, but I owed it to the team to minimize drama. We were risking our lives, and the last thing any of us needed was unrelated interpersonal dynamics getting in the way of the mission. Nonetheless, Kaiden and I had already crossed a threshold by admitting we had feelings for each other that went beyond professional comradery. Neither of us seemed interested in going back to how things were before, so we'd have to find a balance between team morale and our own desires. Since it'd only been a week, we hadn't worked out exactly what that would be.

All I knew for sure is that out of all the people I'd met, he was the only one worth the effort. If that relationship could give me one shred of normalcy amid all the other craziness, I felt I could be that much more effective doing what I'd need to do. The fact that the 'normal relationship' was with someone who'd manifested magical abilities was beside the point.

The shuttle followed autopilot commands across the hangar and through the electrostatic field out into space. Only blackness and distant stars were visible at first, but then the shuttle arced over the bow of the *Evangiel* and the planet of Windau came into view.

Previous worlds I'd encountered that had been consumed by the Darkness had ribbons of swirling black snaking through the atmosphere, muting the normal luminescence of the planets against the dark backdrop of the void. In frightening contrast, I could hardly recognize this world as a planet at all. The Darkness blanketed every centimeter of the world, almost as though ominous clouds from a horrific thunderstorm now covered the entire planet. Unlike a storm, there were no flashes of lightning or calm patches of sky to break it up, only marbled shades of black and dark gray.

"I suddenly feel much less-good about heading down there." I gulped.

Kaiden shook his head. "Pictures couldn't do this justice."

"Why did I ever agree to come?" Maris moaned.

"Because that's the last place anyone should go alone," Toran stated. "We need to look out for each other—that's why we are a team."

"All the same, sorry for talking you into my crazy idea," I said.

"We had no leads about how to stop this thing. You're not wrong that a more hands-on approach might give us a clue," Kaiden replied.

Toran grunted behind me. "And here we thought our role might end when we sealed the Archive."

"Did we *really*, though?" Kaiden countered.

"As soon as Commander Colren said we had a special immunity to the Darkness, I figured we were in this for the long haul," I said.

Maris sighed. "Just my luck to be placed on a team of people who run toward the danger rather than from it."

I smiled. "We have a chance to make a difference. Not many people get the opportunity to save an entire civilization."

"Elle, your hero complex is showing," Kaiden joked.

"Right, like I'm the only one in this shuttle who gets any satisfaction out of saving the day."

"It's true," Toran admitted. "If I can't be with my family, then I want to take an active role in making our worlds safe for them again."

"Yeah, but there's trying to solve a problem, and then

there's going *into that.*" Kaiden made a sweeping gesture toward the planet below us.

"Yet, you were the first to agree to come with me." I eyed him with a playful smirk. "Don't deny that part of you likes the thrill of danger."

"There is something empowering about venturing into the unknown," he admitted.

Maris nodded. "Well, yeah! Why else do you think I came along?"

I chuckled. "All right, so all of us are a little crazy."

"More than a little, by my estimation," Toran replied. "Some might say we have a death wish, visiting a planet like this."

"Nah, we've got this." I grinned.

"Pretty sure that casual dismissal is exactly what would make people call us crazy in the first place," Kaiden pointed out.

"Without that attitude, we'd still be back on the *Evangiel* and the Archive wouldn't be sealed."

"I suppose you're right," he agreed.

"Too late to turn back now," Toran muttered when a glow formed around the shuttle as the nose pushed through the outer layers of the corrupted atmosphere.

The comm on the front console flashed, accompanied by a beep.

"Shuttle 1, the four of you going was *not* the plan," Commander Colren stated tersely.

Kaiden and I exchanged glances. He shook his head and sighed.

I pressed the comm controls. "We decided we were stronger as a team," I said.

"Then you should have maintained that point in our

meeting earlier," the commander replied. "Changing plans without expressing that intent is a great way to get yourselves killed."

"It seemed like a better idea five minutes ago," I mumbled.

"It's reckless. Turn back now," he instructed.

"With all due respect, Commander, no," Kaiden stated. "To beat this thing, we need more information. Our best chance of getting the insights we need is by investigating the planet, and sticking together as a team is how we'll do that safely. Yes, we agreed, and then we went behind your back, which was wrong. However, wasting time arguing isn't going to accomplish what we need to do any faster. We're taking action, because that's what the situation requires. We could have gone about doing that in a more 'official' way, but the outcome would be the same."

Colren sighed. "I suppose I shouldn't be surprised that you take advantage of the fact that I have no direct command authority over you."

"Nothing personal," I said. "We just want to see this through as quickly as possible."

"I can't fault you for that. Just… please don't run off again in the future."

"Yes, sorry. It won't happen again," I assured him with the full intent of keeping my word, though I was well aware that circumstances could change at any moment.

"Be careful down there," the commander added. "We'll be awaiting your safe return." He ended the commlink.

"So it begins…" Kaiden said melodramatically.

The shuttle shuddered as the high-altitude air currents swirled around our tiny vessel.

Toran gripped his armrest. "I must trust in the belief that this is what we're supposed to do."

"Yes, definitely going to keep telling myself that." I cinched my restraints tighter and then gripped my own armrest as another jolt wracked our shuttle.

As much as I did want to be a hero, I couldn't shake the nagging doubt at the back of my mind that I was hopelessly out of my depth. We'd won a handful of fights and had successfully sealed the Master Archive, but those few activities didn't make us seasoned pros. I hoped my grand aspirations would make up for some of what I lacked in practical skills and experience, though I knew my ambition would catch up to me eventually. With any luck, others would be there to help me make it through whatever ordeals I might face.

As we descended through the atmosphere, the oppressive Darkness seemed to close in around us. My heart leaped every time the shuttle jostled in the turbulence. Worse, my inability to see more than a few hundred meters ahead through the black clouds gave me a strange sense of claustrophobia I'd never experienced before.

"How close are we to the ground?" I asked Kaiden.

He shook his head, concern knitting his brow. "I can't tell."

"That seems bad," Maris commented from the seat behind him.

"The ground appears to be quite unstable," Toran reported. I glanced over my shoulder and saw him consulting the workstation along the starboard bulkhead behind me; a planetary model was displayed on the screen. "The mass and density of this world is not what it should be."

"We encountered that before, right?" I said, thinking back to the planet where I'd fought the dragon for my sword Valor artifact. At the time, I'd hoped that the planet had naturally lower gravity than the small handful of other worlds I'd encountered during my brief travels. However, the more we experienced the ravages of the Darkness, the more I was convinced that the infection changed the very composition of the worlds.

"Yeah, but this is far more pronounced," Kaiden said.

"It's been months," Toran replied. "Whatever we witness here is likely a preview for what to expect on the other infected worlds."

"Is the Darkness hollowing them out?" Maris questioned.

I shook my head. "No idea. But I'd really like to know what the end game is." No matter the methods of the planetary transformation, mass just didn't disappear; it had to have gone somewhere. Given everything we'd observed, whatever was controlling the transformation of the infected planets seemed to follow a set of rules. If we could learn enough, we might be able to gain control of that system so we could put everything back to how it was supposed to be. Just as importantly, we could make sure it could never happen again.

Toran didn't say anything more on the matter, which I took as a bad sign under the circumstances. As the most scientifically minded member of our team, I relied on him to be the voice of reason when it came to throwing out random hypotheses related to what alien force we were up against. It was worrisome that he had no commentary on the bizarre conditions, even though geophysics was somewhat far afield from his engineering background. If even he and Kaiden were out of their depth, then anything I might say on the scientific front may as well be pure fantasy.

We continued the descent in silence for another minute until the occasional jolts wracking the vessel turned into constant rattling.

"Nav system is glitching," Kaiden reported. "It's just like what happened on the other worlds—can't maintain a lock."

He took the manual controls.

"We need to set down," Maris said.

"I advise against setting down at random," Toran cautioned. "The ground is too unstable in some places to support the shuttle's weight."

"Plus, the entire point in coming here is to look for clues," I added. "We should try to find one of the crystal monuments."

Toran nodded. "Agreed. Since the Darkness appears to spread through the crystalline network, studying one of the monuments makes the most sense."

Kaiden focused on the controls. "I'm flying blind here, so start searching!"

"Already working on it," Toran replied. "I'm vetting reaction pings from prospective crystals."

I swiveled around in my seat to give him a questioning gaze. "Don't you need Kaiden's or Maris' pendant for that?"

"I've been busy for the past week figuring out how to make it work remotely," he responded without taking his attention from the monitor.

The search method he'd devised using one of the caster pendants and the ship's sensor suite had allowed us to locate sites by pinpointing the concentrated energy signatures associated with crystals. Previously, one of the pendants needed to be placed in a cradle on the device for it to work. Toran's new innovation would certainly make our new searches more convenient.

"There are several strong signatures around the planet, but the closest is ten kilometers to the northeast," Toran continued. "I believe it may be the crystal that serviced the capital city."

"Sounds like a great place to start," I said.

"Let's do it," Kaiden agreed. "Send me the coordinates."

Toran relayed the location to the nav console, and Kaiden identified the point on the holographic map that was overlaid on the front viewport.

"This should be easy to get to," he said while redirecting the shuttle's course toward the new destination.

"It's getting back *out* that worries me," Maris muttered. As much as I wanted to project an aura of self-assurance, I had the same fears.

We sped through the blackness outside the viewport. As we neared the destination, Kaiden decelerated and directed the shuttle toward the ground. However, even as we descended, there was no ground in sight. My heart lodged in my throat as the readings on the proximity sensors continued to jump around.

"Shouldn't we have touched down already?" I asked.

"Yes," Kaiden acknowledged, confirming my worries. "Prior comments aside, we can still bail."

"No, we owe it to our loved ones to vanquish this menace," Toran replied.

"Yeah, no risk, no reward," I said.

Kaiden took a slow breath. "All right." He inched the shuttle downward.

Out the front viewport, the blackness around us began to take on more definition. I squinted into the dim surroundings, trying to make sense of the forms. "What is that out there?"

I reached forward to adjust the overlay settings, hoping to increase the contrast so we could navigate by sight. After fiddling with the slider for several seconds, the view out the viewport took on an amber hint, which brought out previously hidden details in our surroundings. My chest constricted as I realized we had descended into a chasm with steep cliffs rising at least a hundred meters above us.

Kaiden sucked in a sharp breath. "That's not good."

"How did we miss ground level?" Toran mused.

"No idea. Up. Now." I pointed toward the sky.

"Don't need to say it twice." He hit the yoke to gain elevation. The shuttle continued to descend.

My stomach turned over. "Why aren't we...?"

Kaiden paled. "I think we're trapped."

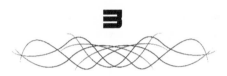

I SWALLOWED HARD. "We can't be trapped."

"Well, the shuttle isn't responding." Concern pitched Kaiden's voice while he continued trying to direct the craft upward. Despite throttling the engine, the vessel continued to descend deeper into the black chasm.

"What's pulling us down?" I asked, panic setting in.

"I don't know!" Kaiden's hands raced over the controls.

Maris' face drained. "Is it, like, a gravity well or something?"

"I don't think it works like that," I muttered in reply.

"The sensors aren't picking up anything in our surroundings to indicate we're trapped in such an anomaly. This shuttle's engines are strong enough to break orbit, so there's no reason we'd be unable to pull away now," Toran explained.

"Unless we've been tethered," Kaiden said.

My heart skipped a beat. "By *what*?"

"I don't know, but see if you can identify anything." Kaiden continued fighting with the controls. The shuttle swayed side to side, but it was unable to gain any elevation.

I used the console in front of me to bring up detailed sensor data around the shuttle, including pressure points on the hull that may indicate a grapple. The aft frame of the vessel did appear to be stressed, though I couldn't make out a singular point where an anchor might be tethered. "Does this thing have a rear-view camera?"

"Not for close-range observation," Kaiden replied.

"Then we'll need to get a look the old-fashioned way." I unbuckled my harness.

His eyes widened. "Where are you going?"

"To look out the rear airlock," I replied, bracing myself on my seatback as the shuttle rocked. "Hold it steady."

"Elle, don't—"

"I convinced all of you to come down here, so I better figure out what's preventing us from going home." I jogged toward the common area with my arms outstretched to either side to catch myself as the shuttle bucked. My heart pounded in my ears. It was my fault we were in the mess. I couldn't let anything bad happen to my friends, especially not before we had a chance to accomplish our mission.

I passed by our packs and the four hazsuits on my way to the aft airlock beyond the sleeping cabins. If things took a turn for the worse, those suits might be the only thing standing between us and the unstable environment... Not that I had a lot of faith that the thin material would last long against the corrosive properties of the Darkness.

At the end of the corridor running the length of the shuttle, the airlock entry door was sealed. I checked the panel to confirm it was pressurized and then opened it. The outside hatch had a one-meter-wide square viewport at its center, and I pressed my face against the thick plastic to see if I could spot whatever seemed to be tethering us inside the chasm.

To my horror, a thick, vine-like structure appeared to be wrapping itself around the shuttle. The vines thickened toward the base, though I couldn't make out the anchor point through the blackness. "Hey, guys! There's a bad thing going on back here," I shouted toward the bridge.

"What do you see?" Kaiden shouted back.

"Black vines, or something," I replied.

A moment later, I heard the heavy thud of footsteps, and Toran came into view down the corridor. He squeezed into the airlock next to me, motioning me aside so he could look outside.

"Stars!" he exclaimed. "What is that?"

"Certain death… if I'm not being overly dramatic."

He frowned. "That's a little too on-point to be a joke."

I looked down, all too aware of my predisposition for ill-timed humor. "We need to detach it," I said to get us back in the right headspace.

"I have no idea what to suggest, given we don't know what that *is*."

"Cut it?" I suggested.

"With what? We need to use a laser cutter from a completely different angle."

"To cut the tendrils from the base, yeah. But what about sheering them off from where they're attached to the shuttle?"

He examined me. "What do you have in mind?"

"What if we make it impossible for the vine-things to grip the hull?"

"Like an electrified fence?"

"Yeah, along those lines."

"That general idea could work if we had time to play around with it, but it's too risky to try as a one-shot."

"What else, then?" I asked.

Before Toran could reply, Kaiden shouted again from the bridge. "What's going on back there?"

"Trying to figure out how to sever the evil, alien vine-things," I shouted back. I returned my attention to Toran. "If we can't science this thing on short notice, then it'll come down to magic."

He nodded. "But how?"

I shrugged. "Giant fireball?"

"Sounds like a job for Kaiden."

"It does, but he's flying." I braced myself as the shuttle rocked. "Do you know enough from your engineering classes to take over for a few minutes?"

Toran scowled. "Not really, but I suspect we may not have another option."

There were two more possibilities—either Maris could try offensive magic, or I could—but neither one of us had Kaiden's degree of control. Given the surgical nature of the task at hand, I decided against voicing the alternatives. "Take over in the bridge and get him back here. I'll get a suit ready."

The large man nodded, then took off toward the bridge.

I followed him as far as the common room, where I started putting on one of the hazsuits and unfurled another so it would be easy for Kaiden to don. He appeared in the common room just as I'd secured my suit up to my hips.

"What are you doing?" he asked.

"Getting ready."

He warily examined the suit. "For what?"

"You use a fireball or lightning, and I slash and make sure the vine-things don't snatch you. Easy."

Kaiden picked up the prepped suit and frowned. "And where are we going to do this from?"

"The back airlock," I replied.

"Elle, that's crazy!"

The shuttle rocked again, knocking me into the dining table. I caught myself and used my hands to steady myself until the ship's internal stabilizers compensated. "Sounds like a better plan than waiting until the tendrils either pull us all the way to the bottom of the chasm or we run out of fuel."

He started dressing. "Point taken."

I slipped my arms into my hazsuit's sleeves. "Gotta say, this isn't what I had in mind when I suggested we come down here."

"Really? Because I figured we'd be screwed."

"Oh, I did, too, but I was thinking more like tar pits or shadow beasts, not giant tentacle monsters."

"Wait, you said vines…"

"Yes, but I have no idea what they're attached to. I thought maybe it would sound better to say we were being attacked by a giant monster rather than being eaten by a demon plant."

Kaiden stared at me with disbelief. "How would that be *any* better?"

"Now that I say it out loud—"

"Never mind." He slipped the hazsuit helmet over his head and then grabbed his magic staff. "Let's try to get free."

I finished securing my own helmet, grabbed my sword, and then quickly followed Kaiden into the aft airlock. We sealed the interior door and then pressurized the compartment to the outside. When the indicator light turned green, Kaiden released the rear hatch.

The roar of the shuttle's engine filled the chamber, and a gust of wind knocked me backward. I gripped one of the handholds near the hatch opening with my right hand and readied my sword in my left. The black vines made no motion in our direction.

Kaiden's mouth fell open as he took in the sight of the alien tendrils writing around our vessel.

"Blast 'em," I urged.

"Those things could take us out in a second!"

"That's why we need to get to them first!"

He shook his head. "No way I can blast them in one go."

"Do your best. I'm here in case they try to counter-attack. We need to try."

Kaiden looked far from convinced, but he nodded. With one hand gripping the wall inside the airlock, he directed his staff toward the most concentrated bundle of black vines. A flaming, blue orb formed on the end of his staff. When it had swelled to twice the side of Kaiden's head, he released the fireball into the blackness.

The orb struck its mark and exploded in a flash, scattering smaller blue flames throughout the vines. In each place touched by the flames, the vines spasmed, but no tendrils appeared to have been severed and none released from the ship.

"Try again," I said.

Kaiden cast another fireball, even larger this time, but it was just as ineffective. "We need to try something else."

"Yeah, you're right." Without hesitation, I locked in my grip on the handhold and then swung my body outward behind the shuttle. Following with the momentum, I slashed with my sword arm toward the nearest vines affixed to the hull.

My blade sliced through the vines, and the severed segments fell away into the blackness below. The ruined ends of the vines, however, lashed out toward me. I swung back into the comparative safety of the airlock just in time to avoid one of the vines whipping toward my sword arm.

Kaiden quickly hurled a fireball toward the vines, and they recoiled.

"Thanks." I smiled at him before taking a cautious look out the open hatch. The ends of the vines were re-forming into points where I had sliced them off. "Stars! These things don't quit."

"Shit, we never should have come down here. No more indulging your crazy ideas!"

"Hey, I wouldn't have suggested it if I expected *this*." I slashed at the vines as they stabbed toward us, slicing them off again.

"Any other ideas for how to get us out?" Fear filled Kaiden's eyes.

We'd faced some terrifying things in our brief time together, but we'd always at least had solid ground underfoot. To have our one means of escaping the planet now grappled by the alien force placed us in a totally new kind of danger. I didn't want this to be the end. We needed to find a way back to safety.

"My blade works against them," I said, trying to suppress my own fear and doubt. "I just need better reach."

Kaiden's eyes widened. "You can't be serious!"

"I need a way to get out there and cut that big one. The shuttle might be able to break free of the others."

"No." He shook his head. "No way. You couldn't hold on through that."

"I won't have to if I'm tied down."

"But the engines—"

"Shut them down, I swing out and do my thing, then use the EVA winch to pull me back in, and Toran punches it."

"Elle…"

"There's no time to argue."

Kaiden swallowed, then activated the suit's comm since he

couldn't touch the integrated comm behind his ear. "Maris, get to the interior airlock door. We need you to cast a protective shell."

"See?" I said. "I'll be in a safe, happy bubble." Despite my attempt to make light of the situation, the notion of swinging out behind the shuttle terrified me. But what scared me more was being drawn down into the blackness where the tendrils were coming from.

"What the…?" Maris' voice filled my helmet as she stared out the interior airlock viewport at the scene.

"Elle has gone mad," Kaiden stated. "But her plan might be the only thing that can save us right now."

I grabbed the end of the winch tether outside the airlock and secured the control belt around my waist. "A shield would be great."

Maris gaped at me for a second, then nodded. She waved her hand and a translucent purple shell appeared around me. "Be careful."

"Yeah, that runs contrary to this entire maneuver." I altered the suit's comm to include the whole team. "Toran, I'm going to need you to cut the engines on my mark."

"But that will—" he started to object.

"I need to sever these vines and I'd rather not be incinerated in the process," I cut in. A new wave of snaking vines were rising from the depths; they'd reach the shuttle within twenty seconds, and then my swordsmanship might not be enough. I prepared to leap from the door. "Kaiden, follow with fireballs behind me so the severed ends can't grab hold while I swing."

"You don't have to."

I looked him in the eyes. "This is our only move." I shifted my gaze down to the approaching vines. "Ready, Toran?"

"Standing by."

"Cut the engines!" The roar ceased. In the sudden silence, I dove from the hatch into a freefall toward the black depths. Ten meters out, I hit the winch's brake using the control belt. The cable went taut, causing me to swing in an arc toward the bundle of tendrils. I slashed through as many as I could reach with my sword as I swung by. The slicing-resistance of the blade slowed my trajectory, and by the time I reached the thickest of the strands, I was only able to cut halfway through. I could only hope it would be enough.

Kaiden's fireballs blasted behind me and the shuttle was losing elevation without its engines firing. There was no way I could try for another pass.

I hit the winch controls to reel me in at maximum speed. Despite the short distance I had to go, the shuttle was falling too fast, and I wouldn't be able to make it back inside before the craft would be snared by the tendrils once more.

"Go now!" I shouted to Toran. Maris' shield had withheld fire breathed from a dragon at close range, so hopefully it would protect me from the engine's wash.

"Wait!" Kaiden shouted, but Toran had already activated the thrusters.

The waist belt dug into me as the shuttle pulled away from the remaining black vines, breaking free when I was still three meters out as the winch reeled me in. Heat from the engines hit me like I'd stepped into an oven, despite the shield and the protective layer from the hazsuit. Fortunately, the winch was positioned far enough from the engines that the cable wasn't in the direct path of the exhaust, and the mechanism was able to reel me in the rest of the way.

Gripping a handhold inside the doorframe, Kaiden extended his free hand to help me inside. "That was some move!" he said as his hand wrapped securely around my wrist.

I grinned up at him while I scrambled inside. "I swear I wasn't trying to show off."

"Nice work and all, but we have other problems," Maris said over the comm.

I looked up at her still staring through the viewport, pointing behind us. Looking over my shoulder, my stomach dropped as I saw the walls of the chasm closing in.

"HURRY!" KAIDEN PULLED me the rest of the way into the airlock. He hit the hatch controls the moment my feet were inside.

"Get us out of here, Toran!" I shouted over the comm.

"I'm trying!" he replied with a frantic tone that made it clear he'd seen the walls inexplicably closing in.

I slammed against the side wall of the airlock as the shuttle apparently changed direction. Out in the corridor, Maris cried out as she toppled away from the door. Kaiden struck the wall next to me. I pawed the side wall, searching for a secure handhold.

The shuttle tilted upward as we started to climb. The shuttle jolted twice, then I sensed smooth acceleration as the black pit receded behind us.

"We're clear!" Toran cheered.

I rose to my feet and released my helmet. "Okay, yeah, that was *not* part of my plan."

Kaiden removed his own helmet and hugged me. "Are you okay?"

"Yeah, I think so." I checked myself over, seeing no apparent injury. "It all happened so fast. I didn't think."

Kaiden's sky blue eyes shone with concern. "Elle, you can't throw yourself out an airlock like that."

"I had no interest in finding out what the tentacle monster had in store for us."

"Well…" He faded out. "I was worried I was going to lose you."

"You won't get rid of me that easily." I leaned close, staring into his eyes until he relaxed. His lips met mine in a reassuring kiss.

The ship shuddered, bringing us back to our surroundings.

I pulled away from Kaiden. "We should get back to the bridge."

"Yes, please!" Toran replied over our ear comms.

My pulse spiked. I checked the comms and realized that we'd left the channel open. Maris and Toran had been free to listen in on our private exchange. "Be right there," I muttered, then muted the channel.

Through the inner airlock door's viewport, Maris smirked at us before turning to walk back toward the bridge.

Kaiden sighed. "They heard that?"

"And saw, apparently." I shook my head. "Well, us being a couple isn't a revelation."

"No, but making out in the airlock in the middle of a mission isn't 'keeping things professional' like we agreed."

"That was hardly 'making out'."

"You know what I mean."

"In all fairness, we just almost died," I stated. "A celebratory moment is allowed."

Kaiden stripped off his hazsuit. "We'll need to do more of that once we're not almost-dying."

I smiled coyly. "I like that plan."

"Again, really don't know how to fly this thing…" Toran said over the shuttle's central comm.

"Sorry, on my way!" Kaiden replied, then hit the inner airlock door. It hissed open and he jogged into the corridor.

"What's the plan now?" I asked, following him.

"We have a decision to make: either proceed with an investigation, or head back to the *Evangiel* and apologize for being foolhardy."

"That second option doesn't sound like our style."

"I figured you'd say that." Kaiden entered the bridge, and Toran rose from the pilot's chair. "Thanks for getting us out of there," Kaiden said, taking over the controls.

"What happened back there?" Toran asked while he returned to his own seat behind mine.

"Angry foliage," Maris replied.

Toran screwed up his face. "What?"

"The vine-things that may or may not have been monster tentacles," I clarified.

"This place is a nightmare," Toran muttered.

"We're going back to the *Evangiel*, right?" Maris asked.

I buckled into my seat next to Kaiden. "We came here to do research, and we haven't learned anything useful yet."

"There was a pretty resounding message of 'this place is terrible'," Maris shot back.

"And what good does that do us for stopping the Darkness? We still need to get access to one of the crystals," I insisted.

Maris crossed her arms. "What's to stop more of the vines from roping us in as soon as we get close to the surface?"

"I think those were just in the chasm," Kaiden chimed in, though his tone was distant. "I can't believe I didn't see it before."

I turned my attention to him. "See what?"

"The pattern of the Darkness' impact isn't random," he explained. "Look at it." He motioned toward the front viewport, which was still tinted amber. "We must have already been down in the chasm when you activated the filter, but seeing it now, it's so obvious."

I examined the surrounding landscape, mystified. There *was* a strange order to it all, and not in the way I would have expected. The chasm we'd escaped was part of a larger canyon that encircled the remains of what appeared to be Windau's capital city. An even larger canyon surrounded the inner canyon, and another beyond that. Each were perfectly formed circles, too precise to appear natural and certainly not random. However, the presence of the mysterious, concentric circles alone didn't catch my eye as much as the way tendrils of Darkness flowed outward from a central point in the city like spokes on a wheel; we had crossed through one spoke and been snared.

"What is it?" I scrunched up my nose.

"I have no idea," Kaiden murmured.

Maris wrapped her arms around herself. "I retract my endorsement for coming here. This is all wrong."

"It's so ordered…" Toran mused, seemingly lost in his own thoughts. "I always thought of the Darkness as chaotic, but the precision of this pattern suggests a high level of refinement and intelligence."

"Great, so whatever aliens are behind it are smart and organized." I sighed. "Question is, can we go to the epicenter of the activity without getting attacked?"

"I guess the only way to tell is the test it out," Kaiden replied. "Maybe we can start by bringing the shuttle into one of the more open areas to see if the vine-tendril things react to our presence?"

"Sounds much better than going into the middle and getting trapped again," I said.

"So, the hypothesis is that the tendrils will find a way to maintain connections through their path no matter what and we just got in the way?" Toran clarified.

I shrugged. "Unless you have any other ideas."

"I do not," he replied. "I can't say I have any solid ideas about anything at the moment. The behavior of our foe has caught me by surprise."

"I'm not sure what I was expecting, either, but I'm with you—I somehow thought it would be more chaotic."

"Exactly. For a bunch of swirling, black smoke, this almost looks like it's programmed."

I hesitated. "But that's crazy, right?"

"No crazier than us manifesting magical abilities. DNA is just a set of biological instructions. Granted, transforming a planet is more complicated than directing the growth of a plant, but the processes are hypothetically the same."

"So, the Darkness is some kind of biotech?" Maris asked.

Kaiden shrugged. "Maybe. It's all speculation until we take a closer look."

"Speaking of which," I frowned at the scene outside the viewport, "how *are* we supposed to do that, given the tentacle-vine-monsters?"

"Well, if our problems before were, in fact, caused by interrupting the energy flow, then we should fare much better if we set down in an open area," Kaiden replied.

"Except, when we visited an infected planet before, creatures came to attack us," I pointed out.

"They were moving before they saw us," he countered. "Maybe we were standing in their travel path and that caused the attack."

"It's a big assumption to think that they'll stay out of our way if we leave them alone," Toran chimed in.

"Not saying they will *entirely*, just that they may be less… aggressive," Kaiden clarified.

"Anything we say is a guess," I stated the obvious. "We already committed to seeing this through, so arguing about whether or not we might die is kinda pointless."

"We, collectively, seem to make terrible decisions," Maris observed.

"As a result, we keep being reckless and doing things no sane person would do." Kaiden sighed.

"Is it crazy, or heroic?" I asked.

Toran shook his head. "I've absolutely no clue."

"Debates for another time. We need to land," Kaiden interjected.

"Right. The part about not dying." I surveyed the landscape. "You said we need an open spot away from the bands of Darkness, right? What about the triangular patch beyond that wall-like structure?" I pointed toward what appeared to be a former field, or perhaps a plaza; it was impossible to tell which, given how much the Darkness had transformed the surroundings. What I could make out, however, was that the city's crystal was at the hub of the twisting, black tendrils which now pervaded the landscape.

"We'll be surrounded, but that also means we won't have to get around those dark tendrils on foot," Kaiden said.

"No need to convince me," Toran replied.

Maris nodded. "Let's get this over with."

"Going in." Kaiden directed the shuttle toward the fairly open area I had identified.

The craft pitched and rolled on the turbulent winds as we came in for the landing. I gripped my armrest while I tried to keep my breathing slow and even. As frightening as the wild shuttle ride was, I suspected that it was nothing compared to the horrors we'd face on the surface; the tentacle monster in the trench had made that clear.

As we neared the landing site, the details in the twisted landscape became clearer. I realized that the dark tendrils fanning out from the central crystal weren't solid objects, as I had thought from a distance, but were rather a steady flow of tiny black particulates—the same fine cloud I'd witnessed in the canyon crystal on my homeworld shortly before I'd been recruited by the Hegemony. In fact, very little in the environment looked to be completely solid, with even former buildings and vegetation appearing to be riddled with holes that resulted in a sponge-like texture. The oddity supported the other evidence about lighter gravity—and reduced planetary mass, by extension—but it still offered no explanation for *where* that extra material had gone. For as thoroughly as the Darkness had consumed the planet, there was no outward evidence of it extending into space or elsewhere.

Kaiden deftly maneuvered the shuttle into position above the plaza and directed it straight down. "Stars willing, nothing will swallow us…" he murmured while descending the final meters.

I held my breath and braced.

The shuttle bumped slightly and then all was still. Out the front viewport, the dark tendrils were unchanged. For now, the Darkness appeared to be ignoring us.

I unstrapped my flight harness and jumped to my feet. "Clock's ticking. This nasty stuff might eat a hole through our ship or clothes."

"I'll get my supplies." Toran raced ahead of me toward the common room.

Kaiden and Maris exchanged glances. "We'll need as much protection as we can get," Kaiden told her.

She nodded. "I'll do what I can."

My stomach flopped. We were out of our minds to enter this kind of environment, but we didn't have any other choice. With no way to learn anything remotely, we needed direct access to that central crystal. Though I wished circumstances were different, it was better to make the most of it rather than dwell on thoughts of alternatives that could never be.

I rushed into the common room to gather my own hazsuit and pack of supplies. "These suits are already tainted," I grumbled while slipping on the garment I'd used several minutes earlier. "There's no way we can retain any sort of contamination containment."

"Yeah, I figured that would be a losing battle the moment we agreed to come here," Kaiden replied with a weak smile.

Maris paled. "Let's hope legend holds and we *do* have an immunity."

I strapped my sword over the hazsuit. "Hey, if nothing else, we'll find out quickly." I wasn't sure if my own words were comforting or not. While a swift death would be preferable in theory, there was no telling what it might feel like to be turned into a column of ash, especially when one's final thoughts would be about how the mission had failed. I shook my head, chastising myself. That kind of thinking wasn't productive.

The others were uncomfortably quiet after my statement, likely running through similar scenarios to my own bleak vision of what our final moments might be like.

"We're going to make it through this," I said. "It won't stop us this easily."

"That's right." Toran looked around the room. "Is everyone ready?"

I checked the seals on my suit. "Ready."

Kaiden and Maris nodded, their suits secured and supply packs slung over their shoulders.

"Let's go." Toran led the way into the airlock and cycled it once we were all inside.

My breath was loud in my ears inside the suit while I waited the ten seconds for the outside hatch to open. Finally, it released with a hiss.

Without the roar of the shuttle's engine to drown out the surroundings, I was struck by how quiet the planet was. Wind whipped through the open hatch, but there were no other audible sounds emanating from the mysterious black tendrils or anything else nearby.

"Be careful out there," Maris said. She waved her hand, and translucent purple shells appeared around each of us.

"Thanks." Steeling myself, I hopped out of the shuttle onto the black ground. My feet sank in five centimeters as the aerated ground compressed beneath my boots. I took several firm steps to make sure I wasn't going to sink in further, and it appeared to be solid enough. "This is weird."

Toran paced next to me. "I have no idea what to make of it."

"I'm pretty far beyond trying to make scientific sense of this," Kaiden said. "Let's get to the crystal." He set off in the direction of the monument two hundred meters to the north.

Maris wrinkled her nose as she followed. "If I could smell anything right now, I bet this would reek."

Toran nodded. "I'm inclined to agree."

"That other world didn't," Kaiden pointed out while he forged ahead.

"But that one had *just* been infected. This one has had months to marinate in its own destruction," Maris countered.

I kept careful watch on our surroundings, looking for any signs of movement by creatures that could attack us. "What a delightful thought."

"Doesn't matter. Let's get out of here before we become one of the permanent fixtures." Kaiden picked up his pace.

I jogged ahead to walk abreast to him. Catching his gaze as I approached, I gave him a reassuring nod. It was clear his nerves were starting to fray; we'd need to support one another and not give in to our imaginations' worst case scenarios.

Kaiden's outward demeanor didn't change, but he took a slow breath and nodded back. Nerves or not, he was still there in the moment with me. I had nothing to worry about.

The first hundred meters from the shuttle, our path toward the crystal was fairly clear. We plodded across the black ground, leaving a path of footprints behind us. As we neared the destination monument, however, small tendrils of the Darkness started to sprout from the black ground.

"I didn't notice these from the air," I admitted.

"Neither did I." Kaiden frowned at the pulsing energy pathways of the dark particulates.

"Let's try to step around them." I eyed our path ahead, but I couldn't tell if the ground closest to the crystal monument was the black spongy material we had been walking on, or if it was a mat of the tendrils.

It was possible that it didn't matter either way. However, given our working hypothesis that we were attacked because we'd interrupted the energy flow of one of the larger tendrils, it was reasonable to assume that the attributes would scale down, as well. My companions had all instinctively stepped around the small tendrils when they'd first appeared in our path, so I definitely wasn't the only person thinking in those terms.

By the time we'd gone another twenty meters, it was clear that avoiding the small tendrils might be unavoidable. I slowed my pace. "Decision time."

Kaiden looked at the path ahead and then back to me. "We can't give up now."

"Agreed, but we should be prepared for a fight if the ground turns on us," I replied.

Maris groaned. "How in the stars are you supposed to prepare for *that*?"

I shrugged. "I don't know, but I have a sneaking suspicion it's about to happen."

"Elle," Kaiden took a step backward and a fireball appeared in his palm, "move!"

I TENSED AS my gaze shot down to my feet. Four of the slim, black tendrils had started to wrap around my boots. I tried to raise my right foot, and the tendrils elongated but didn't let go.

"Stars!" I took two rapid steps back the way we'd come. The tendrils maintained their hold.

"I'll get it!" Kaiden said, bringing back his arm to throw a fireball.

"No." I held up my hand. "If we start attacking, everything around us might go on the offensive."

I took several slow, cautious steps, and the tendrils continued to let me move, though the Darkness remained wrapped around my boots up to my ankles. "Look, it's not stopping me."

"We should just let it latch onto us?" Maris didn't look convinced.

Kaiden took a hesitant step into the patch of tendrils that had snagged me, and they flowed over the toes of his boots. "We might not have another choice."

Maris refreshed the protective shells around us, but the

new magical barrier appeared to have no effect on the tendrils or ground. "You're all out of your minds."

"Takes one to know one, Maris." I smirked.

She rolled her eyes and stepped forward into the now-writhing tangle of dark tendrils. "Just go already."

Without further delay, I continued toward the crystal monument, taking slow, gentle steps to avoid disturbing the ground too much. The tendrils seemed content to wrap around my feet and then move aside as new tendrils rose to take their place. I kept watch on the behavior as I pressed onward to make sure it wasn't getting any more aggressive.

Toran brought up the rear of our party, looking extremely concerned about the risky strategy. As the strongest of us, I'd expect him to be less worried about being snared by something as narrow as my pinky finger. Nonetheless, the strange properties of the Darkness were enough to put even the largest warriors on edge. And, despite his appearance, I needed to remind myself that Toran was an engineer and family man at heart, not a veteran fighter.

We shuffled our feet across the ground like we were wading through ankle-deep water. By the time we were thirty meters from our destination, the strange ground covering had wrapped us up to our knees. It took all my concentration to keep from panicking. So long as we could move, there was nothing to worry about... though that could change at a moment's notice.

"Almost there," I said. "Toran, you ready to hook into the control system?"

"Assuming it still works, yes," he confirmed.

The crystal monument loomed before us, standing nearly three stories. Though it should have been glowing blue, the crystal was now off-white and was filled with a swirling cloud of the dark particulates. Dark tendrils seemingly flowed out from the crystal, thickening and merging into the apparent energy conduits crisscrossing the landscape. What had once been a chrome enclosure surrounding the crystal with a touch-surface access panel was now dull black and beginning to crumble.

I scowled at it. "That doesn't look like it's in very good shape."

"It's not." Toran swung his pack forward on one shoulder so he could root around inside. He retrieved a screwdriver and proceeded to prod at the interface panel; the corroded metal flaked away. "These wires are shot."

"Dead end?" Kaiden asked, his brow tight with concern.

"Didn't say that." Toran dug deeper into the ruins. "The components next to the crystal still look functional—I need to cobble together a bypass around the typical interface protocol."

My concerns receded the slightest measure. "But it will work?"

"It should." He got out more tools and started chipping away at the corroded metal until the salvageable interior components were exposed.

There was nothing for us to do but wait. I moved my feet on occasion so the tendrils wouldn't work too far up my legs.

"This is so eerie," Kaiden said under his breath while he paced next to me.

"I'm kind of getting used to us being the only ones roaming around an alien world," I replied, trying to bring some levity to the situation.

"This was a thriving colony," Maris shot back. "We're not alone."

"There's no one here anymore, Maris," I said.

Her face reddened. "Those dark columns over there? I think those used to be people."

My heart skipped a beat. I'd been so focused on the ground and the crystal up ahead that I hadn't been paying attention to the other features in the surroundings. The columns Maris had pointed out had seemed like any of the other mass of dark tendrils stretching in every direction, but I could now make out the heads and shoulders atop the vertical shapes. They were posed in combat, some with arms up for an attack while others were bent over, shielding their heads with their arms. At first, I thought that they were defending the crystal. As we got closer and I was able to assess the arrangement, it instead appeared that they were in the process of fighting something coming *from* the crystal.

"I'm sorry, I didn't mean to diminish anyone's sacrifice," I murmured.

"Don't think about that now." Toran said.

Kaiden swallowed. "Everything is backed up in the Master Archive. That's the important thing."

"Let's focus on what we're doing now." Toran cast me a cautionary glance before pulling his interface equipment from his pack. I rarely saw strong emotion from him, and I definitely wasn't eager to be on the receiving end of a reprimand in the future.

I kept my distance while Toran continued to work. Not knowing what may be lurking in the Darkness around us, I rested my hand on my sword hilt, ready for action.

Kaiden shuffled over to stand next to me, then turned sideways so he was facing me while also being orientated away from Toran's and Maris' sightlines. "Everyone's on edge," he said over a private comm channel. "You didn't say anything wrong."

"I could have phrased it better," I replied over the same private link.

"Even so, Toran is having an especially rough go of it because today is his daughter's birthday."

My chest constricted. "Oh, I didn't know."

"He mentioned it to me while we were walking to breakfast. Don't say anything to him about it, but I thought that context might explain some things for you."

"Thanks."

Kaiden brushed his gloved hand down my arm. "Hang in there. We'll be back to the ship soon."

"Yeah." I glanced over my shoulder at Toran, who appeared to be finished hooking up his equipment. I switched to the general comm channel. "Were you able to access the crystal interface?" I asked.

The large man grunted. "Sort of. The connection is working, but I haven't been able to decipher the data logs."

"Will you be able to?" Kaiden asked.

"If this is just a security safeguard, then yes," Toran replied. "If it's because the data is corrupted, then there's nothing I can do."

I looked out at the Darkness swirling around us. I wasn't sure if my eyes were playing tricks on me, but I thought I saw movement in the shadows. "And how long before you know either way?"

"I have absolutely no idea, which I know isn't helpful," Toran replied. "It'll take as long as it takes."

"Can't fault honesty." I kept my attention on the place where I'd seen movement before. "Work as quickly as you can." I realized just how stupid the obvious statement sounded as soon as I heard it out loud, but no one called me on it.

Two minutes passed in the unnatural silence of the world. At last, Toran made a satisfied huff. "I think I'm finally getting somewhere."

I perked up. "Really? What have you found?"

"No specific *what* yet, but maybe part of a *how*," he replied. "It traces back to my vision."

"About how the Darkness spreads through the crystalline network?" Kaiden asked.

Toran nodded. "I believe I may have identified the signal that controls the Darkness' spread."

"That's huge!" I exclaimed. "Now we can counteract it, right?"

"Maybe eventually, but that would take so much more research that it's not worth thinking about yet."

My excitement faded. "Okay, what *do* we know, then?"

"I'm copying the records to a portable drive, but at first glance, this signal looks to have segments similar to the records used for crystal backups," Toran revealed.

"Wait, you know how to read the backups?" Kaiden interjected.

"I can't decode it myself, no," the other man clarified. "There are maybe three people alive who know enough about the storage medium to decipher a fraction of a backup record without the crystal interface. I've just seen enough interfaces to recognize the organizational structure of the code when I see it."

"That's weird that it's coded," I commented. "I always thoughts the records were a physical thing... You know, crystal-y."

"Yeah, me too," Maris agreed, looking over Toran's shoulder. "Really, can you even call that a 'code'?" She tilted her head.

Toran held up his tablet so I could see the contents of the screen. From a distance, it reminded me somewhat of a complex molecular model from chemistry class. "It's a code in the sense that it's an alphanumeric representation, though there's also a relationship component. Really, it's too complex for a person to understand—even super computers only know how to interact with the crystal storage medium, not recreate it."

"What does that mean for the Darkness—or alien tech, however we want to refer to it?" I questioned.

"I know too little to say," Toran replied.

"And if you had to guess?"

He hesitated. "My hunch is that this alien code taps into the crystalline network's reset ability and overwrites it with its own instructions to restructure the physical reality inside each crystal's zone."

I let the words sink in. "That's pretty out there, but it weirdly does explain everything."

"I don't like that hypothesis," Kaiden said. "That means that these aliens understand the tech on a level that is far beyond ours."

"Not liking the implications doesn't make it incorrect," Toran replied. "But, like I said, it's a wild guess."

I took a slow breath, sorting my thoughts. "This confirms some of the ideas we've been tossing around about what the Darkness is and its purpose, but that doesn't get us much closer to stopping it. We somehow need to trace where the signal is coming from."

"Well, I can tell you for sure that it's being sent via the crystalline network, so it's a planet somewhere in this galaxy," Toran replied.

"Narrowing it down to a whole galaxy, that *really* helps." I sighed.

Kaiden thought for a moment. "Come to think of it, does anyone actually know how big the crystalline network is?"

I shrugged. "No idea. Does the Hegemony have a map?"

Maris activated a comm link to the *Evangiel*. "Commander Colren," she greeted when the communication connected.

"Is everything okay?" the commander replied, sounding anxious through the static on the link.

"Ran into a bit of trouble, but we're unharmed," she continued. "We've reached the central crystal and are extracting the data logs now. Say, do you know about any sort of map of the crystalline network?"

He was silent for several seconds. "Why do you ask?"

"We need to trace a signal being transmitted via the network. Knowing how far-reaching it is might help us narrow down where it's coming from," Toran chimed in.

"We have a partial map, yes," Colren replied. "It was extracted from the Master Archive using the interface system on the *Evangiel*. Now that the Archive is sealed, though, there's no way to get updated records."

"A partial map is better than nothing," I said.

"Maybe, but I don't know how useful this one will be. There aren't any outer boundaries to the network—it's as expansive as known space," the commander clarified.

My sense of hope that had been building over the past several minutes crashed. "It really could be anywhere…"

"There might be answers buried in the signal," Toran said, his enthusiasm returning even as mine dwindled. "We won't know for sure until I get this data back to the *Evangiel*."

"Then get back here," the commander instructed. "I don't want the four of you down there for a second longer than necessary."

"Just another minute or two and this download will be complete," Toran acknowledged.

"We'll be waiting for you. Central Command out." Colren ended the commlink.

"One step forward, two back," I muttered.

"I don't know, we may have actually had a net gain of half a step forward with this one." Kaiden smiled.

Maris snorted. "This is really testing the definition of small victories."

"Yeah, I guess it's something to investigate, at least," I realized. "Leads are better than dead ends."

Kaiden nodded. "For sure."

Toran checked on the transfer. "We can be on our way soon. Just another minute or so until—" He cut off. "What's that over there?" He set down the tablet on the monument's edge and brought up his fists in a defensive pose.

I noticed the approaching figure a moment after him. The creature slinked through the black tendrils with the grace of a cat, one moment on four legs and the next on two. Its sleek pelt and powerful jaws reminded me of the creatures we'd encountered a week earlier after I'd retrieved my Valor artifact. Given that I'd watched those other creatures birthed, I could only draw one conclusion. "Is that what those things from the Valor world grow up to be?"

Kaiden readied a fireball. "An alien hybrid."

"This day just keeps getting better." Maris refreshed the protective shells around us.

"We need to hold it off for another minute," Toran said. "As soon as the transfer is complete, we can make a run for the shuttle."

"Yeah, except the ground might eat us," I pointed out.

The shadowcat snarled and bounded toward us, ending any hope of avoiding an engagement that might aggravate the vines.

Kaiden released a fireball as soon as the alien made its move. The blast struck the shadowcat in the center of its broad chest, but the creature barely missed a stride.

I ripped my legs free from the nest of vines as quickly as I could, not worried that I may aggravate them. I needed to move; my sword had proven to be one of the few effective weapons against similar shadowcreatures in the past.

Wading through the dark tendrils, I raised my blade, its magical blue flames rippling around the steel. After six strides, I was within striking distance. The shadowcat reared to maul me, and I ducked, thrusting my blade into the base of its ribcage and slashing downward.

The alien beast roared with pain and fury as it struggled to distance itself from my attack.

"Hit it now!" I shouted.

Fireballs launched from the end of Kaiden's staff as I ripped my blade free and dove to the side. I rolled over my left shoulder and jumped back to my feet to face the creature, which was still standing but looked weakened.

Kaiden struck it with an electrical attack, which branched into three separate beams to simultaneously hit its head, torso, and hindquarters. Smoke rose from the charred hide at the points of impact, and the creature swayed on its feet.

I needed to finish it off while it was stunned. I ran forward until I was a pace away, then swung my sword downward at the base of its skull. The flaming blade sliced clean through the flesh and what must have been the equivalent of bone in the alien hybrid. Its jaws flexed wide as it sucked in a dying breath. Knees buckling, it crumpled to the ground. The moment it fell, the black tendrils blanketing the ground began to encase it; within minutes, it would be nothing more than an unrecognizable mound.

I lowered my sword and released a relieved sigh. "I really hate these things."

6

"YOU OKAY?" KAIDEN asked me, lowering his staff.

"Didn't even touch me," I replied, checking myself over. It was then, however, that I realized my moves during the fight had foolishly exposed most of my suit to the infected ground. I quickly checked myself to make sure that none of the tendrils had latched onto my torso, and at least I seemed to be unscathed in that respect. What might happen to my suit remained to be seen.

I flicked my blade and then wiped it off using a cleaning cloth from a pouch next to my scabbard. "Are we ready to get out of here?"

"Yes, transfer just completed," Toran confirmed as he detached his equipment from the interface.

"Good, let's go." I shifted anxiously on my feet while Toran finished packing. Dark forms kept darting through the shadows around us. As much as I wanted to hope I was just on edge from the last engagement, I knew better; we were being hunted.

Once Toran had secured his equipment and the data backup in his pack, we began making our way back through the tendril-covered plaza at a steady pace. Though the way toward the monument had been easy going, I now found that the tendrils were beginning to tug more at my feet whenever I tried to take a step.

"Is anyone else feeling a little restricted here?" I asked.

"Then it's not just me." Kaiden frowned at his feet as he continued to plod forward. "I don't think it wants us to go."

"That might be the most disturbing thing I've heard all day—and there've already been some doozies." Maris shook her foot as one of the tendrils threatened to climb up her leg. In response, the vines already around her feet and ankles cinched tighter. "Agh!"

"Don't fight it!" I cautioned, trying to keep my own movements measured despite my pulse spiking. "Relax. See if they let go."

Maris paled, her breath quavering over the comm. "It's getting tighter."

"Shit." Kaiden glanced from Maris to the shuttle a hundred fifty meters away. The last two-thirds of that distance were relatively open ground, but we still had another fifty meters of the tendril field that now seemed intent on keeping us as part of its personal collection.

"I don't think we can make a run for it without turning this entire field against us," I said. "Let me see if I can cut it off. Keep moving."

I shuffled over to Maris with far more difficulty than I would have had even a minute prior.

Kaiden and Toran continued along the path to the shuttle, watching me over their shoulders.

"Stay calm," I told Maris when I reached her.

"Easy for you to say when a demon-plant isn't cutting off the circulation in your foot," she replied through gritted teeth. Terror filled her eyes in the light cast from the hazsuit's facemask.

I pointed my sword blade toward the ground and slowly pressed it through the knots of black tendrils at the side of Maris' right foot. The steel sliced straight through the vines, but they recoiled from each severed point and snapped back in an attempt to re-snare her legs. A new tendril snaked up her thigh.

Maris conjured a fireball in her palm. "Stand back, Elle."

"Maris, don't! This whole field might turn on us."

She looked me in the eyes through the facemask of her hazsuit. "It already has."

A beam of fire streamed from her palm toward the dark tendrils closing around her. I brought up my arm to shield my eyes against the blaze, regaining my vision just in time to see a wave of the black vines rising up before me.

I took a hasty step back and sliced at them with my blade. "Run!" I shouted to Kaiden and Toran, hating that we might fail in the mission after being so close to succeeding. It might be too late for Maris and me, but maybe the two men could make it back to the shuttle before they were snared.

Only, rather than the sound of receding footsteps, my attention was drawn by a fireball thrown by someone other than Maris. The orb hurtled past Maris, who was still desperately trying to beat back the vines attempting to weave their way around her.

"You missed!" she yelled at Kaiden.

"I wasn't aiming for you."

Then, behind Maris, I saw his intended target—a pride of six shadowcats slinking from the shadows of the city ruins.

Their expressionless black eyes were impossible to read, but their inky lips were curled back to reveal three rows of needlelike teeth.

"Great, that's all we need." I sliced the black vines at my feet and bolted back toward Maris.

She was still rooted to the ground, casting weak fireballs in an attempt to get free. "We're not going to make it." Her tone had gone from frightened to defeated, not a good sign.

"Don't even start." I glared at her. "Buck up and fight back. We're the heroes, remember?"

Maris worked her mouth while she no doubt searched for the right objection, but instead she nodded. "You're right. Screw this planet."

Our eyes met and I suddenly knew what we had to do; I couldn't explain where the feeling had come from, but Maris' eyes lit up. She cracked a smile. "Ready?" I asked on instinct.

"Do it."

I slashed my sword around her and she spun, simultaneously casting a continuous beam of fire from her hands. As the movements unfolded, I couldn't shake the feeling that we'd done it before, even though it hadn't occurred to me until a moment earlier. Wherever the idea came from, the move worked. My sword severed the bonds holding Maris in place, and the vines recoiled from the heat radiating from the flames. As Maris spun, she picked up her feet and jumped to a new patch where the vines appeared to be dormant; they certainly wouldn't stay that way for long, but a half-second delay was everything with the tools at our disposal.

My world tinted orange as Maris cast haste magic on our party. My own movements appeared in real-time to me, but everything except for my companions in the outside world now looked like it was moving in slow motion. The vines unfurled from the groundcover like a time-lapse video, and I carefully stepped around the tendrils slowly extending toward my feet.

"Stars, this would have been really handy earlier!" Kaiden exclaimed.

"Sorry, I was distracted," Maris replied, flushed. "Stop complaining and fight!"

Our banter ceased and two of the shadowcats parted from the others to circle around behind us. Their movements were swift, even with our altered perception from the haste magic. We wouldn't have any advantage, but this at least gave us a fighting chance.

I got into battle position. Just one of the shadowcats had proven to be a reasonable foe for our group, but I had my doubts about half a dozen. While physically I knew we could take them on, the real challenge came from six individual targets. We needed a way to keep them working together as a unit so we didn't have too many separate fronts to track.

"Maris and Kaiden, keep those four distracted," I ordered. "Toran, those two will be coming up behind us. We can't let them catch us by surprise."

"Okay, we'll try," Kaiden acknowledged.

I wanted to correct him that 'try' wasn't an option, but I decided that went without saying. We were about to fight for our lives, and we all knew it.

With our backs to Kaiden and Maris, Toran and I arranged ourselves so we'd have full visibility of the area around us; there was no way the two shadowcats could sneak up behind us without us knowing. One of them was bound to make a move at any moment, we just had to wait.

Except, nothing happened.

"Where are they?" I asked in a low voice when thirty

seconds had passed with no sighting.

"I don't know," Toran replied.

"How long are we supposed to distract these things?" Kaiden called out.

I kept my feet moving to avoid being snared. "Until these two aren't behind us."

He grunted "Well, these four are getting impatient."

It didn't make any sense. The other shadowcat had pounced on us the moment we saw it. Why had these two disappeared?

The orange tint faded from my vision, the haste spell having expired. "Maris, time to—"

My vision spun and a sharp pain radiated from my right shoulder. I struck the ground, my vision black as tendrils washed over me in one horrifying wave. My arms were bound by the vines in an instant. I was trapped.

Heat radiated above me. I couldn't see it, but I could feel two taloned paws pinning my shoulders to the ground. The shadowcat's jaws must have been centimeters from my face. "It's got me!" I shouted into my comm, not sure that anyone would hear me or know where I'd fallen. I needed to free myself.

My arms felt impossibly heavy with the vines wrapped around them, but I yanked my sword hand with all my might. The vines had just enough give to free it a little, and then I used the slack to see the movement through the rest of the way. I pivoted my wrist as much as I could to stab the end of my blade upward into where the shadowcat's abdomen should be based on it pinning me with its front legs. Unable to raise my shoulder, I knew the attack would be weak, but the flaming blade of the sword would do the work for me.

Just as the blade met resistance, the world tinted orange

around me again. The weight released from my shoulders and I sat upright. As I rose, some of the tendrils that had covered my facemask fell away, and I saw the shadowcat stumbling backward, viscous black blood spurting from a wound in its side. Amazingly, I'd hit it right where I'd intended.

A smile played on my lips. "You messed with the wrong group." I leaped to my feet, slicing back the vines around me to keep them at bay.

The shadowcat I'd wounded snarled, but when it tried to lunge toward me once more, it stumbled. I took the opportunity to deal it a lethal blow, severing its head at the base of the skull like I'd done with the first. Its lifeless body collapsed, the pool of blood invisible amid the bed of vines.

"Well, that wasn't so bad." No one replied to my quip. I pivoted to face my friends and was horrified to see that four shadowcats were racing toward Maris and Kaiden while Toran was gripped in the talons of the fifth.

My heart dropped. I couldn't aid in both defenses at the same time. Toran was closer to me, but I also had more faith that he'd be able to beat the solitary shadowcat into submission. A fight of four against two—especially given Maris' weak offensive capabilities—was where I was needed the most.

I bounded across the intervening terrain, still under the influence of the haste magic. Kaiden's and Maris' fireballs appeared to have almost no effect on the attacking shadowcats. The creatures' movements were almost as quick as ours, but I could still close the distance in time.

"Jump clear!" I shouted when I was right behind Kaiden and Maris.

They looked over their shoulders, then quickly took a step to the side as I charged past them.

"What are you—" Kaiden started to ask.

In response, I jumped over the head of the middle shadowcat and flipped midair. When I was directly above it, I plunged my sword into its back and used it as a pivot point to kick the shadowcat on its left, and then swung back around to the right. As I completed the rotation, I removed the sword, bringing it around at an angle to decapitate the other middle shadowcat as I flew horizontally through the air. I didn't have enough momentum to repeat the move on the fourth, but I was able to embed the tip of my blade as I passed over its back, opening up a gash that stretched from its shoulder to the center of its ribcage on the other side.

I landed on my side and then rolled up to my feet in one motion. By the time I was upright, the first shadowcat I'd stabbed had fallen to the ground and was disintegrating, and the decapitated creature was already halfway turned to soot. The remaining two shadowcats looked worse for wear but were still standing.

"Holy shit…" Kaiden whispered in stunned disbelief.

"Don't just stand there!" I lunged back for the shadowcat nearest me, which I'd slashed across its back. Just as I made my move, the orange tint faded from the world around me, along with the protective purple shell.

The shadowcat seemed to sense the change, and it rose on its two rear legs, bearing its teeth and flashing the dark talons on its front paws. I thought it was just a display at first, but then it compressed its hindquarters and sprung toward me. I tried to dodge it, but the talons had latched onto me before I fully registered the movement. The hazsuit's fabric ripped. I sensed pressure on my back, but there wasn't the searing pain of the nails in my flesh that I expected to follow; my coat beneath the hazsuit had done its job once again. The shadowcat, however, wasn't deterred by the thin fabric.

It snapped at my facemask, wrapping its jaws around the transparent plastic. The faceplate fogged from its warm breath and smeared with slobber. Rancid air leaked in through the tear in my hazsuit's shoulder. There was no telling it if would hasten the corruptive properties of the world on my equipment, but at least there was still oxygen I could breathe.

I struggled to get my arm into position to stab at the beast, but my sword was too tangled in the tendrils covering the ground for me to get it free from my current position. Instead, I kicked up with my right knee, aiming for the wound in its side. I couldn't connect. I was pinned, and it was only a matter of time before the creature broke through my remaining defenses.

A sudden glow of energy surged through me, and I balled my right hand into a fist to punch at the creature. As I brought my hand up, my eyes snapped shut on reflex as a fireball smashed into the shadowcat's side. I opened my eyes to see Kaiden holding his staff. Several seconds earlier would have been nice, but I appreciated his help all the same.

The shadowcat recoiled from the fireball, loosening its hold on me just enough to roll free. The tendrils on the ground slithered over me, and I bolted to my feet as quickly as possible to keep them from getting any purchase. As I stood, I noticed that my three companions had disposed of the other shadowcat already, leaving us the one final foe.

Kaiden launched a series of fireballs at the shadowcat as soon as I was out of range, and it cried out. When he paused his attacks, I made my move to end the fight.

I took a running leap toward the beast and flipped over it, swinging my sword at its neck as I passed overhead. The shadowcat shuddered, its legs buckling. I landed on my feet on its other side as it started to dissolve into soot.

"Just like that!" I cheered. But my celebration only lasted for a moment.

The ground covering, which had remained fairly subdued during the fight, now looked intent on finishing what the shadowcats had been unable to do. The tendrils had all straightened up to almost waist-level, and they were reaching for us.

"Run!" Kaiden shouted, casting a solid stream of fire from his palm in an arc around us. The tendrils shrank back just enough to leave a path. He took the lead, clearing the way, the intentions of making a quiet retreat now a distant memory.

I took the third position after Maris, with Toran at the rear. I kept enough distance between myself and Maris to hack at the tendrils with my sword after Kaiden thrust them back. We ran at full speed toward the relative safety of the open area around the shuttle. Just another twenty meters to go.

The tendrils tugged at my ankles, but I wasn't about to let anything stop me. I checked over my shoulder to make sure Toran was safe, and he nodded to me.

We were almost to the end of the black field. The ground covering was shorter and sparser now, allowing Kaiden to ease up his flame attack. After another ten meters, we were free from the last of the tendrils.

Maris let out a relieved chuckle. "And *that's* why I didn't want to come with you."

Toran patted his backpack over his shoulder. "We got what we came for."

"Yeah, but I expect the rest of this world will turn on us at any moment." I looked back at where we'd come from. The tendrils were still writhing on the ground, and some were beginning to snake toward us.

Kaiden continued running in the direction of the shuttle. "What are you waiting for?"

We picked up our pace and closed the final hundred meters to the craft. Kaiden was the first to arrive, and he halted two meters from the back airlock.

I stopped short when I saw the look of horror on Kaiden's face. "What's wrong?" I asked.

He pointed at black pits in the shuttle's thermal plating. "We have another problem."

7

"NO! IT CAN'T have corroded this quickly." My stomach turned over.

"I don't know what to tell you." Kaiden took an unsteady breath.

Maris gulped. "Is it flyable?"

Kaiden shrugged. "No clue. It might be superficial damage, or there might be no structural integrity whatsoever."

Toran cautiously approached the craft. "As long as the support structure is intact, it will be space-worthy. We'll just need pressurized suits."

"Are the hazsuits enough?" Kaiden asked.

"Perhaps, for a short time, but the emergency EVA suits would be better."

I pointed at the tear in my shoulder. "I'll definitely need one of those."

Kaiden's eyes widened. "Elle! Why didn't you say you were hurt?"

"I just did. I've been a little preoccupied with not dying. And, I'm not hurt—just my suit."

"That means you're contaminated directly, not just the outer layer," Toran said.

I shrugged. "I already took off my suit once inside. We lost containment a long time ago."

Toran took a slow breath a nodded. "We'll deal with it once we're back on the *Evangiel*. Come on."

He opened the exterior airlock hatch and beckoned us inside. We squeezed in, and Kaiden cycled the interior airlock. The door opened with a hiss.

"I'll get it started up and see what kind of damage we're facing," Kaiden said, rushing toward the bridge. He began stripped off the hazsuit.

"Maris, help me with the EVA suits. They should be in storage back here," Toran instructed.

"I'll help Kaiden with the inspection," I said and followed him toward the bridge. I paused in the common area to remove the hazsuit, then jogged the rest of the way to the front of the vessel.

Kaiden was seated in the pilot's chair and was busy looking over the preliminary system scans. "...Yes, Commander. Understood." He ended the comm link.

"What's the word?" I asked.

He didn't glance up from his work. "It's not looking good."

"Was that Colren? Is he sending help?"

"I told him to hold off. We have a shot at being able to achieve orbit even with the damage; the reduced gravity works in our favor."

"I'm sorry I got us into this," I mumbled.

"We needed that information. It was worth the risk."

"But we haven't gotten it back to them."

He shook his head. "We have a datalink. Central Command is waiting for an upload."

"That's great the data will be safe, but *I* don't want to get stuck here," I replied. "Things were just starting to get good."

"Me either."

"But if this shuttle is too damaged, they can send another, right?"

He didn't respond.

"Right, Kaiden?" I pressed.

"That's what I was talking about with Colren. I had to manually pilot us down here. I don't know that the automated systems could do it. Any pilot without our resistance to the Darkness would likely only last a few minutes here, even with protective gear, based on what Colren said."

"So, even *if* they could make it here, it'd be a one-way trip."

"Yeah. Let's hope it doesn't come to that."

I'd never placed one life at a higher value than any other, but when it came down to it, we have unique skills that would be difficult to replicate. I had no doubt that Colren would send someone to their death if it meant saving us, and I didn't want that on my conscience. "Is there anything I can do to help you?" I asked.

"I'm getting a warning error on the amidships starboard bulkhead next to the side hatch. See if there's any corrosion visible on the inside yet," he replied.

"I'm on it." I headed back toward the corridor, then paused and turn around. "We're going to get out of here, Kaiden."

He glanced back at me. "I know we will."

I returned to the common room to find Toran and Maris donning EVA suits. "Good, you found them!"

Toran moved stiffly in his, the outfit far too tight on his broad frame. "They'll keep us alive, provided the ship can fly."

"Kaiden thinks we have a shot," I replied. "He said we still have a datalink, so you can upload the info you pulled from the crystal."

"Oh, good. I'll do that right away." Toran rushed toward the bridge.

"Did Kaiden talk to Central Command? Are they sending a replacement shuttle?" Maris asked.

"That's complicated," I replied. "Short answer is that we're on our own until we have no other options."

Maris frowned. "But won't we not know this one isn't space-worthy until we're, you know, up in space?"

"That's my worry, too."

"I mean, these suits are just a precaution, right? We won't actually need them inside the shuttle…"

I didn't want to lie to her, so I instead turned my attention to the bulkhead Kaiden had sent me to inspect. "Just make sure your suit is sealed, Maris. We'll be fine."

The other woman worked her mouth. "I really shouldn't have gotten out of bed this morning."

"You're tellin' me." I turned my attention to the problem bulkhead. Leaning in until I was only a few centimeters away, I looked for any signs of the dark corrosion we'd witnessed outside.

My initial assessment didn't reveal any concerning patches, and I was almost ready to breathe a sigh of relief. Then, I noticed a dark area with small pits in the metal at the base of the hatch. "Uh oh."

"No. No 'uh ohs'!" Maris exclaimed while she hurriedly donned her suit.

"Would you prefer 'that doesn't look good'?"

Her face flushed. "How screwed are we?"

"I don't know." I turned toward the bridge. "Toran, how important is the starboard-side bulkhead?"

There was only silence for several seconds, then the rapid thud of footsteps. Toran came into view down the corridor.

"What did you find?"

I pointed to the problem patch.

He approached and crouched down, frowning at it. "This might be superficial or the interior of these walls might be as brittle as charcoal."

"Yeah, that's what I was afraid you'd say." I took a steadying breath. "I didn't see anything else over here, but I haven't looked over the rest of the shuttle."

"Well, conditions are guaranteed to deteriorate. We should probably try to take off while we still have functional engines," he replied.

"We're all going to die," Maris moaned.

I cast her a silencing glance. "No, we're not."

"Finish suiting up," Toran instructed. "The upload will be complete in two minutes."

"That's way faster than it downloaded from the crystal," I said with surprise.

"This connection actually works properly."

Maris took a deep breath. "I'll try to cast a shield around the shuttle in the meantime." She clasped her crystal pendant in her left hand and closed her eyes.

I bit my tongue to keep from questioning her about why she didn't do that the moment we got back; it hadn't even occurred to me, but it wasn't my responsibility to do her job for her. Instead, I turned my attention to putting on the EVA suit.

The garment was, thankfully, straightforward to secure, even for a novice spacefarer like me. However, as I brought it over my right shoulder, which had taken the brunt of the shadowcat attack, I had to hold back a grimace of discomfort. While I was used to having limited shoulder mobility, it was always my left arm; to be injured on the other side was disorienting and annoying. I was fairly confident that I was only banged up, though, and the discomfort would be temporary.

By the time I was finished dressing, the upload was complete and we were ready to go. I sealed everything below my neck, then picked up the helmet and returned to my seat on the bridge to strap in.

"All sensors indicate we have structural integrity," Kaiden announced over the front speaker on his EVA suit.

I clicked my helmet into the neck collar and switched to the interior comms. "This is the part where we ignore the maybe-hole back there, isn't it?"

He kept his gaze straight ahead. "Yep."

"Nothing could possibly go wrong." I tightened my restraints.

"Let's get out of here." Kaiden made the final necessary entries on the front control panel, and the shuttle lifted off the ground.

"So far, so good." Maris sounded more cheerful than she had all day.

Toran and Kaiden remained silent, watching the readouts on their respective stations. I kept my gloved fingers wrapped around the end of my armrests while I focused on staying calm.

When we were at an elevation of five hundred meters, the comm chirped, indicating an incoming call.

"Glad to see you're off the ground. Wishing you a safe return flight," Colren said.

"Thank you," Kaiden acknowledged.

"We're already recoding the data you gathered," Colren continued. "It's invaluable."

"Glad to hear it. I look forward to reviewing it myself," responded Toran.

"We'll see you soon." The commander ended the link.

"That totally felt like he was calling to say goodbye," Maris said.

I rolled my eyes. "Everything's fine. We're off the ground—that was the hard part."

Kaiden glanced over at me, his expression telling me that wasn't the case.

"What else is there?" I prompted.

"I haven't kicked in the main boosters yet to get us up to the *Evangiel*'s orbit altitude."

My stomach dropped. "That's what will stress the structure."

"Yeah." He took a slow breath. "We're about to find out if it will hold." He activated the controls.

Sudden pressure pinned me against the back of my seat. I ran through the scenarios in my head for what I'd do if the shuttle started to fall apart around me, contriving an epic plan to leap from the doomed craft and somehow make it safely to the ground, where I'd defeat any enemies that dared to mess with me. In reality, I figured that if anything went wrong, we'd be goners before we realized what'd happened.

Even as my mind raced with disastrous possibilities, there was no sign of trouble. Once we made it past the first critical minute of the boost and the pressure eased, I started to relax. "So far, so good."

Kaiden nodded, but he was still tense. "We're entering the upper atmosphere now. We should be past the worst of it."

"I don't like what I'm seeing on some of these structural readings," Toran chimed in. "This isn't my area of expertise, but some of the integrity measures are getting close to their warning levels."

I was even less of an expert, but Toran's tone told me

everything I needed to know: we were in trouble.

My heart thudded in my chest as the EVA suit closed in around me. If the hull failed, the suit's thin fabric would be the only thing separating me from the void. "What do we do?" I asked, panic pitching my voice.

"It might be fine. Hang on," Kaiden replied. His own tone was still calm and level, but his frantic movements belied inner worry.

Through the front viewport, the planet's atmosphere dissipated, and pinpoints of light from distant stars greeted us.

"We're almost to the *Evangiel*, right?" I asked tentatively.

"Yeah, out of the atmosphere—they can pick us up?" Maris added.

Kaiden and Toran remained silent.

"*Right*?" I emphasized.

"We're out of the atmosphere, but we're still in the gravity well," Kaiden said at last. "I don't know how much maneuvering I'll be able to do before we lose structural integrity."

"The corroded components are right around the mid starboard thruster," Toran explained. "It's the main boost we need for landing. If it fails while we're coming in, part of the infected material could break off and hit the ship. Without being able to decontaminate it properly..."

My chest constricted further. "What are you saying?"

Toran took a shaky breath. "It's too dangerous to land, but if we don't land soon, the shuttle will fall back to the planet's surface and we'll be stuck for good, assuming we don't burn up in the process."

"No. Nope." Maris shook her head, squeezing her eyes shut.

I looked to Kaiden. "There has to be another way."

His gaze flitted between the shuttle controls and out the

viewport. "Maybe."

"What do you have in mind?" Toran asked.

Kaiden swallowed. "We can't use the maneuvering thrusters too much, but I may be able to feather them enough to get us *close* to the hangar entry."

I tightened my grip on my armrests. "Close enough to land?"

"No. Close enough to make a jump for it."

"You *have* to be joking!" Maris exclaimed.

"There's still risk of contaminating the outer hull of the *Evangiel*," Toran pointed out.

"Not if we're coordinating with them," Kaiden countered. "They just need to pull away to avoid the craft colliding—that's way easier to avoid than thousands of tiny fragments from the ship disintegrating."

"This is completely insane," I muttered under my breath.

"Well, we either make a break for it or let the ship fall apart around us. Want to vote?" Kaiden asked.

"I don't think there's any room for contention," Toran replied. "Are you thinking the side starboard hatch?"

The other man nodded. "Angles wouldn't work with the rear airlock."

"But the corroded area is around the side hatch!" I looked over my shoulder at Toran. "Won't it—"

"There's a way to work the angles and approach so the hatch and debris will eject away from the *Evangiel*," Toran said. "The nav computer can handle the calculations and piloting."

I shook my head. "It couldn't possibly have been designed to do that."

"It was, actually." Kaiden's hands raced over the controls. "All sorts of emergency evacuation procedures are embedded in the system. We almost crashed one time as a kid and the disaster protocols saved us."

My mind raced, trying to think of any other way to get out of the predicament. But I couldn't kid myself. I knew nothing about what we were facing, only that I wanted to live. I had no choice but to trust the opinion of the two people on my team who knew what they were talking about when it came to ships.

"Tell us what to do," I said.

"Stars! This can't be happening," Maris moaned.

"Seals on your suits are good?" Kaiden asked. He began to gently turn the shuttle toward the *Evangiel*.

"Yeah," I confirmed, followed by acknowledgments from Maris and Toran.

"Okay, unstrap and brace yourselves in the common room," Kaiden instructed. He hit the comm controls while I released my harness. "Commander, we have a situation."

I worked my way down the short corridor while Kaiden briefed Central Command on what we were planning. I listened in on the conversation, though I glazed over when they got into the technical jargon. To my surprise, the commander supported the proposed approach, agreeing that it was too risky for the shuttle to make contact with the larger ship given its level of contamination. It would be left to burn up on reentry into the atmosphere where the Darkness would claim it.

They rapidly completed the planning, and Kaiden made the necessary entries to the nav system to enable Central Command to remotely control the shuttle. He joined us in the common room, his face drawn with worry. "I know this sounds nuts, but it's going to be fine."

"I've never been in a spacesuit. This—"

Kaiden gripped my shoulders. "You've got this, Elle."

I looked out the side viewport at the *Evangiel* rapidly approaching. "It's so far away."

"It won't be by the time we make our move. Just consider it hands-on training for that Tactical School you were so eager to attend," he shot back with a forced smile.

"Well, *I* didn't want to be a Ranger," Maris said, it almost turning into a wail.

"Put that worry to good use and conjure us up a protective shield," Toran suggested.

"Hey, I'll take anything." I hugged myself. But, another thought broke me from the worries about my mortality. "Stars! Our gear."

When we'd donned the EVA suits, I'd set down my Valor artifact sword and my other armor, thinking that it would be safe in the common room until we landed. However, if we were to abandon the shuttle, the items would be lost with it. A quick glance at Toran confirmed that he'd, likewise, set down his gauntlets. Only Kaiden had been able to wear his artifact—the delicate, silver circlet, inside his EVA suit's helmet.

"Forget about the clothes, just get the artifacts," Toran said, racing toward his gauntlets.

I ran for my sword. Just as I took my first steps, the shuttle lurched. I stumbled sideways, and Kaiden caught my arm. "What was that?"

"Shit! The thruster didn't fire how it was supposed to," he replied, looking at our approach out the viewport.

"Shuttle 1," a female voice said over our ear comms, "we'll compensate for your flight path. We'll get you. Don't worry."

"Right, 'don't worry'!" I finished my dive for the sword and wrapped the scabbard's waist strap around my hand. "Really helpful."

Toran grabbed his gauntlets and shoved them inside his backpack. He looped the pack's straps around his arm. "Better than 'you're probably going to die, but good luck anyway'."

Maris gaped at us. "You're all terrible!"

"Look at us, still bantering even in the face of death." I couldn't help cracking a smile.

"Yep, we've officially lost our minds." Kaiden shook his head.

The shuttle lurched again, and I stumbled back toward where I'd been bracing against the port bulkhead. "When is this thing happening?"

"Any second," Kaiden murmured, keeping his attention out the viewport. "The *Evangiel* is turning now."

"But, what's the plan?" Maris asked. "We're just leaping from here to the ship, or…?"

Kaiden shook his head. "Not exactly. We'll blow the side hatch, and the sudden pressure change will suck us out. If we've timed everything right, that will put us on a trajectory to pass through the electrostatic shield into the hangar, and then the *Evangiel* can pull away from the contaminated shuttle."

"Then we get scrubbed down along with all of our stuff?" I completed.

"That's the idea."

I eyed him. "You're making it sound too easy."

"Am I? Sounds pretty tricky to me," he replied.

"But totally doable, right?" Maris pressed.

Kaiden shifted on his feet. "Yes, absolutely."

I wanted to call him out for lying to our faces, but I figured that wouldn't do anyone any good. The commander had signed off on the plan, so that meant it was the best course of action under the circumstances. "Just tell me when to let go and I'll follow." I said.

Kaiden took my hand in his. "Get ready."

KAIDEN AND I gripped handholds along the bulkhead in our free hands and prepared to make our move. Toran and Maris also took each other's hands for extra stability, and Maris cast a purple shell around us to hopefully offer added protection against debris or radiation the EVA suits might not shield against.

After a tense forty seconds, we finally got the signal from Central Command over our comms. "Remotely releasing the hatch in three... two... one... breach!"

My perception tinted orange around me, and I realized a haste spell had been cast the moment the countdown ended. The hatch across the shuttle from me released in slow motion, sending a cloud of oxygen into the void as the common room rapidly depressurized. Kaiden let go of his handhold and allowed the pressure change to suck him toward the opening. Reluctantly, I released my own handhold and we careened toward the opening. Toran and Maris were only a meter behind, and the four of us flew into the open void.

With my altered perception, I was able to take in the unobstructed view of space for the brief moment I passed between the shuttle and the *Evangiel*. The stars were even brighter than they seemed from inside a craft, and for that instant I felt the true vastness of space. I was a speck in the universe. Yet, my purpose made me an important speck, and I needed to do everything I could to survive.

Our course was true as we hurtled across the void toward the large ship. The shimmering gold of the electrostatic field raced toward me. Kaiden's firm grasp offered my only sense of grounding as I cartwheeled on an uncontrolled vector through the barrier. The energy passed over me in a wave and bright light assaulted my eyes.

Artificial gravity kicked in the moment I passed all the way through, pulling me toward the hangar floor—which happened to be above me based on my awkward entry angle. I thudded to the deck face-first. Kaiden released my hand the moment before impact, allowing me to catch myself a little and absorb the worst of the fall.

Cries of surprise and relieved chuckles sounded over the comms as my teammates settled on the deck. We carefully rose and checked ourselves over.

"Everyone all right?" Toran asked.

Remarkably, the event had left me no worse for wear. "I'm alive. That's good enough for me," I said.

Maris brushed herself off. "I am *never* doing that again."

"I don't know, it wasn't that bad." Kaiden cracked a smile.

I raised an eyebrow. "You really do have a hero complex, don't you?"

He shrugged. "I mean, I suppose it was me who got us back here safely."

"Right, yeah, the Central Command crew had nothing to

do with that."

"Elle," he leveled his gaze on me, "I'm just messing with you. This was a team effort."

I popped off my helmet and brushed my hair back from my face. "Right, sorry. Guess I'm still on edge."

Toran smiled. "We accomplished our mission. We got the data we set out to retrieve."

"We should go—" I cut myself off as I looked down at my EVA suit. We still needed to go through decontamination. The tents where we'd need to scrub down were waiting for us on the other side of the hangar.

"Are you okay?" Tami shouted from my left.

I turned to face her. "Think so."

The engineer stopped seven meters from us. "Were you... exposed?"

"Unavoidable," Toran replied.

She nodded. "All right, you know the drill."

I began stripping down to my white base layer shipsuit. "Yep."

Kaiden pressed behind his ear while he started to undress. "Commander," said to the comm, "we're back on board. We'll come see you as soon as we've finished the decontamination procedure."

"Glad all of you made it back," Colren replied in our ears. "I want a full med eval, as well. We're working through the data you gathered and should have a summary of the preliminary findings to share once you've finished."

"Okay, see you soon," I acknowledged.

We filed into the decontamination booths and completed the scrub-down. It was just as unpleasant as I remembered, but I gladly took it over the chance of having some of the corrosive Darkness remaining on me. Unlike the previous time in the booth, however, duplicates of our custom-sized shipsuits were waiting for us. After dressing, we were directed from the decontamination booths into a temporary medical examination area next to it. A nurse looked me over inside the tent, pausing on some bruises forming on my limbs and torso from the fights, but everything checked out to her satisfaction.

When I emerged from my medical screening, Kaiden was waiting for me. "You have a radiant glow about you again," he teased.

"You too. I think this time the chemical scrub took off an extra layer."

"We were right up in it on the planet. I won't complain about anything that keeps the Darkness far away from us."

I nodded. "Think we'll finally be able to get answers about what it is and where it's from?"

"Stars, I hope so! The longer this drags on, the more antsy I get." He crossed his arms.

Toran emerged from the tent next. "I would like to second Maris' vote to avoid corrupted worlds in the future."

"If that information is as good as you made it sound, we won't have to," Kaiden replied.

"Here's hoping," Maris said as she stepped out from the tent, her hair still perfectly styled through some mysterious magic she'd no doubt deny using.

"Let's get up to Central Command and find out," I suggested.

Kaiden held out his arm for me to lead the way.

The bridge crew snapped to attention as soon as we arrived. They'd always examined us with curiosity, but this was one of the rare moments that their professional regard bordered on awe. We'd just successfully come back from a planet that would have destroyed anyone else. While part of me appreciated the attention, it was awkward to be idolized for something I didn't have any control over. We had been called to fulfill our role—that didn't make us special, we were just performing our duty.

Colren beamed at us from next to his seat at the center of the bridge. "Welcome back. I'm almost willing to forgive you for disobeying our agreement considering what you managed to retrieve."

My cheeks flushed slightly. "Sorry about that."

"It's done now. Let's talk in the conference room." The commander led us into our standard meeting space, then took a seat on the far side of the table.

The four of us sat down facing him with Kaiden and me in the center.

I folded my forearms on the tabletop and leaned forward. "Did you get anything good from the data Toran extracted?"

Colren nodded. "We're still working through exactly what it means, but the preliminary findings are promising."

"What have you learned?" Toran asked.

"Well, the signal embedded in the data is quite curious." Colren tapped on the touch-surface tabletop and an ethereal melody began to play. Underneath the enticing tones was a dissonant hum that caused everyone at the table to scowl. The commander silenced the recording and continued. "At first we thought it was a specific set of instructions, like a looping set of orders. But when the techs looked deeper, they realized that there were actually multiple layers to the signal."

Kaiden tilted his head. "In what way?"

"Well, there does appear to be a high-level message on one layer, but there's also a complex code we were able to pick up from other parts of the world that were well outside the vicinity of the crystal you accessed. In some manner, it appears to be a control system for the Darkness."

Toran nodded. "I suspected that might be the case."

"How did you arrive at that?" the commander asked.

"Based on how everything behaves on infected worlds, I thought maybe the Darkness was tapping into the crystal's unique properties—to use them as a means to re-form a world." Toran spread his hands on the table. "Now, I can't be certain that's how the crystals work, but that's been the prevailing hypothesis."

I hadn't fully processed what Toran had said down on the planet's surface, but now that I didn't have the black tendrils snaking up my leg, I allowed the words to properly sink in. "What are you saying... that a reset is actually rearranging matter?"

"As far as anyone can tell, yes," Toran replied.

"How?" Kaiden asked.

Toran bowed his head. "Scientists have debated that for decades—arguing everything from nanotech to a controlled release of hyperdimensional energy. The important part has always been the outcome, not the mode. However, if the Darkness is interrupting the process and inserting its own variations for how to restructure the environment, then we might need to dive deeper."

Matter rearrangement. I'd always taken the crystalline network for granted, never thinking about what actually happened during a reset. Having it spelled out, though, it all made so much more sense—why materials needed to remain within the crystal's zone in order to come through after a reset. It wasn't so much that the raw material needed to be the same, as I was certain state changes happened, but there needed to be enough material and energy present for the crystals to recreate the physical state from when the reset point was set.

What still didn't make any sense to me, though, was why an alien race would want to tap into that process to alter a world, let alone how they could accomplish such a feat. It was clear they had access to ancient technology that was well beyond our comprehension, so that would suggest they would have the firepower to wipe our worlds if they saw fit. Why go to the trouble to taking worlds one by one through the Darkness?

Commander Colren seemed to have similar thoughts as he leaned back in his chair with steepled fingers. "What might the aliens want with these worlds?"

"Clearly, they want us gone," Maris said.

"Yeah, that much is obvious," I agreed. "Everything on those worlds is designed to kill us."

"But maybe not intentionally," Kaiden chimed in.

Colren tilted his head. "Go on."

"Well," Kaiden continued, "I tend to look at everything the way I would with an agricultural problem. There's the natural state of the world, and then there's what happens when some outside force starts directing the natural progression—like when there's an infection. For example, a virus that attacks blood cells isn't trying to kill the host, per se; rather, it is trying to redirect the hosts' resources to fulfill a different role. Though that can result in death, that wasn't the virus' specific aim. I think the Darkness may operate in a similar fashion."

"Like the animals," I realized. "Not all of them died. Some were transformed into those other creatures that attacked us."

He nodded. "Exactly. And the plant life and other things turned to soot, but then new forms took their place. It might not be intended as an attack, but rather some sort of bio-optimization."

"Perhaps transforming the worlds to match the aliens'

preferred habitat?" Colren posited.

"That's my best guess," Kaiden replied. "Especially since the gravity of the planets has been altered somehow. I can't think of another explanation that covers all the things we've observed."

"The ships," Toran murmured.

The commander's brow furrowed. "Pardon?"

"In Kaiden's vision, there were ships," he explained. "If they've been preparing these worlds for habitation, then…"

"Eventually the beings themselves will come," I completed for him. A chill gripped me as I thought through the implications. We weren't just up against the faceless Darkness—an entire invasion force of unknown beings might be coming for us.

Colren snapped to attention. "We have little chance of standing up to an adversary we know nothing about—especially one with the kind of skills these aliens seem to possess."

"We must be able to learn more from the code," Toran said. "Trace it to an origin."

The commander made several entries on the touch-surface tabletop, and a holographic star map appeared above it. "The techs have been unable to trace its origin, but they did observe something interesting. The full code has never been recorded before, but when it was broken down into its components, they realized that part of the signal had appeared on the other worlds."

"All parts, or only some of them?" Toran asked.

"There wasn't an apparent pattern," the commander replied.

Toran held out his hand toward the holographic model. "May I?"

Colren inclined his head with assent.

"Where do you have the data stored?" Toran asked.

The commander navigated to a directory, and then Toran began sifting through the information displayed on the tabletop in front of him.

I leaned over Kaiden to watch him work, but it was all foreign codes and graphs that made no sense to me. To my left, Maris took one glance and then leaned back in her chair with a mystified sigh.

After two minutes, Toran's hands stilled. "That's curious."

"What is?" Colren prompted.

"The fragments of the signals you recorded—there isn't a pattern, exactly, but there are two instances of some of the same code segments." Toran's brow knit as he stared at the data. "It may well be that duplicates of other segments of this full pattern may appear at other locations in the future."

I massaged my temple. "You mean, the signal was broken into pieces, and each world has one part of that larger signal?"

"Sort of. Rather, there are six instances where the same signal segment appears on two different worlds."

"Adjacent locations?" Colren speculated.

Toran shook his head. "Quite far apart, by the look of it. Let's see how they map." He manipulated the star map to display each of the locations of infected worlds with lines drawn between the six worlds that had emitted a signal that duplicated part of the full pattern they had retrieved.

As soon as the red lines were in place, it was clear the seemingly random arrangement of impacted worlds wasn't so random at all—the lines all intersected through a single point two systems over from Yantu, Maris' homeworld. I had no doubt where the other lines would pass if the worlds with no duplicated signal-segment had their doppelgängers identified.

"What's over there?" I asked.

Maris shook her head slowly. "Nothing. It's empty space."

"This arrangement is too consistent and widespread to be a coincidence. I can't believe we missed it," Colren murmured.

"In all fairness, you've only had this data for, what, half an hour?" Kaiden said. "Toran has spent more time analyzing signals related to the crystals than anyone else on the ship."

"It was a lucky, educated guess." Toran took a deep breath. "The relationship between the worlds is certainly clearer now, but I have no hypothesis to offer about the significance of that intersecting location."

The commander crossed his arms. "It's important in some way—I can't imagine any other reason why these paths would all converge in the same place."

"Could there be a planet there we don't know about?" Kaiden asked. "The source of the signal?"

Toran zoomed in on the location using the holographic display. True to Maris' assertion, there was nothing nearby.

"Maybe it's so corrupted by the Darkness we can't see it?" I suggested.

"Perhaps." Colren nodded. "In any case, this is the lead we had hoped to find. We should investigate it and see if we can learn anything more up close."

Kaiden leaned back in his seat. "There is another possibility. What if this is where the aliens are going to appear?"

INTENTIONALLY JOURNEYING TO the location where advanced aliens might emerge was simultaneously thrilling and terrifying.

I'd always been one to fantasize about meeting other intelligent life. The Hegemony had never made direct contact, as far as I knew, but I'd heard about discoveries of ruins that suggested we weren't alone in the universe. Whenever I heard about such things, I'd always pictured a glorious, peaceful meeting where we'd share our greatest developments and be welcomed into the fold of another interstellar civilization. Knowing what little I did about the Darkness, however, I suspected that the aliens we could potentially be meeting in the near future were almost certainly aggressive and probably weren't out to make friends. Being on the frontline for that first contact sounded like a surefire way to have things end badly.

All the same, my friends and I had been touched by the Darkness propagated by the aliens, and that connected us to them more than anyone else. If anyone had a chance of successfully interacting with them, it was probably us.

Still, as I left the meeting with Commander Colren on the bridge, I couldn't help but feel like we were about to fly into a trap.

"Just when I thought this day couldn't get any crazier…" I muttered to my companions.

"I know, I'm not crazy about going there, either," Kaiden agreed. "When the best case scenario is that we find a planet no one has observed before, you know you're in trouble."

"What if a whole alien fleet appears around us?" Maris asked, looking a little pale. "This isn't a warship."

"Like the whole Hegemony fleet would do any good against these guys." I took a deep breath.

Toran cast me a stern glance. "That attitude won't get us through this."

"Hey, I know, I didn't mean it that way." I looked down at the deck as we walked down the corridor toward the lift.

Maris held her hands at waist level. "Let's just get some rest before the jump."

"Yeah, good plan." I kept quiet for the remaining journey to our residential area, lost in speculations about what we might find at our destination.

When we reached the lower deck, Toran and Maris headed straight for their quarters. Kaiden took a slower pace, and I hung back when he motioned to me.

"Are you planning to go to sleep right away, or do you have a few minutes?" he asked when we were alone in the corridor.

I smiled coyly. "I could be persuaded to stay up for a bit." I opened the door to my quarters and beckoned him inside.

We stood together in the narrow space between the bed and side wall. A flutter of nerves hit me as he took a step closer.

"It's been quite an eventful day," I said to break the tension.

He laughed. "Yeah, you could say that. Those were some

pretty impressive moves."

"I held my own."

He eyed me. "Come on, Elle. I know you're dying to gloat. Let it out."

My anxiety from earlier dissipated as I thought through everything I'd done that day—feats I never would have dreamed were possible. I tried to contain my excitement for a few more seconds, but it burst out. "That thing with the rope? That was insane! I still can't believe it worked. And then, when I took out those four shadowcats in one pass—"

"Shadowcats?"

"Yeah, I figured we should name the alien things. I thought it sounded cool." I placed my hand on his toned chest. "You had some shining moments, yourself. That was some good thinking with the shuttle escape—jumping from there to the ship."

"I can't believe it worked."

My mouth dropped open. "You told us it would be fine."

"Well, yeah. That's what you're supposed to say to get people to go along with a crazy plan."

"Colren supported it."

Kaiden shrugged. "We didn't have another choice. It was the best out of a series of bad options."

"So, we really did almost die today?" My momentary excitement faded as the reality sunk in. Despite all the remarkable things I'd been through in the last couple of weeks, I hadn't been able to shake my conditioned thinking that there were always reset points and experts were in charge to make sure something terrible didn't happen. Even facing mortal danger, part of me felt invincible—that it was all part of the plan and things would work out even if I screwed up. I knew that was foolish and naïve, but such a radical shift in thinking took time. Maybe now, with so many dire events occurring in rapid succession, it was finally enough for me to see that the stakes were real this time, and the outcome permanent. We no longer had a safety net of local resets, now that the Master Archive was sealed.

"I think we had at least three proper near-death moments today," Kaiden replied. "I hope the universe continues to side in our favor."

I chuckled. "Yeah, right? Let's see, the tentacle monster, the insane shuttle ejection back to the *Evangiel*..."

"And the shadowcat things," he filled in. "I didn't really think they'd do us in, but they *could* have, so I figure it counts on the list."

"Yeah. Thanks again for fireballing that shadowcat. I wouldn't have gotten away if you hadn't."

Kaiden looked down. "About that... That wasn't me."

"Who, then? Maris?"

He shook his head. "No, Elle. It was you."

My heart skipped a beat. "Me? But—"

"You cast magic on Crystallis. This wasn't the first time."

"Yeah, but that..." I still couldn't wrap my head around the idea that I had fragments of abilities from all three disciplines. I'd chalked up what happened on Crystallis to the pressure of the situation, the imperative to defeat the dragon guardian so we could seal the Master Archive. The notion that I could still tap into those abilities... I wasn't sure I was ready to wield that level of power.

"Why are you so hesitant? It's amazing you can do those things," Kaiden said.

"And I bet Hegemony scientists will have a field day studying me for years to come as soon as we're not in crisis mode."

"They wouldn't do that."

"Since when does a one-of-a-kind person *not* become the center of attention? Stars, I didn't even realize I'd cast that magic! If Colren finds out what I can do, there's no telling how he might react."

Kaiden looked down. "This is a big thing to keep secret."

"Can I trust you to do that?" I asked. "Whatever anyone pieced together about what happened on Crystallis, I want to leave it at that. As far as anyone is concerned, that was a one-time thing."

He hesitated, then nodded. "I have your back, Elle. And that's not just because of what's going on between us. You're right that Colren might single you out, and I don't want there to be anything to mess with our team dynamic."

"We're already throwing that off enough as it is."

He smiled. "Well, *that* part is okay."

"You would think so."

"I've gotten the distinct impression you don't disagree."

I tilted my head and shrugged playfully in response. The movement sent radiating pain down my right arm, and I winced.

Concern spread across Kaiden's face. "Hey, are you hurt?"

I brushed it off. "Just a little bruised. Medical cleared me."

"Why didn't you say anything?"

"I can handle a few bumps and scrapes. It's nothing to worry about."

He caught my gaze. "I'm going to worry all the same."

Admittedly, I knew I'd react the same way if I found out he'd been hurt. And, furthermore, I knew that part of the reason I'd gone for the four shadowcats rather than helping Toran was because Kaiden was at risk. We'd vowed to not let romance get in the middle of duty, but I knew that was impossible; subconscious desires were too powerful.

"It's happening," I said.

"What is?"

"The thing we said we wouldn't let happen. I like you, and now I'm thinking about *you* rather than the *mission*."

He took my hand. "I like you, too, Elle. I'd be lying if I denied being more concerned about you than the others."

I shook my head. "But this is crazy! We just met two weeks ago."

"Sometimes that's all it takes, especially when you've been through the kind of stressful situations like we have. That kind of thing can bring people together."

"What are we going to do? Isn't this some kind of huge liability putting everyone else at risk?"

"Why? Because we like each other as more than casual friends? I don't think that's going to destroy civilization." He raised an eyebrow.

"But the Hegemony is counting on us to be focused. And if we're distracted by non-mission things, then—"

Kaiden placed his hands on my shoulders. "Elle, take an objective look at what you're saying. This isn't a disaster that's going to compromise the team; it's a chance for us to be closer so we can work even better together. And, you told me a few days ago that you wished you had something constant in your life, knowing that even once we defeat the Darkness, you're still moving away from your family and friends. Well, maybe this thing with us could be that for you."

I gazed up at him. "Isn't it a little soon to be thinking about that?"

"Maybe. Probably. But all I know for sure is that I've been lonely for a really long time. I thought it was because I'd moved around too much, so settling on a world would give me a sense of grounding. When it didn't, I figured I just hadn't been there for long enough. Except, in the brief time I've known you, I feel more fulfilled than I ever have before."

"I do, too, but—"

"Then why question it? Relationships don't have to be a distraction, they can be an asset."

A thousand thoughts filled my mind, about how I'd always been more of a loner but had been secretly envious of the couples around me. How I'd watched my parents while I was growing up, and how I'd always hoped I'd find my own partner who complemented me as well as my parents worked with each other. And how I was sick of being alone, but I was afraid to get close to someone because I wasn't used to being vulnerable, and I was worried that once someone saw the inner me, maybe there'd be something that they didn't like.

As much as those worries swirled inside, there was still a sense of calm deeper down. What I felt for Kaiden wasn't a superficial crush like I'd experienced before, but was instead the kernel of what could grow into a lasting bond. If there was anyone worth overcoming my fears for, it was him—not *in spite* of our larger team efforts, but *because* of it. To get through that, we needed to trust each other.

I swallowed. "You're right. I guess I'm just nervous."

"About what?" He smiled. "It's not like some switch flipped when we admitted we have feelings for each other and now you have to do anything different."

"But it *is* different. I don't know how to do this relationship thing."

"As you've said. But you know how to be a friend, right?"

"Well, yeah. I mean, I have friends, and we've hung out for years."

He nodded. "Right. Well, I'd say we're on our way to being

friends, too."

"Agreed."

"Okay, that's pretty much it. Dating is essentially just being friends, but with some other physical stuff added on. All the serious stuff comes with time, and there's never a guidebook for that. It's something you have to discover as a couple."

"And you know this from experience?" I eyed him.

"No, but living in close quarters on freighters growing up, I watched a number of relationships go from stolen glances in a corridor to people starting families. In all those cases, the friendship bond is what saw them through the rough patches."

I chuckled. "You know, my mom would really like you."

"If I can get a therapist mom to approve of me, I must be doing something right."

"A lot." I inched closer, gazing up at him. "I like that you're honest and speak your mind. I have a bad tendency to bottle things up when I get uncomfortable, but you help me want to face those things head-on."

Kaiden brushed my hair away from my eyes. "That's what friends do."

The gentle touch of his fingertips on my face sent an excited shiver through me. "Thank you for being here with me. I mean, I know we were all randomly assigned to this team, but thank you for wanting to take a chance on 'us'. I'd probably lose my mind if I didn't have you as a friend through this."

"I think I'd be feeling pretty lost without you, too." He leaned closer, his breath warm on my cheek. "You really are incredible."

"You're not bad yourself."

Our lips met. He entwined his fingers in my hair at the base of my neck and wrapped the other around the small of my back. We'd kissed several times since our first a week prior, but those had mostly been passing pecks—touches to gain familiarity and comfort. This was different, passionate in a way I'd never experienced. I gave into the desire, happy to let him direct me to the bed so we could lie together and forget the troubles in the outside universe.

I reveled in the contact as he kissed down my neck and caressed me. The soft touch set me at ease, never pressuring for it to be more than the next progression in the gradual process of getting to know one another. Based on these initial impressions, I liked where things were headed.

Faces flushed and breath heavy, we eventually settled into a cuddle with one of my arms on his chest and my head nestled on his shoulder.

"Well, that was nice," I said, breaking the silence.

He chuckled and stroked my hair. "Yes. Yes, it was."

"I take it that was some of the 'other physical stuff' bonus one gets from dating as opposed to other friendships?" I winked.

"Just a preview, really."

"That is definitely something I am eager to explore further."

Kaiden pivoted to face me. "Eager, huh?" He gave me a light kiss. "I have nowhere I have to be until the jump, so I am all yours until you say otherwise."

"Is that so?" I kissed him, scooching my hips closer to his.

"I could do this all day." He kissed me back, slower and deeper.

The desire that had just started to subside came back full force, and I pressed against him as our arms wrapped around each other once more. His hand traced down the side of my shipsuit. Suddenly, the garment felt far too restrictive—

"Dark Sentinel Team, report to Central Command," a

female voice said over the intercom.

Kaiden pulled back from me slightly. "Really? *Now*?" He sighed.

I frowned. "This better be for something meaningful with real action items."

"Action to offset the interruption of other action?" Kaiden smirked.

I rolled my eyes. "I guess I should probably get used to your terrible word play."

"I have it on good authority that you love it, and, in fact, probably would have said something very similar yourself."

"No comment." I slid off the bed.

"Uh huh. Thought so."

We smoothed our mussed hair and then entered the hallway after checking that Maris or Toran weren't already in the corridor. I'd gotten used to the idea of holding Kaiden's hand around them, but I didn't want to share much more than that about the state of our relationship just yet.

When we began walking toward the lift up to Central Command, Toran and Maris emerged from their cabins.

"Calling us back already?" Toran said as he jogged to catch up to us.

"I'd *just* fallen asleep." Maris sighed. "I guess we'll all need a pick-me-up."

A moment later, a green wave passed over me, leaving me refreshed. "Thanks, Maris."

She smiled. "Anytime."

The healing magic wouldn't sustain us long-term, but it would buy extra hours in between proper sleep. Not knowing what we were about to walk into, I'd take any advantage I could get.

We were buzzed through the entry door to the bridge when

we arrived, and Colren was talking with the helm officer. One of the techs motioned for us to wait in the corral of workstations near the entry door.

After concluding his conversation, Colren turned around to acknowledge us. "I know I promised you some rest before the jump, but we've uncovered some new information buried in the signal."

"We're ready to help in any way we can," Toran replied.

"It may be nothing, but I wanted to get your impression of something since you're the only ones to have visited a world in Darkness." The commander swept his hand, and the front viewport changed from the view of a starscape to a split screen image depicting the darkened surface of three infected planets from a high elevation. "We left probes at the worlds we visited with you," he continued. "We just received footage from Yantu, Erusan, and the Valor artifact world. In and of itself, the footage isn't that remarkable. However, when we synced the time stamps and compared it to your combat log, it took on new perspective."

He waved his hand again and the three videos began to play. At the same time, an audio clip played. I instantly recognized my voice and the sounds of fighting during our engagement with the shadowcats earlier. The images of the planets were each of dark, swirling clouds. On the surface, tendrils of dark energy like we'd seen on Windau flowed across the landscape. The moment I slayed the final shadowcat in battle, however, there was a shudder in the energy flow on the other worlds—almost imperceptible.

My eyes widened. "That's not a coincidence, is it?"

"Was there anything significant about that battle?" Colren asked.

I flashed to my use of a fireball, but quickly shoved it aside.

Kaiden has used plenty of magic before. Unless... "Were there any other instances like this in the recording?" I asked.

"Nothing from during your most recent mission. We haven't checked others," the commander replied.

That confirmed it wasn't the use of magic itself. But me wielding it couldn't be all that different. At least, that's what I insisted on telling myself. There were plenty of other explanations.

Kaiden glanced at me, but he said nothing.

I swallowed. "We were tapped into the crystal at the time. Maybe that augmented whatever natural link exists between the worlds through the crystalline network." Logically, that made more sense than the odd behavior being the result of me casting magic. The timing, though... I couldn't explain why the Darkness has reacted at the moment it did rather than showing constant signs throughout the sync when the other shadowcats had been slain.

"Given that the signal seems to be everywhere, that makes sense," Kaiden agreed.

Toran nodded thoughtfully. "If we can learn how to tap into the crystal's controls ourselves, we may be able to fight back against the Darkness."

"It's something for us to observe further, I suppose," the commander said after a pause. "Nothing more we can do at present. Now, I've kept you from your rest for long enough. I'll see you after the jump."

We bid our farewell and filed out from the bridge.

"Really, they had to wake us up for *that*?" Maris grumbled.

"It was a very strange observation indeed," Toran stated. "I can't think of anything that stood out in that moment compared to any other."

"Definitely strange," Kaiden said quietly. He caught my

gaze again, and I gave a subtle nod.

Whatever was happening with my abilities, it may have given me more of a connection to the Darkness than anyone realized.

10

I STARED OUT at the alien starscape, hoping for a clear sign of why the signal had pointed to this specific location. The aftereffects of the spatial jump still clouded my mind, but the adrenaline rush from reaching our destination was quickly bringing me back to full awareness.

Next to me, Kaiden frowned at the void. "Something doesn't feel right about this place."

"I know what you mean," Maris agreed, arms crossed. "I feel like I'm being watched."

I wanted to tell her it was all in her head, except I wasn't sure she was wrong. The aliens *could* be watching us, waiting to strike. I hated feeling like I was waiting in a trap. "How long are we going to hang out here?"

Toran shook his head. "At this point, I believe the commander intends to wait until we make contact."

My heart skipped a beat. Was I really going to be on the welcoming committee for the first alien contact in generations? "How long might that take?"

"Stars if I know." Kaiden sighed. "Say, doesn't this ship

have some sort of interface with the Master Archive?"

"That won't do any good now that the Archive is sealed—same reason we didn't use it to get any leads over the last week," Toran replied.

Kaiden waved his hand. "Not for new leads—looking backward. Before the Archive was sealed, did they extract any more information about which worlds would be affected?"

"Pretty sure Colren would have mentioned if they had anything like that," Maris said. "Sounds like the information source was cut off as soon as we were done."

"But they knew there were blank points in the Archive," Kaiden insisted. "So, they must have *some* information beyond what was real-time a week ago."

Maris screwed up her face for a couple seconds, thinking. "I dunno. Maybe, I guess."

"Well, if there *is* something the commander didn't share with us, it might be in the same directory as data we extracted since it's all connected to the Darkness," Toran suggested.

"Do you remember where that is?" I asked.

"I think so." He stepped over to the table in the center of our lounge room and began navigating through the computer network.

"Why haven't we gone looking for this info before?" Maris wondered aloud.

"Probably because we thought we were being told everything," Kaiden muttered.

She tilted her head. "And what makes us think they're keeping anything from us now? We were promised last week that we had been told everything the Hegemony knows."

"As much as I want to believe that's the case, Colren was way too casual about coming here into an unpredictable situation facing likely alien contact," Kaiden replied. "Do you really think we'd be here with no backup if the circumstances were as uncertain as they seem?"

"That's a good point," I realized. "What do you think they're keeping from us?"

Maris' eyes widened. "Do they know what the Darkness is?"

"Doubt it. Colren has seemed genuinely surprised by every bit of information we've brought him," I said.

"Then what else?" she prompted.

I looked to Kaiden. "Any thoughts?"

"I think it has something to do with the Master Archive or the records," he began slowly. "Every time he's been especially cagey, it's been connected to records of past events—or the things that are in the record that haven't happened yet."

Maris frowned. "I still don't get how that's possible. If it hasn't happened, it can't be history. Time travel isn't a thing."

"Not time travel. A reset," Kaiden said.

"Yes, the Archive appears to exist in a different plane that might not be subject to the physical resets," Toran stated while he browsed through files via the tabletop interface.

I eyed him. "Meaning, there *has* already been a universal reset."

"I'd believe that sooner than I would time travel," he replied.

"If there's been a reset, then why don't we remember it?" That was how it always worked—our cognition remained intact.

"It could have been well before our lifetime," Kaiden replied. "Resets don't have to be limited to going back only hours or days."

"But decades or centuries would mean…" Maris massaged her temples. "Nope, can't do it."

"Makes my head hurt, too." I rubbed my eyes. "But it's all speculation. We might be reading way too much between the lines."

"Except, we're not," Toran murmured. He fanned out a set of documents on the touch-surface tabletop. "Bandwidth issues in the crystalline network could explain the memory issues. And, they *do* have evidence of a prior reset."

"Wait, really?" I came to attention. "From when?"

Toran released a long breath. "That's not clear—but a long time ago. They also noted something strange, like the same record had been overwritten multiple times... and that anomaly matches up with the present, as near as anyone can tell."

My chest constricted. "Are you saying that we might have gone through a reset we don't remember?"

"It's possible," Toran replied. "There are scientific models to support it, but it's still in the realm of theory."

I groaned. "I'm getting really sick of speculation. We need *answers!*"

"Let's take a step back here," Maris cut in. "The reason we were looking into this is so you could see if there's talk about the alien fleet, or whatever. These other potential resets are another matter entirely."

Kaiden huffed. "There are too many threads to chase."

"You're right, Maris," Toran conceded. "We need to focus on clues related to what we're about to face—the distant past isn't important right now."

"And what *can* you glean about that?" asked Kaiden.

Toran laughed. "Absolutely nothing."

I did a double-take. "You're joking, right?"

He held out his hands to encompass the tabletop. "When I said they have evidence, I mean there's a single note on this file where someone circled some weird data points and scribbled, 'Universal reset???' with, yes, three question marks." He pointed to it.

Sure enough, the red text stood out from the jumble of nonsense displayed on the screen. Dots and bars formed lines, which had gaps and intersecting branches, but each of the points could mean anything. Codes were attached to some of the lines, though it was unclear if that was a product of the data extraction procedure or if Hegemony researchers had added the notations. My head swam as I tried to wrap my mind around the implications of resets on top of resets, but I didn't know where to begin.

"Can you make any sense of this?" Toran continued. "I hate to say it, but I think Colren is just following whatever clues we give him. There is no grand strategy here. They weren't truthful in the sense that they *do* know there was a universal reset at some point and didn't tell us, but they don't know anything else about it. The code from the Archives may as well be random splatters of paint on a wall."

I stared at the data he'd spread out in front of us, and I was inclined to agree. "So, that's it? We just have to sit around and wait again, hoping that everything works out okay?"

My friends' shoulders rounded.

"The only thing I can tell you is that, like Colren told us before, there are records indicating events past our present time," Toran said. "Assuming that's true, then at least some people must survive whatever's coming."

"But if everything works out okay, then why was there a reset?" I asked.

Kaiden's brow knit. "Yeah, that's a good point."

"There's too much about this that we don't understand," Toran said. "We may be looking at this all wrong."

"Then what are we supposed to look at? I have no idea what to suggest we should do." Kaiden sighed.

"The commander thinks we should wait and see," Maris pointed out.

I nodded. "But he'll listen to us if we bring another suggestion."

"I still think we must be missing something in the signal," Kaiden insisted. "The commander may have come here on faith alone that things will work because of what's recorded in the Archive, but that's not good enough for me."

"Yes, there is still the question of *why here*," Toran stated. "With so many systems to choose from, there must be significance to why the aliens selected this location."

"That's assuming the intersecting lines *do* have any significance," I said.

"It was all too perfect," Kaiden countered. "You saw it—there was nothing random about it."

Maris paled. "What if it was a test?"

I looked at her. "What do you mean?"

"What if they embedded all of that in the signal as a test to see if we were smart enough to figure it out. Create a map, see if we follow it."

"And if we show up here, we pass?" Kaiden asked.

"Or lose, depending on what they might be trying to measure," Toran replied.

I swallowed. "If that's the case, this wasn't us hacking into their secret plans at all… we might be playing directly into their hands."

Kaiden bit his lower lip. "If so, what do they want?"

"Well, it gives them information about our reasoning ability as well as technological capabilities," Toran said.

A chill passed through me. "None of that matters when

we're delivering a whole ship. An investigation of the unknown—any civilization would put their best foot forward. They may have been trying to bait us into handing them the Hegemony's best tech, signed, sealed, and delivered."

"Stars, if that's the case—" Kaiden cut off as a warning claxon sounded.

My heart leaped into my throat. "No…"

"Spatial anomaly seven thousand kilometers to port. Crew to battle stations," a woman announced over the central comm.

Maris' face twisted with terror. "What do we do?"

I looked down at my white shipsuit—hardly battle-ready attire. "We need to get our gear."

"Tami's going to be a little preoccupied," Toran said.

"Do you want to only be wearing this is we're boarded?" I gestured to my onesie. "Yeah, no."

"Can't argue with that. Let's go." Kaiden headed for the door.

"We should stay here and wait for instructions, not go wandering around the ship," Toran insisted.

"Sure, I'm all for waiting this out—*after* I have my sword in hand." I followed Kaiden to the exit. Foolish or not, I wasn't about to leave my fate entirely in others' hands. It seemed especially prudent for me to retrieve my weapon considering our 'no magic' rule on the spaceship, but I also suspected those rules might be bendable under the new circumstances.

As Kaiden and I entered the corridor, Toran and Maris jogged to catch up. Though I never had any doubt that they'd accompany us to the hangar, it was still a relief to have the team sticking together. Now, more than ever, was the time to make sure we didn't get split apart.

The corridors, which were typically devoid of too many passersby, were now abuzz with activity as crew members ran toward their various posts. Most individuals barely seemed to notice our presence, but now and then, I caught a sidelong glance from the occasional higher-ranked crewman. On the fourth such instance on our way to the lift, a dark-haired man with a petty officer insignia held up his hand as we passed by.

"Where are you going?" he asked.

"To retrieve our gear," I replied.

His dark eyebrows drew together. "That can wait."

I stood my ground. "Can it? What's the reason for the alarm?"

"A spatial anomaly—"

"Yes, we heard the commander's announcement. But if that anomaly turns out to be an alien ship, we need to be ready."

"We're under orders to keep you secure," the petty officer replied.

"Great, then that supports our objective of being able to defend ourselves. We'll come back here as soon as we have our gear."

The crewman looked like he was about to protest further, but Toran cut him off, "We can look after ourselves."

"Fine, just stay out of everyone's way." The man continued to jog down the corridor.

I pressed forward. "I kind of feel like we could get away with anything on this ship."

"We do seem to have more freedom than I'd expect," Toran agreed.

"No complaints from me." Kaiden pressed the call button for the lift when we reached it.

"I guess the 'last, best chance designation' does afford some autonomy to do things 'our way'," I said.

Maris chuckled. "Which appears to be getting in the

middle of the mess and then miraculously finding a way out."

The lift doors opened and Kaiden stepped inside. "The part about overcoming the challenges is key."

"Sounds like we're about to face a whole new mess," I replied. "We've sort of gotten a handle on fighting the Darkness creatures planetside, but how in the stars are we supposed to fight something in *space*?"

"Assuming the aliens behind the Darkness are anything like those creatures," Toran countered.

"Why else would they make those changes to the planets if it wasn't to make it hospitable to them? Yeah, they might not be exactly like those black monster things, but I bet some of the attributes carry over." The lift arrived at the hangar level and I led the way out.

"That's true, the form of the creator often does transfer into design," Toran agreed while we hurried toward the hanger. "Like, our bipedal robots."

Kaiden frowned. "Let's hope that they didn't make those shadowcats to be cute little pets in the way we'd breed hamsters."

"Yeah, nope." I shook my head. "Not going to think about it." I knew from experience that I could have an active imagination and assume the worst, so there was no way I could let myself start thinking about what a guard dog might look like if the shadowcats were the equivalent of little fuzzballs that liked to munch on carrots.

We entered the hangar to find it more crowded than it ever had been since our arrival on the *Evangiel*. Crew members were busy inspecting all the fighters lined up on the far side of the hangar deck, and two of the remaining three shuttles were being prepped. I tried to pick Tami out of the forty or more people darting around the cavernous room. After thirty seconds of observation, I spotted her at a control station near the port bulkhead.

"Let's find out where to get our stuff," I said, jogging toward her.

We slowed to a walk as we neared the control station.

Tami was absorbed in her monitor, but as we walked up, she pivoted to one of her techs. "Have you completed the initialization sequence?"

"Yes, the P-85s are idling. Awaiting the launch order."

"How about—" Tami cut off when she saw us, her face flushing. "What are you doing here?"

"We came to get our gear," I replied.

"Your—" She sighed and it turned into a swear under her breath. "All right, fine. The decontamination cycle should be finished. It's over there in the tent."

"Thank you." Toran paused. "Is there anything we can do to help you?"

She laughed. "Tell me what kind of loadout I should give to our fighters? Stars, we may as well be staring into a blank black box."

"What's going on out there?" I asked her.

"All I know is that the engagement protocol Colren issued is for the highest risk scenarios with likely loss of life."

Maris sucked in a sharp breath next to me.

"We need to find out what the commander knows," I said.

"Whatever it is, I don't want to know. I just keep the ships flying," Tami muttered.

"It will all work out," I told her. I hated generic platitudes, but it was all I could think to say in the moment.

She nodded. "Thanks. We'll do what we can."

"Incendiary rounds," Kaiden said as he headed toward the decontamination tent.

"Hmm?"

"The loadout for the fighters. Incendiary rounds," he repeated to Tami. "The creatures in the Darkness don't like fire."

11

GETTING MY SWORD and other gear hadn't set me at ease the way I'd hoped it would. We were still on a ship, reliant on the craft and crew.

"I want to see what's going on," I stated.

"Didn't we agree to go back to the lounge and wait this out?" Toran protested.

I smiled. "Since when do we stick to the plan?"

"And things have gone *so* well for us whenever we improvise." Maris rolled her eyes.

"I think we'd all like to understand what's happening. It's not like we're reinterpreting orders this time," I replied.

"I'm not confident they will let us on the bridge, but I'd like to try," Kaiden agreed.

"Only one way to find out." Hand on my sword's hilt, I strode toward the hangar exit.

"Colren is totally going to yell at us," Kaiden murmured, walking abreast.

"Yeah, but maybe we can learn something in the process."

"You know," Toran said behind me, "we might be able to

tap into the feed from the front viewport and the general sensor suite. Given the directory I accessed earlier, I'm pretty sure I have the right permissions."

I smiled back at him. "But what's the fun in that?"

"For the record, I have no problem observing from a distance," Maris interjected.

"Noted. Now, let's go find the middle of the action." I continued forward with renewed purpose.

As much as I pretended to be the reluctant hero, I loved being in the thick of it. I'd dreamed of being a Ranger on the Space Force, and this was my chance to skip Tactical School and live out my fantasies. Granted, the mortal danger wasn't ideal, but I couldn't imagine sitting back and watching from afar while more worlds were consumed by Darkness. As we stood on the precipice of direct contact with the aliens behind the attack, I wanted to see it firsthand.

Kaiden and I led the way up the lift to the command deck. The corridors had cleared out while we retrieved our gear, giving us a straight shot to our destination. At the entry door to the bridge, Kaiden pressed the buzzer. We were normally buzzed in almost instantaneously, but this time, no response came.

"I don't think they want to talk to us," Maris said.

Toran nodded. "Let's go back to the lounge room."

"Not yet." I tapped the comm activation point behind my left ear. "Commander, we're here to help."

"Elle, I'd expected your team to remain in your quarters."

"Well, you *didn't* say that, and we're here now, so…"

The comm cut out for a few seconds. "Honestly, we could use another set of eyes on this." The door buzzed open.

I disconnected the comm link and smiled at my team. "See?"

Toran shook his head. "I can't believe that worked."

Kaiden eyed me. "Have you always been this assertive?"

"Stars, no! But having a badass magic sword is a major confidence booster." I was still somewhat surprised by the ongoing changes in myself. I'd done reckless things and always had a bit of a rebellious streak, but outright standing up to authority and making myself heard was a new attribute. At one time not long ago, I hadn't even wanted to tell my parents that I wanted to attend Tactical School; now, I was expecting a Hegemony commander to include me in decision-making. The changes seemed to become more pronounced every time I tapped into my new abilities. Eventually, I wondered if I'd even recognize myself.

We entered the bridge, and the crew members didn't even glance at us. Commander Colren's attention was glued on the front viewport.

At the center of the starfield, an almost imperceptible distortion warped the appearance of the stars behind it. I squinted, trying to make it out. "What is that?" I whispered to Kaiden.

"Must be the 'anomaly'."

We slowly approached the back of the command chair, waiting for Colren to acknowledge us. He finally turned around, looking more openly distraught than I'd ever seen him in our two weeks on the *Evangiel*.

"We've never seen anything like it," he murmured.

I gestured at the distortion. "Was it here when we arrived?"

The commander nodded. "We didn't notice it at first, but when we scanned the area, it showed up on all of the non-visual displays. What you see on the screen is augmented with a holographic overlay; there's nothing to see with the naked eye."

"I *knew* this place felt wrong," Kaiden said to me.

"Is it related to the Darkness?" Toran asked.

Colren stood up from his seat. "Considering we can't see it against the void, in some ways it seems like *pure* Darkness. The anomaly is disturbing because it's radiating gravity like a black hole, but there is no event horizon or debris field."

My stomach flopped. "If it's not a black hole, could this be the location of a system that was completely consumed by Darkness?"

"If it was, we'd have no way to verify it," the commander replied.

"But we *do* know our tech came from another civilization. This may have all happened before," I said.

Kaiden nodded. "We saw what looked like weapons fire on Crystallis, remember."

"Yes, remnants of past wars could be all around us," Colren said. "But whatever this is, it's not dormant. It's emitting a signal that's made up of components from the others we've observed."

I tilted my head. "But not the same?"

"Not exactly, no. There's another code segment we haven't observed before."

"May I see it?" Toran asked.

Colren accessed a panel next to his command chair, bringing up a hologram in the open area between the seat and the forward bulkhead. "Can you make any sense of this?"

Toran stepped forward toward the projection, his eyes flitting around the displayed data.

As usual, it was all nonsense to me, though I did pick out waveforms that I recognized as components of the signal emitted from the crystals, which we'd also observed coming through the infected crystal on Windau. "How is a signal coming from a thing that's essentially nothing?" I asked.

"Probably a wormhole," Kaiden replied.

"There's a hyperdimensional connection between the crystals, which exists outside of our normal spatial perception; that much has been clear for a long time," Colren stated. "Whatever that link is, we might be witnessing it here in its true form without a crystal to enclose its terminus."

That concept stopped me cold. There was much we didn't know about the technology we took for granted in our everyday lives, but I'd always associated the crystals with connections between the worlds. It hadn't occurred to me that any connections might extend beyond the known crystalline network.

"I'm not sure what to suggest," Toran said. He took a deep breath. "The signal we picked up on Windau was only detectable through a hard connection, and other signals can be picked up in the vicinity. I don't know where this one would be coming from."

"From whatever the anomaly is connected to." I looked at him. "I mean, it has to be connected to someplace else, right?"

"That is the only explanation," he agreed.

"How do we find out *where* that is?" Kaiden asked.

Colren placed his hands on the back of his command chair. "I was hoping you might have some suggestions."

"I don't—" Toran began.

"What I meant is that you developed the detection system using the crystal pendants. Could that be adapted for longer distances?" the commander clarified.

Toran shook his head. "It's only a proximity indicator. I don't see how we'd use it to trace the signal anywhere."

"Maybe you don't need that approach at all," I said in the ensuing pause. "Why go after the aliens at all when we can have them come to us? Force the engagement to be on our home turf."

"Preemptive strikes have an advantage," Colren replied.

"But only if you know what you're facing, right?" I countered. "Even if we *did* trace this signal back to somewhere, that probably wouldn't give us any more details about the aliens who sent it out. We're here to study and assess the potential enemies themselves, not just where they might be from. Right? So, let's observe, find a weakness."

"Wait for them to come to us?" Colren asked.

"For now. All signs point to this being a hub of some sort for them. My guess is they'll show up here eventually—and probably soon. The *Evangiel* and whatever other ships you want can be waiting here."

He considered my statement. "The only reason I'd shied away from that approach is we have no way to predict what kind of ships they'll possess or how many they'll send."

"What I saw in my vision was an entire fleet," Kaiden said. "Not that those visions necessarily reflect reality, but there's at least potential for more than a hundred ships."

"Topping those numbers would be a huge commitment for the Hegemony's resources. Our fleet is stretched thin with evacuation efforts on the infected worlds," the commander responded.

My heart skipped a beat. "Evacuations? You never said anything about that before."

"That information was outside the scope of your responsibilities and activities," Colren stated.

"Yeah, wait, you never mentioned any ships being around to get people offworld when we went to get Elle or Maris," Kaiden said.

"There weren't any there," the commander said.

"Then who? Where?" I pressed.

"Certain high-asset individuals and their families have

been taken to secure locations," he said slowly.

"Meaning government and military personnel," Toran filled in.

The commander nodded. "Those decisions are made well above my paygrade. Most evacuations have been from the Capital as a preemptive measure."

"I hope they at least threw in a few scientists," Toran said. "I'm out of my depth with all of this—I've just gotten lucky."

"More than luck," Colren replied. "But yes, there are scientists who've been briefed on our latest developments. We'd hoped to rendezvous with them after the investigation here, but it looks like we may be sticking around here longer than I'd anticipated."

Toran tilted his head. "We don't need to meet in person. A vid chat via hyperspace relay would allow us to share ideas."

"Good thinking," the commander agreed. "I'll talk with the admiralty about making a stand at this location against a potential invasion force. In the meantime, I'll put you in contact with the research team so you can compare notes."

"Sounds like a reasonable approach to me," I said.

"What are the rest of us supposed to do?" Maris asked.

"Stay vigilant, but you're free to pass the time however you see fit," Colren said. "We'll be at Threat Imminent status until further notice."

"And, when things go down, should we... wander up here?" I asked.

He sighed. "I have a feeling that even if I said you should remain in your quarters you'd show up here anyway."

"Most likely."

Colren shook his head. "Then we may as well just make it your standing instruction to report here if and when any alien craft appear."

I cracked a smile. It looked like we'd get a front row seat to the next show after all.

THE RED WARNING lights had changed to yellow by the time we were back in the corridor outside the bridge. "Anyone else have an overwhelming feeling of impending doom?" I asked my team.

Kaiden chuckled. "That's been a pretty constant state for the last few weeks."

"It just doubled down," Maris replied. "I don't know how we're supposed to relax."

"I, for one, will be trying to learn everything I can about this anomaly and how it works," Toran stated. "I suggest you find your own ways to contribute."

I wanted to help, too. It was the reason I'd wanted to venture down to Windau and was the same reason I'd embraced my transformation rather than trying to run away. But I felt like I was backed against a wall with my hands tied in this moment. Everything I'd learned about my new abilities related to skills that I'd be unable to exercise on a spaceship. So long as we were here, I had no idea what kind of 'contribution' I might be able to make.

"I guess I'll head back to the lounge," I said at last.

Kaiden nodded. "I'll join you, unless some space plants appear that you need analyzed."

We reached the lift and stepped inside.

Maris eyed us. "Would it cramp your style if I joined in?"

"Of course not," I replied on reflex, only afterward realizing that it would have been nice to get some more couple time with Kaiden. However, maybe it was for the best we slowed things down a bit, especially given the new complication related to the potential alien fleet.

Momentary disappointment flitted across Kaiden's face, but when his gaze met mine there was understanding in his eyes. "I still feel awkward just sitting around waiting."

"Me, too. But, we don't have the right skills to bring to this one. We need to leave it to the scientists," I said.

Maris nodded. "I'm *definitely* out."

The lift doors opened, and we stepped out into the corridor on the level housing our cabins and lounge.

"Well, you three sort that out. Reach me on my comm if you need anything. I'll be in my cabin." Toran walked quickly towards his cabin.

I sighed, plodding behind him at a slower pace. "More waiting. I had enough of that last week."

"You know, we don't *have* to wait in the lounge," Kaiden said after we'd only gone a few steps. "We could get in some combat practice."

Maris crossed her arms. "I thought there was a 'no magic on the ship' rule?"

"In all fairness, that was self-imposed rather than any official ruling from Colren," Kaiden clarified. "If we can find an interior storage room or something, it might be a good opportunity to keep working on our combat skills."

"Toran would say that's a terrible idea," I replied.

Kaiden smiled. "Toran isn't with us right now, is he?"

Maris evaluated us. "I get the impression it's a bad idea to ever leave the two of you unsupervised."

"Nonsense! We're completely responsible one hundred percent of the time," I lied.

"Right, like when you dove out the back of the shuttle earlier," she countered, missing the irony in my statement.

"Hey, I *saved* us." That was the truth. The move was dangerous, yes, but we hadn't had a lot of options. If I was going to be berated, it should be for doing something genuinely reckless—like when I climbed up the rock titan's arm without a plan.

"I promise to not use any of the strong magical attacks," Kaiden stated. "Besides, we made that rule when we were just starting to learn about our abilities; we all have a lot more control now."

Maris smirked, looking us up and down. "You two have lost control in other ways." She sauntered back to the lift and pressed the call button. "Are we going to practice, or what?"

Face flushed, I followed her back to the lift. "I'll check with the commander."

I'd prepared myself for some gentle ribbing about the new relationship, especially from Maris. She had always struck me as the kind of young woman who'd get wrapped up in other people's relationship drama. Just like I had a tendency to joke around when I was stressed, she was seeking her own distractions to ease anxiety about the terrifying unknowns. Nonetheless, the teasing was annoyingly out of place amid our present bid for survival.

After a quick call to Colren about our desire to practice, he directed us to use an unoccupied storage room on the hangar level. After exiting the lift, we headed to the right, past the fighter pilots' quarters, until we reached a series of larger doors labeled numerically as cargo holds. All the nearby doors had a biometric lock, currently in red 'locked' mode.

I frowned at the lock on the first door. "I wonder if our credentials will open it?" I extended my hand to the scanner and placed my palm flat against the surface. The device let out a harsh beep.

"That would be a 'no'," Kaiden observed. He peered down the hall. "Hey, I think I see a green light further down."

The three of us continued another twenty meters to a door that did not appear to be locked like the others. Kaiden brushed his hand over the control panel, and the door opened with a hiss. Beyond, a five-meter-by-ten-meter storage room was completely empty.

I smiled. "Now we're in business."

Kaiden stepped inside. "Point any attacks toward the inside. We don't want to blow a hole in the outer hull."

"What if there's something combustible on the other side of these walls?" Maris asked.

Kaiden and I exchanged glances. "Well, let's not bust through any walls, then," he replied.

Maris was silent for a moment. "Maybe this is an opportunity for me to try something out. We've needed a lot of shields around us, right?"

I nodded.

"This might be a good time for me to practice some of that defensive magic," she continued. "Like, put a shield around this entire room."

Kaiden placed a hand pensively on his chin. "You know, that's not a bad idea. It would contain my magical attacks so we wouldn't have to worry about damaging the ship."

"Except, we'd be trapped in the shell *with* the fireballs or lightning or whatever," I pointed out.

Maris' eye lit up. "Unless I can maintain different sets of shields—one around the room and individual ones around us."

I raised an eyebrow. "That's kind of a jump from what you've been able to do in the past, isn't it?"

"We're down here to learn new skills, aren't we?" She strode confidently into the center of the chamber.

"We are, indeed." Kaiden followed her inside. "Elle?"

I sighed. "Guess the only way to find out is to try." I stepped inside and spotted an interior control panel next to the door. After flipping the lights on and closing the door, I joined my friends in the center of the chamber. "Have at it, Maris."

She took a slow, deep breath and closed her eyes. "Okay, a shield. A big shield."

Purple sparks danced around her hands, casting a cool glow on her form-fitting clothing. The sparks shot upward toward the ceiling and arced in all directions to form a circular dome. With the rectangular shape of the room, the dome's edges brushed up against the side walls while open floor space remained in front and behind.

"I don't think it would be a good idea for the bubble to extend into the other storage rooms," I stated.

"Can you do anything about the shape of the shell, Maris?" Kaiden asked.

"I'm not sure." Her brow furrowed with concentration. Slowly, the shape of the shell began to elongate to better fit the proportions of the chamber, reaching almost to the ceiling and stretched into a curved oval footprint that covered most of the deck space.

I smiled. "Hey, not bad!"

She grinned. "It's actually not that hard now that I'm doing it."

"See how else you can augment the spell," Kaiden suggested.

A second wave of sparks passed over Maris' hands, but as soon as they reached her fingertips, the larger shield began to shudder. "Gah!" she groaned. "So much for this being easy."

"It's just like when you have the individual shells around us," Kaiden said, though I suspected he was making it up to keep Maris from giving up. "Since Toran isn't here, pretend the room is him."

Maris raised an eyebrow. "He's big, but he's not room-sized."

"Then make this one smaller and work up from there," he replied. "Practice the nesting and then bring it to scale."

She took a steadying breath. "Okay."

The shell brushing the confines of the chamber shrunk until the dome was only five meters wide. Then, Maris' hands glowed once more with purple sparks. They extended from her fingers and fed into three smaller domes, one around each of us.

"It's working!" she exclaimed with a giggle.

"Shed the self-doubt, Maris." Fire danced across Kaiden's palms. "Now make this area bigger so we can start to play."

Maris fed the larger shell until it filled the room. "I'll just have to keep it simple for now."

"All right," Kaiden agreed. "Now, we need to let attacks pass through our personal shells and get blocked by the room shell and the other personal shells."

"And how am I supposed to do *that*?" Maris sighed.

"I don't know. The same way we can do anything else." Kaiden sent a tiny fireball toward the side wall—no bigger than the end of his thumb, but enough to help Maris focus on controlling the properties of each shield. The lower-temperature orange flame passed through both barriers and struck the wall, leaving a black smudge. "That's what we *don't* want to happen."

Maris rolled her eyes. "I got that, yeah."

"Again." Kaiden repeated the move with another tiny fireball. The orb shot through the inner defensive shield but then sputtered when it reached the outer layer.

Maris grinned. "Just need to picture what I want it to do!"

"While you two keep up with that, I'm going to work on my flips." I drew my sword in preparation for my own practice activities.

We spent the next half-hour playing around with our various skills. Maris was only able to maintain each shield for two minutes initially, but she eventually improved her concentration enough to keep the large one active for nearly five minutes at a stretch. I hoped we wouldn't need those skills in the future, but it was comforting to know it was an option for any prospective engagements.

Kaiden eventually grew tired of practicing with scaled-back fireballs and stood back to watch me practice my forms. "You're looking like a seasoned pro with that sword."

I smiled over my shoulder while I continued to practice lunges. "Feels like it, too." I flourished the sword over my head and pivoted on the ball of my right foot to face him. "This ancient muscle memory or whatever it is we got from the artifacts is awesome."

"Some of these skills we woke up with in the bioprinter, which is even weirder," he replied, tossing a loose flame between the palms of his hands.

"It doesn't make any sense, but this magic is a part of me," Maris said. "I can't believe I went most of my life without it."

I stopped my exercises. "Looking back, it's like something

was always missing."

"I know what you mean." Maris swelled the latest iteration of the outer shield until it touched the side walls. "After this practicing, I feel even stronger." The sphere continued to expand, its edges passing through the bulkheads into the adjacent chambers.

"Whoa, Maris, dial it back," I cautioned.

Her faced paled. "I'm trying" she exclaimed. "It's like something else is fueling it." Purple sparks danced on her fingertips.

The flame Kaiden had been playing with suddenly flared to the size of his torso. "Stars! What…?" He threw his hands wide and the flame dropped toward the deck, fizzling out.

Maris' shield, on the other hand, continued to grow. Hoping to break her concentration, I ran over and grabbed her right wrist, twisting her arm behind her back as gently as I could.

She sucked in a sharp breath, and the purple shields dissolved. "What just happened?"

I shook my head. "It was like an energy surge or something."

Kaiden frowned. "I've never had that happen before."

A chirp sounded in my ear, startling me. "Dark Sentinel team to the bridge! We have contact."

13

I RACED DOWN the corridor toward the lift with my comrades. "Contact with *what*?"

"The aliens?" Kaiden speculated.

My heart skipped a beat. "Is that what caused the magical energy surge?"

His frown deepened. "If it was, then we know even less about them and their capabilities than we imagined."

"I can't believe this is happening," Maris moaned.

I couldn't, either. Not only was my civilization about to meet genuine aliens for the first time in recorded history, but I was going to be a part of that experience. No matter how many times I thought about it, I couldn't help feeling giddy despite the danger. No longer was I some anonymous girl from a backwater world—I would be in the history records as someone who was present during what would no doubt be a landmark moment in our civilization, no matter how the events unfolded.

Taking a deep, steadying breath, I tried to mentally prepare myself for whatever was about to happen. "We need to say something about the magical surge."

Kaiden nodded. "Yeah, I was thinking the same thing."

We took the lift to the bridge level. As we exited, I spotted Toran marching down the corridor ahead.

"Hey!" I called out.

He glanced over his shoulder then halted when he spotted us. "Good, you got the summons."

"Do you know anything about this 'contact'?" Kaiden asked.

The large man shook his head as we reached his position, and we continued down the hall toward the bridge. "I've just been going over the data about the anomaly. I was about to have a conference with the team working on it in the Capital, but then the alert sounded."

"I kind of thought we'd have to wait a long time for something to happen," I admitted. "There are still several unpaired worlds, so I was thinking that pattern would be complete before the aliens appeared."

"Maybe our presence here has altered the plans," Kaiden suggested.

"Let's hope the aliens are happy to see us," Maris said.

"Yeah, here's hoping." I didn't have any faith that would be the case.

We reached the entry to the bridge and were buzzed through the door. The usually calm techs were visibly rattled, eyes darting and a slight tremble to their hands. Colren stood in front of his seat, dividing his attention between the holographic data display and the enhanced image overlaid on the front viewport.

The previously faint anomaly was now a bright point of light. When my eyes adjusted to it, my breath caught in my throat as I realized that the light wasn't the only change. An object was coming through. "Stars!" I gasped. "What is that?"

Kaiden tensed next to me. "I think it's a ship."

The craft was recognizable as such only because of its present location and behavior. From its appearance, I would have thought it a clump of organic matter, like moss viewed under a magnifying glass. Thin tendrils looped around each other to form a roughly cylindrical shape, and the craft's dark coloration was only visible because of the bright light from the anomaly behind it. The more I looked at the form, it reminded me of the tentacle monster and ground covering we had encountered that morning.

"Is it alive?" I murmured.

"I don't know, but that's what I saw in my vision," Kaiden said. "It's coming true."

I swallowed hard. I couldn't get a clear sense of scale from my vantage, but I got the impression the ship was nearly a kilometer in length—far larger than our own vessel, and with unknown firepower. All the same, seeing it put me in an aggressive mood. "We can't let them invade. We need to stop it!"

"They've already begun the invasion, Elle," Toran said with uncharacteristic grimness in his tone.

"It's not too late to turn them back." I stepped forward to the dais with the captain's seat. "Commander, we're here."

Colren didn't take his gaze off the ship as the final section of it cleared the anomaly. "This is the moment that will define our future."

"Whoever they are, they mean us harm," I said.

He nodded. "I know."

The alien ship had no visible engine wash, but its movements made it clear that it wasn't traveling on inertia alone. It moved away from the anomaly, looking like it was coming for us, but then halted twenty kilometers from where it had emerged.

"Helm, pull back to fifty thousand kilometers and hold," the commander ordered.

"Aye," the helmsman acknowledged, and the front view began to shrink as the ship pulled away.

"We're just going to let them hang out here?" I questioned.

"Of course not," Colren replied. "We'll do our best to drive them back through whatever that anomaly is, but the Hegemony fleet hasn't arrived yet. We thought we had more time to prepare."

My heart pounded in my chest. "What if the rest of the alien fleet comes before our backup?"

"We'll evaluate our options at that time," he replied.

I took a deep breath. "Commander, there's something else going on. We were practicing magic on the lower deck, and there was some sort of magical energy surge. It happened right before we got the alert from you."

Colren's scowl deepened at the end of my statement. "We noticed some strange activity, too, in the device we use to interface with the Master Archive."

"What *is* that, anyway?" Kaiden questioned.

I'd been curious, myself. The commander had mentioned it on several different occasions, but never more than a reference in passing. Considering that he had disclosed there were only four such devices known to our people and this ship had one of them, I would have thought he'd make a bigger deal out of it.

Colren glanced out the front viewport, the site of the anomaly now only a bright point in the distance. "I suppose it's time I showed you." He led the way off the bridge. "I must admit that I wasn't entirely forthcoming about this device and its supposed capabilities."

"We can't help you if you don't share information with us," Toran said.

"And that's why I'm showing you now. It wasn't necessary before," the commander replied.

Kaiden brushed his hand across the small of my back as we turned to follow the commander out. "We'll get through this," he whispered just loud enough for me to hear.

I flashed a slight smile. "I know we will."

Colren led us back in the direction of the lift and then continued past it. I'd originally thought the corridor dead-ended just after the lift, but the commander touched the wall panel and a compartment opened to reveal a biometric scanner. He placed his palm on the device, and a portion of the wall slid to the side.

I exchanged surprised looks with my team members. "A secret passageway on a spaceship?"

The commander cast me a cautionary glance. "And it will remain need-to-know." He stepped through the opening into the chamber beyond and we followed him inside.

The room had a similar aesthetic as the bridge, with control stations situated around the perimeter of the seven-meter-wide round room. At its center was the device that was clearly the main attraction—a transparent orb suspended on a chrome pedestal. The meter-wide orb glowed with soft blue light.

"Is this crystal?" I asked.

Colren sealed the entry door behind us. "All analyses point to yes, but we have never been able to carve crystals. This device and the three others like it are the only instances we've ever seen the crystals in a form other than their natural shape."

Kaiden twirled his pendant in his fingers; the crystal at the end of the chain glowed brightly with proximity resonance. "What does it do?"

"More than you could ever imagine." The commander approached the orb and placed his hands on either side of it. As he made contact, the intensity of the glow increased momentarily, then darkness filled the center of the sphere.

"Stars! It's infected," Maris exclaimed.

"No," Colren replied. "This is a 'no signal' notification, of sorts. Before the Master Archive was sealed, this is how we extracted information."

"How?" I asked. It looked more like a giant crystal ball than anything capable of downloading information about past–or, potentially, future–events.

"There's a visual interface for the hyperdimensional link," Colren explained. "The user would navigate through a series of visual cues. For example, a digital maze with multiple branches, and at each turn, a world. The selected planet could be spun backward through thought commands to view its past states at the saved reset points."

"Thought commands? Like, telepathy?" Kaiden asked.

Colren nodded. "The crystal forms a sort of cybernetic connection with the user so long as they are in physical contact with the sphere."

"Just like how we make a reset point by touching the crystal," I realized.

"*Any* world can be viewed?" questioned Toran. "Even uninhabited worlds without a crystal interface?"

The commander inclined his head. "There appears to be a passive record stored at regular intervals, though we'd have no way to access it for a reset without the interface. Anyway, this system sounds more interesting than it was useful in reality. Over the years, researchers figured out how to translate the visual feed into raw data for analysis. That's how we observed the record gaps we eventually connected to the Darkness."

As crazy as it sounded, all of the questions that had been floating in my head for the past two weeks were slowly getting answered. Colren *had* been telling the truth earlier when he said he'd told us everything, just not enough details for us to understand the full extent of his statements.

"Okay, so, this device doesn't work now that the Archive is sealed," I said. "You said there was some strange activity with it earlier. What happened?"

"We received a momentary data feed, but it was jumbled—like data had been overwritten multiple times on the same file, so only fragments were readable."

"What did they say?" Toran asked.

Colren turned around to access the workstation behind him. "It was only a few minutes ago, so we haven't run a full analysis. What little information the techs could make out looked like code snippets."

Toran joined him by the monitor integrated in the wall. "These look similar to the waveforms I was analyzing, actually."

The commander perked up. "Can you plot them?"

"Maybe." Toran took over the controls. After a minute of entering commands, he shook his head and frowned. "No, these are too incomplete for the results to be accurate. I could easily extrapolate and plot *something*, but there'd be too much guesswork involved to trust the result."

I drummed my fingers pensively. "It's strange… this seems to be the origin point for the signal, but there isn't a crystal here. I don't know how it would interface at all."

"We *assume* there's not a crystal here," Toran interjected.

"What if there's one inside that anomaly?"

"I guess there could be, since it's all… anomalous," I stated awkwardly.

"But what about everything else going on here?" Colren prompted. "Why would the aliens have interest in this place if there's no world to consume?"

I thought through everything I had learned about the crystalline network over the past two weeks and how everything operated. It *didn't* make sense that the aliens would select this as a staging ground for their fleet when there were more than a dozen worlds they had already shaped to their specifications using the Darkness. But, when I failed to rationalize the actions using my conventional understanding, I flipped it around. Suddenly, the pieces started to fall into place. "You said the gravity was high here—meaning there could be dense mass we can't see?" I asked, breaking the silence in the room.

Colren nodded.

"So, what if the signals we keep picking up are instructions for that matter? On the other planets, the crystals were used to rearrange matter to create whatever environment the aliens want for their bio…"

"Bio-optimization," Kaiden supplied for me.

"Right. And that process could be done anywhere there's sufficient raw material, correct?" I asked, and Toran nodded. "So, what if the ships aren't coming through that anomaly, but that they're being *manufactured* in it?"

Toran paled. "That's all the crystals do—follow a set of instructions and use whatever is at their disposal to complete the structures."

"Stars! If that really is what's going on…" Colren raced to the door. "We need to shut it down!"

14

"COMMANDER! ADDITIONAL ALIEN craft inbound," the helm officer announced as soon as Colren returned to the bridge with my team following close behind.

"It might not be inbound at all," Colren muttered.

"Sir?"

He shook his head. "Set ship to combat-ready. Move into high-precision firing range of the anomaly."

"Aye!" the helm officer acknowledged.

"This could totally backfire," I whispered to Kaiden.

"If your idea is correct, then there aren't a lot of other options. The longer that thing is active, the bigger the enemy fleet we'll be up against."

"What's the ETA on our backup?" Colren barked.

"Jump logs indicate they should arrive in six minutes, sir," the comm tech replied from one of the rear stations near where I was standing. She was the most composed of the support staff, but I could still plainly see the worry in her eyes.

"Ten kilometers to engagement range," the helm officer announced.

"When you have a lock, fire a Class I barrage at the anomaly," Colren ordered.

My hand found Kaiden's, and we entwined our fingers. The warmth of his presence took the edge off my worry as we braced for combat.

"Target in range. Commencing Class I barrage," the helmsman announced.

"May the stars be with us," Colren murmured.

Twenty torpedoes launched from the bow of the *Evangiel* and streaked toward the anomaly. It still seemed too far away to fire on, but I had to remind myself that the physics of space battles are different than on a planet. In terms of this environment, we were practically breathing down the enemy's neck.

Four excruciating seconds passed while we waited for impact. As the torpedoes neared their mark, the single alien craft that had fully emerged from the anomaly fired what looked like an inky cloud, visible only thanks to the visual overlays on the front viewport. The black cloud intercepted the torpedoes two kilometers short of the anomaly's event horizon, and the twenty bombs vanished.

"Report!" Colren demanded.

"The torpedoes are gone, sir. No detonation," the helmsman replied, a quaver in his voice.

Kaiden's grip on my hand tightened. "They can command the Darkness," he whispered.

"No. This can't be happening!" My throat constricted as tears stung the corners of my eyes. We had been making progress, we had a plan. Now, all of those efforts seemed to be meaningless. How could we stop an enemy who makes weapons vanish?

Colren seemed equally at a loss.

"Sir?" the helmsman prompted when no further orders were given.

"Plasma cannons," the commander instructed.

"That gets us too close," Toran murmured.

"What do you mean?" Maris asked, drawing the four of us into a huddle.

"Plasma cannons are a short-range engagement weapon," Toran clarified. "If we're close enough to fire at the anomaly, we would be well within range of their Black Cloud of Death."

"Yeah, I don't want to go anywhere near a thing you'd give that nickname." I glanced at Colren. "Should we say something?"

"He is no doubt aware of the risks already," Toran said. "My guess is that this move is to determine which strategy will be best for the rest of the fleet to follow. Torpedoes appear ineffective, so we need an alternative means of attack."

"Then saying something won't help." I sighed. "For being here on the bridge, we're not doing much."

"We're civilians on a military vessel. It's a wonder we're here at all," Kaiden replied.

With a sudden and horrific death now too near a reality for comfort, I was beginning to agree with Maris' assessment that I should have never gotten out of bed that morning. Agreeing with Maris... the end really was nigh.

No, thinking like that wasn't going to accomplish anything. "Come on," I said, beckoning my friends toward the exit.

"Where are you going?" Toran asked.

"Back to that special room," I said. "If that thing can pick up signals from the aliens, maybe we can learn something about them during the attack."

"Wait, we'll need a way to see what's going on out here,"

Kaiden countered. He jogged up to Commander Colren and whispered something to him, which I assumed was my plan.

The commander nodded. "I'll give you access and patch through the feed."

Kaiden bounded off the dais and headed for the door.

"It's not as fun now that we have permission," I jested, jogging up next to him.

He cracked a smile. "Only you would say something like that at a time like this, Elle."

We dashed down the corridor to the secret entry.

Toran placed his palm on the hidden biometric scanner, and the door opened. "This is why we ask for permission."

"Oh, right." My cheeks flushed. "I wasn't thinking about that part."

Once inside, we sealed the door and then turned our attention to the various stations around the room. Toran began fiddling with one to get the live feed from the bridge's viewport while Kaiden examined the sphere.

"I can't believe Colren trusts us with this," he said.

"In all fairness, we have more experience with this ancient tech than anyone, after we went through the artifact-gathering," I pointed out.

"I guess there is that. We haven't broken anything yet."

I smiled. "That we know of, anyway."

"The cute banter can wait. Figure out how this thing works!" Maris cut in.

"Sorry." I inspected the device. There were no obvious controls. "Colren said the viewing was controlled by thought, didn't he?"

"That's right, he did." Kaiden eyed the device. "Should I...?"

"Be my guest." I held out my hand.

Kaiden placed his palms on either side of the sphere. The glow intensified for a moment before the blackness returned. However, one of the idle workstations along the wall sprang to life.

"I think we have a link!" I ran over to it. "Try to focus on the anomaly, Kaiden."

"Great, that's the *last* thing I want to think about."

"Hey, you volunteered to do this part." I checked the workstation's monitor, which had code scrolling across it. "How are you doing getting the feed set up, Toran? I'll need you over here."

"Almost ready," he replied.

I looked over my shoulder to see what he was working on just in time to see the video stream from the bridge appear on the monitor at his station. The *Evangiel* was rapidly approaching the alien ship and the anomaly. By my estimation, we had to be getting close to firing range for the plasma cannons. Any nearer and it would be a suicide run; maybe it already was.

"Come, on they'll fire soon!" I urged.

Toran ran over to my position, immediately locking his eyes on the monitor. "Okay, good, this is steady and matches what I was observing earlier. If there's any change when we strike, we'll know why."

"They'd better make a move soon." I took an unsteady breath. I had no interest in finding out firsthand what it felt like to be disintegrated by that black cloud.

With Toran focusing on the code, I went back to the station with the feed from the bridge. Four additional alien ships were starting to appear in the anomaly, and two earlier ones were almost complete. The tapered noses of the vessels protruded from the bright glow like they were predators rising from a pond, elegant and sinister.

A new glow appeared on the screen, originating from the *Evangiel*. With a sudden flash, two blinding plasma beams crackled across the blackness toward the anomaly. The beams struck one of the half-formed ships, sending a ripple of lightning over its hull. At first, it appeared the energy blast was dissipating without causing any damage, but then the tendrils that comprised the hull slowly began to unfurl from their proper places. The black bands dropped and began to shrivel, eventually disintegrating. With gaps in the structure, the rest soon fell apart.

"Hey, it worked!" Maris cheered.

I kept my own glee at bay, knowing this was only the beginning of the engagement. We were still within range of the completed alien craft. "What does the readout say, Toran?"

"There was a marked spike at the time of impact," he reported. "One of the waveforms dropped in amplitude."

"Does that mean the more ships there are, the stronger it is?" I speculated.

"As good a guess as any at this stage." Toran pressed behind his ear. "Commander, the signal changed when the ship was in distress. We'll keep an eye on it."

"That's a relief to hear. We'll take care of the rest of these in short order," Colren replied. The comm link ended.

"How can we use this information to our advantage, though?" Kaiden chimed in. "It's obvious the ship was hurt when it fell apart. Does this thing with the waves and signal actually help us?"

"What if the impact *hadn't* been so obvious? The waves would have told us something," Toran replied. "And now, even if a ship shows no exterior damage, we know we can assess the health of their fleet using this method."

"Well, we better take out the rest of those ships before it becomes a proper fleet," Kaiden said.

New ships popped onto the screen with a blue flash. Information tags popped up above each on the screen. "The Hegemony fleet is here!" This time, I did cheer.

Colren no doubt had relayed the information about the plasma cannons because the new Hegemony ships were accelerating toward the anomaly. I counted at least three dozen craft—a sizable fleet to take on the four remaining alien vessels and the anomaly itself.

When the Hegemony ships were close enough, plasma beams lanced out from the bows of the ships toward the targets. The beams rippled over the hulls like they had when the *Evangiel* fired, and the dark tendrils began to fall away from the ships' forms. However, the attack had placed the Hegemony ships close to the completed alien vessel, which obviously wasn't going down without a fight.

"It's getting ready to fire!" My heart pounded in my ears. If its weapon could do to a ship what it had to the torpedoes, the Hegemony fleet could be leveled in a matter of minutes.

"Why aren't they pulling away? Didn't Colren warn them?" Kaiden's voice was pitched with concern.

"They're getting ready to fire again—waiting for the plasma cannon to recharge," Toran replied. "I don't know if they have enough time…"

Everything seemed to fall silent around me as the scene unfolded on the screen. The mouths of the cannon glowed in preparation to fire, but before they could, a black cloud engulfed the forward line of ships. I could barely make out the alien attack itself, only brief explosions as the destroyers lost integrity. Within seconds, there was no evidence the ships had ever been there.

The cloud of Darkness was all but invisible against the starscape, and it wasn't until the next wave of Hegemony vessels began disintegrating before my eyes that I could make out its path of destruction.

"Stars! They have to get out of there," I choked.

"They can't outrun it," Kaiden murmured.

Three of the Hegemony vessels that had been farthest from the alien ship attempted a hasty retreat, but before they'd gone four ship lengths, another cloud of the Darkness enveloped their hulls, each glowing for a moment before falling dark.

Tears glistened in Maris' eyes. "The crews…"

I wanted to honor them for their sacrifice, but we had more pressing issues. New alien vessels were beginning to form within the anomaly, and the *Evangiel* was now the only ship standing in between the enemy front and the Hegemony worlds. There was no reason to believe our ship would fare better than the warships the Darkness had already dissolved as if the reinforced hulls were tissue paper in a sandstorm.

"There's no way out of this," I realized. The rest of fleet was annihilated and we were next. We were all going to die.

Kaiden swallowed. "At least we tried."

I opened a comm channel with the bridge. "Commander—"

The view on the screen changed as the *Evangiel* rapidly pulled away from the anomaly.

"We have to retreat," Colren confirmed over the comm. "Stars help us. Those ships were the most advanced in our fleet."

My stomach turned over. We could run now, but to what end? Any future engagements couldn't possibly have more promise with our lone ship against such a formidable enemy. The war was over before it had truly begun.

I slowly shook my head, not wanting to believe. "This can't

be it."

"We'll regroup with the reserve fleet at the Capital. We need to consolidate resources," Colren stated. "Prepare to jump."

Maris turned to leave the chamber to head toward our jump pods. "If only we could start over," she murmured

Except, there *was* a way to start over...

"We can!" I exclaimed. "The shard."

"Elle, we have no idea what that will do," Toran cautioned.

"Can it be any worse than this? We're dead, our worlds are lost. Us dying here would very likely doom the rest of our civilization, too. If we have any chance for a do-over, I think we need to take it."

The commander didn't say anything over the comm at first. "Yes, we do need to take that chance. Come to the bridge."

Kaiden shook his head. "This is nuts."

"It is, but it might be the best shot we have," Toran replied.

"If we go back far enough, we can save our worlds," Maris said while we jogged down the corridor to the bridge.

"We'll find a way to do that no matter what," I told her.

The bridge door was standing open in anticipation of our arrival, and Colren was in his customary position at the center of the domed command area. He bore a grim expression, but a sliver of hope shined in his eyes as he turned to face us.

"Our fate falls to you." He pulled out a locket hanging from a black chain underneath his uniform jacket. The spherical locket reminded me of a multi-pointed star, crafted from an exotic blue-tinted metal. He pressed one of the spikes and the sphere split in two, revealing the crystal shard inside. He handed it to me. "If I don't remember any of this, thank you in advance."

"How do we use it?" I asked, taking the crystal from his outstretched hand.

"If the lore is correct, bring it to the viewing device and merge it with the crystal," the commander said. "You hold our future in your hands."

"We won't let you down."

I ran back to the viewing room with my team, not bothering to close the door since this physical reality was about to vanish. We huddled around the crystal orb.

"We just stick it in there?" Maris asked.

"I guess so." I looked between the shard in the palm of my hand and the orb.

Worry filled Kaiden's eyes. "How will it know when to reset to? If it only goes back five minutes, we're still dead."

"The cybernetic link!" I hovered my hands side-by-side two centimeters above the crystal. The shard felt tingly and warm in my palm so close to the sphere. "Maybe if we all think about where we want to reset to, it'll do that."

"I don't know what else to suggest," Toran said.

"It needs to be sometime when we were all together and we weren't about to die," Kaiden said, his brow knit.

"What about right after we sealed the Archive?" I suggested.

"Yeah, that could work." He nodded.

"Why not go back before that?" Maris said. "If we could see into the Archive for clues."

"Going back to an older reset point might not un-seal it," I said. "In fact, the point was made that the Archive exists outside of our reality."

"Wouldn't it be worth trying?" she insisted.

"For that matter, go back to before the Darkness appeared," Toran said.

"But we weren't in our new bodies yet," I protested. "It needs to be after we met."

A shudder wracked the ship.

"There's no time to argue!" I continued. "We'll go with right after we sealed the Archive."

"Okay," the others agreed.

With thoughts of the significant moments from the past two weeks still drifting through my head, I prepared to merge the shard. My friends each held their hands above the crystal's surface like mine.

I looked each of them in the eyes. "See you on the other side." I pressed my hands against the sphere, and the shard held against my palm was absorbed into the orb.

The crystal was warm against my hands, radiating not only heat but also an aura of power I couldn't fully comprehend. All I knew was that the sphere was my connection to both past and future. I needed it to save me and my friends while there was still any hope.

I pictured the moment we finished sealing the Archive—the elation and relief I felt having accomplished a task that had seemed impossible. I tried to envision the cavern with the seemingly endless rows of crystals. In that moment, I was thankful for my family, my new body, the artifacts, and the skills that had enabled me to accomplish those things. I had been born anew, and that moment was affirmation that I had become my full self.

Blackness closed in around me. I held the images in my head as best I could, trying to trust in the crystalline network—that it would detect our good intentions and aid us in accomplishing our goal. I floated in nothingness in the way I had after the reset on Erusan before I awoke on the *Evangiel*. As much as I wanted to remain confident, part of me wondered if this time I wouldn't wake up, that I might be trapped in the darkness forever.

15

THE MOMENT STRETCHED on. I sensed myself drifting away, pieces fading into the surroundings.

Just when I was worried there might not be anything of myself left, light crept in at the edges of my vision. I pulled myself toward the bright point in the distance.

At last, I sensed air in my lungs and my vision cleared. I was standing in front of a meter-tall crystal column, and a small crystal shard was in my hand. The crystal was at the center of a ten-meter-wide platform inside a giant cavern covered in millions of crystals. I was overcome with a sense of joy as I took it in.

"We did it!" I said. "We sealed the Archive." There was something else nagging at the back of my mind, like I'd forgotten something.

"We should get back to the *Evangiel* and give Colren our report," Kaiden said.

Colren... there was something I was supposed to tell him. I looked at the crystal shard in my hand. It had something to do with that.

Toran led the way back to our shuttle while I tried to remember whatever it was I had forgotten.

"You okay, Elle?" Maris asked me.

I looked around at the eerily familiar surroundings. "Have we been here before?"

"Well, yeah, on the way in," she replied.

Kaiden placed his hand on my back. "You sure you're feeling all right?" His touch was familiar, setting me at ease in a way I didn't expect.

"Yeah, just worn out, I guess," I replied.

We exited the Archive, pausing only to clean the monument we'd defaced earlier in our quest. As we stepped outside into the diffused purple light of Crystallis, I was overcome again with the feeling that I'd been in that place before. The towering crystals scattered throughout the two-kilometer-wide valley were alien to my eye, yet I couldn't shake the impression that I'd stood in that exact place admiring the view. I shook my head slowly, hoping the déjà vu would pass.

"It's a magnificent sight, isn't it?" Toran commented.

"Yeah. Don't think I could ever get tired of it," I replied.

He nodded. "All the same, I hope we never have to come back here."

"With you there." I followed him down the scree slope toward the shuttle.

We entered the craft and got situated on the bridge. My friends were visibly relaxed compared to the tension we'd been under for the past week, and it warmed me to see genuine smiles on their faces.

Kaiden, in particular, had a lightness about him I had only witnessed in the briefest moments during our time together. As he secured his flight harness, his gaze caught mine. "I can't believe we actually pulled that off."

I smiled back. "Never thought I would slay a dragon."

"First time for everything." His gaze lingered on me for a moment longer, then he turned his attention to the flight controls.

Jovial small talk continued during the flight back to the *Evangiel*. By the time we entered the hangar, I had convinced myself that the odd feeling of familiarity was just the adrenaline from the days' events coloring memories of the other missions with my team. So much had happened in such a short time, it was no wonder that the experiences had started to blur together.

After being greeted by a joyous maintenance crew, we took the central lift to the command deck. As we passed by the ancillary pod room across from the weapons vault in the corridor, Kaiden caught my eye and nodded toward the door to the pod room. "Elle, hang back a minute."

Toran glanced over his shoulder with a raised eyebrow.

"We'll be right there," Kaiden replied to the silent query.

My heart skipped a beat as we waited for the others to go ahead, and I followed Kaiden inside the pod room.

When the door had closed behind us, Kaiden took a step closer to me. "You were amazing today, with the dragon and everything. I'd say that in front of them, too, but there's something else that's more... private."

"What's that?" I stared into his sky-blue eyes.

"When I was lying there on the floor of that cavern, thinking it was all over, all I could think about was that we'd left things at a 'maybe someday'. But we have no idea what's coming tomorrow or a minute from now, so what's the point in waiting?"

Those same thoughts ignited in my own mind. Or, they felt like my thoughts. Somehow, it was almost more like a memory.

"There will always be another reason to wait."

"Exactly. And I don't want to miss the chance to see what we could have." Kaiden stepped toward me until we were almost touching. Gently, he brushed the fingertips of his right hand along my shoulder and then cupped the side of my face in the palm of his hand.

"I don't, either." A tingle of desire surged through me as I stared into his eyes. I slid my left hand behind his head and locked him in a passionate kiss.

We melted into each other, the stress and uncertainty of the previous week fading into the background. I was eager to lose myself in him and forget what we had been through. In that moment, it was only us, and I'd want it no other way.

Even though we'd never done more than hug or hold hands before, I somehow felt like I knew him—how to touch, how to move. As I followed my instincts, I could feel him respond how I sensed he would, and he somehow knew exactly how to caress me even though I didn't consciously know myself what I wanted.

Eventually, we separated, breathless.

Kaiden's lips parted in a stunned smile. "Wow."

I grinned. "Good wow?"

"Definitely." He paused. "That didn't feel like a first kiss."

"It really didn't." While I didn't have much experience on the matter, my friends back on Erusan had talked about enough awkward encounters for me to know that instant physical sync was rare, to say the least. There should have been some level of awkwardness or uncertainty. Either we were soul mates, or… I gnawed on my lower lip. "*Was* it our first?"

He chuckled. "Considering we were interrupted by Maris the last time we almost did—"

"No, not then." I shook my head. "Never mind."

Kaiden cocked his head. "You can't start a statement like that and not finish."

I sighed. "I dunno, ever since we left the Archive I just can't shake the feeling that we've done all of this before."

"Yeah, I remember what you said earlier."

"I know it sounds crazy."

He swallowed. "It would, except being with you just now, I couldn't help thinking the same thing."

I took an unsteady breath. "How would that be possible?"

"The only thing that comes to mind is a reset."

"But we remember those."

"We're *supposed* to remember them."

I tugged on the end of my braid. "I wonder if Toran or Maris have had any of these same feelings?"

"Only way to find out is to ask," Kaiden replied. "And they're probably wondering where we are."

"Oh, right! Colren." I glanced toward the door. "Should we say something?"

"About a potential reset or what we were doing in here?"

"Both."

He linked his fingers with mine. "Regarding this, I think we can drop a few subtle hints and they'll figure it out. As for the other thing, let's give it a little bit and see if anything else unusual sticks out."

"Works for me."

Still holding hands, we exited the pod room and continued down the corridor to Central Command. When we entered, we found that Toran and Maris were already with Commander Colren in the conference room. Kaiden and I rushed to join them, dropping our hands to our sides as we entered.

"Nice of you to join us," Colren stated, his gaze fixed on us as we found our seats.

"Sorry, Commander." My cheeks flushed.

Maris smirked. "We were just getting to the part about the rock titan outside the Archive."

"Yes, that." I nodded.

Kaiden and I interjected bits about our battles with the rock titan, spirit elemental, and dark dragon while Toran took the lead on the explanation. When Toran finished the description of the Master Archive and our talk with the mysterious voice, Colren leaned back in his chair.

"That explains so much," the commander said, shaking his head with amazement.

"Unfortunately, the information doesn't help us know how to stop the Darkness and whatever beings are behind it," Toran said. "All we can say is the records are safe."

Colren nodded. "That's what we hoped to achieve. Also, now we know this assault on our worlds was a first wave and ships may be coming next. That's more information than we had before."

Maris crossed her arms. "Even after *all* of that, we still don't have any other hints about what to do next? For a place that was supposed to hold all the answers, we didn't get many."

"There was nothing else?" Colren asked.

I snapped to attention. "Well, there was one other thing." I pulled the crystal shard from my pocket. It tingled in my palm, almost like it was resonating with the magical energy inside of me.

The commander carefully took the crystal from my outstretched hand. "Where did you get this?"

"It's a piece of a crystal in the Archive," I replied. "The voice said it would aid us in the trials ahead."

"Stars!" Colren exclaimed. "Could it be...?" He examined the tiny crystal fragment with awe in his eyes.

"Do you know what it is?" I asked.

Colren cracked a smile. "It appears to be a shard from a Master Crystal. I didn't think we'd ever get access to one."

I tilted my head. "What it is, exactly?"

"If there's any truth to the legends, it's connected to the Master Archive," Colren explained. "Such a shard provides a direct hyperdimensional link to allow backups beyond our inhabited worlds."

Kaiden frowned. "And what does that mean for us?"

The commander's eyes shined with renewed hope. "This is the tool we needed. It gives us a control point."

"It would enable a universal reset," I murmured, meeting Kaiden's gaze.

"That's right." Colren nodded. "With this, you could access the Master Archive from anywhere and use it as the locus of the reset event."

"Even with the Master Archive sealed?" Kaiden asked.

"With the Master Archive sealed, a shard like this would be the *only* way to conduct a reset, as I understand it," Colren replied. "But, as powerful as this tool is, there are so many unknowns that I'm not sure if it's viable."

Toran nodded. "A last resort, then."

Kaiden and I exchanged glanced again. "So, if we did use it, there could be side effects?" he asked.

The commander shrugged. "I couldn't even begin to predict what might happen. Controlling the timeframe of the reset would be a challenge even with the tools at our disposal. Furthermore, there's no telling how a reset on an interstellar scale would work." He stared at the crystal in his palm. "I look at this and see a way to restore the worlds that have already been lost, but it could also mean going back in time before any of us exist. As much as I want to use it, we need to try to find another way."

I shifted in my seat. "I guess we would have to be pretty desperate if we decided to use it, then."

Maris smiled. "That's for our future selves to worry about. For now, I say we should call today a victory."

"Indeed, it was," Toran agreed.

I forced a smile. "Yeah, totally."

"Take the rest of the day to celebrate and rest," Colren told us. "We'll regroup in the morning and figure out our next steps."

"Thank you, Commander. See you then." Kaiden rose from the table.

The bridge crew offered us thanks and congratulations as we passed through, but I barely heard the words. All I could think about was the potential side effects of a universal reset and wonder if what I was experiencing might be related to that. Based on Kaiden's intense expression, I suspected he was thinking about the same thing.

"So, how are we going to celebrate?" Maris asked as soon as we were in the corridor outside Central Command.

"Not sure if I'm up for much of a party," I replied, far too preoccupied with other thoughts.

Maris eyed me, an amused smile playing on her lips. "Just hoping for some alone time with Kaiden?"

"No, that's not—" He started in response then cut off. "Yeah, we've grown close, but there's something else going on."

I nodded. "You know earlier what I asked if we'd been in that cavern before? Well, those same feelings of familiarity keep happening."

"I started noticing things, too," Kaiden added. "We were talking about it before the meeting. That's why we were late."

"Have you experienced anything out of the ordinary?" I

asked Toran and Maris.

Toran frowned. "Nothing specific."

"But there's a feeling, right?" I pressed. "Like we've had these conversations before. Not *precisely* the same, but similar."

Maris sighed. "Next you're going to say that this has something to do with that crystal shard thing."

"It might," Kaiden replied.

"Colren said there could be side effects after a universal reset," I continued. "What if there was one and we don't remember?"

"That would mean something went wrong and our consciousness didn't reknit correctly," Toran said.

"We have nothing to go on other than a hunch," Kaiden continued. "It might be nothing—just a bizarre byproduct of being in the Master Archive. But what if we *did* do a universal reset? What had happened to make us try something so extreme?"

"Maybe we learned how to control it?" Maris speculated.

Toran inclined his head. "Perhaps. Or, we were so desperate we'd try anything to get another chance."

I swallowed. "Whatever the circumstances, what we do next will dictate whether we go down that same path or have a different, better outcome."

Maris' brows drew together. "How can we have things turn out differently if we don't remember what we did the first time around?"

"We need to *try* to remember," I implored. "Keep track of all of those little things that seem familiar. Assemble the pieces."

"We should bring this to Colren," Toran suggested.

"And we will, as soon as there's anything actionable," I

assured him. "Right now, all we could say is that we think we get into trouble at some point and resort to a universal reset. That sounds more stress-inducing than helpful."

Maris glared at me. "You don't say?"

"Elle is right. The commander has enough on his mind right now without piling on an issue this vague," Kaiden agreed. "The four of us need to figure out what we can so we have something solid to bring him."

"Very well," Toran conceded.

Maris sighed. "All right, fine. Where does that leave us with the celebratory party?"

Kaiden shrugged. "Well, if we hadn't had this something-isn't-right realization, I expect a party would have been in order."

I still wasn't thrilled by the idea of having to be social while I was working through what kind of problem we were up against, but I did have to agree with Kaiden's logic that we should try to recreate the circumstances as much as possible. The more similar we could make it, the more we might be able to jog our memories about the alternate reality from which we had potentially reset.

"Something in the Mess, maybe?" I suggested.

"Oh, *now* you're in the mood for a party?" Maris cast me a sidelong glance.

"I think other-me would have been, that's all."

"Trying to guess what we would do under other circumstances is a recipe for madness," Toran cautioned. "We shouldn't try to overthink this."

Maris got a devious glint in her eyes. "I know one surefire way to help you relax."

16

NOT SURPRISINGLY, BARTENDER Maris' solution to our worries revolved around shots. However, we soon learned through various inquiries that, being a military starship, the *Evangiel's* booze selection was limited to a single bottle of whiskey in Colren's quarters, which was a rare vintage and declared to be strictly off-limits.

With that plan thwarted, we instead found ourselves gathered around one of the tables near a viewport in the Mess. We'd each taken extra helpings of the least offensive variety of gruel on the menu, the orangey-brown one. When I didn't think about it too much, I could almost convince myself it was proper chili.

"Really festive, guys. Definitely pulled out all the stops with this one," Maris muttered as she gathered a portion of the paste onto her spoon and dribbled it back into the bowl.

"Okay, so we didn't take into account that everyone else is still on duty," Kaiden said.

"Think the original celebration was like this?" I asked.

"I can't imagine significantly different circumstances,"

Toran replied. "After all, the rest of the crew remains unaware of our situation."

I set down my spoon. "You know, that's a good point. Do you think anyone other than us is having the déjà vu thing happen?"

Toran nodded thoughtfully. "True. If we keep this to ourselves, we won't know if the phenomenon is limited to us."

"Some subtle question-asking might be in order," Kaiden said. "Wasn't that the plan anyway?"

"It was." I pushed my mostly empty plate away. "Sitting around here isn't exactly festive, as Maris said. Why don't we go mobile?"

Maris raised an eyebrow. "Bring the party to those who can't leave their stations?"

"That's good thinking." Kaiden smiled. "See people in their element where they're comfortable, find out if anything feels off to them."

I nodded. "Precisely."

"This would be way better with a party tray." Maris sighed.

"Booze isn't necessary to get people to talk, Maris," Kaiden said.

"No, but it certainly makes things easier."

I stood up and grabbed my meal tray to bus it. "We're not trying to get people to spill their deepest secrets here."

"Okay, so maybe I want the drinks for *me*," Maris admitted. "Come on, it's been a rough day! We were almost eaten by a dragon."

I placed my leftovers in the receptacle. "Well, we *weren't* eaten, so there's that."

Kaiden laughed, joining me at the bussing station. "My list of 'things to be thankful for' has gotten incredibly strange."

"Best not to think about it too much." Toran rose to take

care of his own plate.

While the others finished clearing the table, I scoped out the rest of the Mess. Only three other tables were presently occupied. The diners at two of the tables were completely absorbed in their own conversations, but those at the third kept glancing over at us. I decided they might make a good warmup for our planned investigative discussions.

"Let's start over here," I said, leading the way to the target table with the two men and a woman.

"And these are…?" Kaiden whispered.

"People who seem to have an interest in us." I whispered back. "Hopefully that means they'll talk."

I plastered on what I hoped was an approachable smile as I neared the table. "Hey, I couldn't help but notice you watching us. What's up?"

"Real subtle, Elle," Kaiden said under his breath behind me.

The first of the two men, a crewman in his late-thirties with dark hair and amber eyes, folded his hands on the tabletop and tilted his head. "Why might have we taken an interest in you?"

"We *are* the heroes around here, after all," I replied in a smug tone. "I'm actually surprised no one else wanted to join us in our celebration."

"Oh, that's what that was?" the red-headed woman asked. "Looked like any other meal."

"We had hoped for some company, but everyone is busy," Kaiden chimed in.

Maris squinted. "Not to mention, how do you get by without a stocked bar?"

The fair-haired second man raised his water glass. "Cheers to that!" His two companions cast a stern glance in his direction and he lowered the glass.

"Some of these days really start to blend together, you know?" I continued. "I don't know how you do it."

"You have no idea," the dark-hair man replied. "Sometimes, I could swear I'd already processed the same readings."

"Oh, is that so?" That sounded remarkably like the situation we were presently facing, but his phrasing made it sound like it was an ongoing situation, not a recent development.

"I've been doing practically the same thing for seven years. You've got to expect the days to run together now and again." He cracked a smile, though it didn't seem heartfelt.

"Already happening to me and I've only been here for two weeks," Kaiden chimed in.

The blond man snorted. "I don't know how anything could feel routine for you while you're off galivanting on those planets."

"It's usually more 'trying not to die', if we're being honest," Maris corrected.

"Sure, whatever you want to call it," the first man replied. He swirled the purple contents of his glass. "In any case, we were wondering what's going to happen to the rest of us when you do get yourselves killed."

The breath left my lungs like I'd been kicked in the chest. "Pardon?"

"You heard me. It's only a matter of time your lack of experience catches up with you and you don't come back from one of your little missions," he continued, sweeping a lock of dark hair from his eyes.

The woman at the table crossed her arms. "Sorry, does it come as a surprise to you that everyone on the ship doesn't worship the deck plates you walk on? The commander has put his faith in you for whatever reason, but some of us would prefer to place our trust in seasoned soldiers who don't play dress-up and play with swords."

I had half a mind to draw my blade and see what she thought of it up close, but Kaiden placed a calming hand on my elbow.

"Why were you watching us, then? Taking bets on which one of us would die first?" he asked the three crew members.

"More or less. We were wagering a weeks' worth of dessert about which one of you would crack under the pressure first," the blond man said. "My bet is on her." He nodded toward Maris.

While I didn't disagree with his assessment that she was the potential weak link on our team, I wasn't about to let anyone get away with talking about my new friends that way. I glared at him. "None of us asked to be placed in this position. No, we don't have a lot of experience, but so far we've already accomplished things no one else has been able to do. If we end up dying on a planet, at least it won't be for lack of trying—for stepping outside of what's safe and familiar. This isn't a conventional enemy, so maybe an unconventional team is *exactly* what's needed."

He inched back in his chair as I spoke, fear evident in his wide eyes. It surprised me that I could come off as so intimidating, but I realized that the attack glove I normally wore on my right hand had started to glow even though it was only hanging at my side rather than on my hand. I suppressed my concern about the remote activation; right now, I was busy defending the honor of the Dark Sentinels.

"I told you not to bet against this one," the woman said to the dark-haired man, seemingly unfazed by the magical item clipped to my belt.

Kaiden rounded on the man. "What happened to make you so hostile?"

"What happened?" The dark-haired man laughed bitterly. "Our worlds have been destroyed, and yet we're chasing down so-called 'legendary artifacts' and letting a handful of kids call the shots."

"I'm not as young as I appear," Toran spoke up for the first time, his booming voice grabbing the crew members' attention.

"Doesn't matter. Why aren't we fighting back against the Darkness?" the blond man said, leaning forward in his chair. "Why haven't we done anything to reclaim our worlds?"

I narrowed my eyes. "We *are*. We've done nothing but try to find a solution for the last week. Just because you don't know everything we're up to, don't assume nothing is happening."

The woman shook her head. "I work in Communications. I know exactly what you've done, and it amounts to sealing the Archive—the thing we need to restore the worlds. You haven't made any progress, it's just been a giant step backward."

"That's not an accurate assessment," Toran said, his voice still level and calm.

The dark-haired man downed the remaining contents of his glass. "The Hegemony is doomed if they truly believe in placing their faith in the likes of you. The sooner you aren't around, the sooner they'll get back to solving this problem with soldiers like they should have all along."

Acrid annoyance welled in my chest as I thought about how much was wrong with his statements. The Hegemony *had* tried a direct physical approach and all those people had died. Even though it might look like we hadn't accomplished much, we'd made sure the records of our worlds were safe. Without that, there never would have been a hope for a reset to fix everything. We'd made a tangible contribution for the better, even if these people didn't want to see it.

I wanted to yell at the three crew members and set them straight, to show them that I wasn't a helpless teenager who didn't have the guts to fight in a war. I was putting my life on the line, and they needed to see that I took it seriously. My friends and I were a formidable team, and we would stand together to the end.

But I held my tongue. These people didn't want to have their opinion changed; escalating the conflict wouldn't solve anything.

"I guess we'll just have to show you why we're the best team for the job," I said as calmly as possible. "Oh, and for the record, swords and capes are awesome." I spun on my heel and stormed out of the Mess.

I didn't turn back to see the reaction on the crew members' faces, but a snort from Maris suggested that they were at a loss for words.

Once in the corridor, I took a slow, deep breath. "Okay, so maybe talking to people outside the inner circle was a bad idea."

"Yeah, no way around it, that could have gone a lot better," Kaiden said.

"I had no idea anyone had resentment toward us," I continued. "Tami and Colren have been so welcoming, I thought that carried through to the rest of the ship."

"High-tension times aggravate people's fears," Toran replied.

Maris frowned. "They weren't just afraid, they were angry."

"I'm angry, too," I admitted. "This is a terrible situation. Our worlds might be lost, we don't know what to do, and now we might be stuck in a reset loop without knowing it."

"Our very presence here asking questions has changed things," Toran said. "Perhaps it is better we return to our quarters as we would have otherwise."

Maris stifled a yawn. "Fine by me."

"Yeah, we can do more investigating in the morning," I agreed.

We took the lift to our area and moseyed down the corridor. As we neared the common room, I slowed my pace. "I'm not quite ready for bed. I think I'll hang out for a bit and enjoy the view."

"Mind if I join you?" Kaiden asked.

"Of course not."

Toran gave us a knowing smile. "Stay out of trouble, you two. See you in the morning."

"Good night," I bid him and Maris, then wandered into the lounge.

The planet of Crystallis was just visible out the viewport, approaching the leading edge of dawn. White light flared from behind the planet's shoulder, creating a dramatic aura above the purple-hued atmosphere.

"I don't think I'll ever get tired of viewing a planet from space," I murmured while taking it in.

Kaiden came to stand at my left hip. "Even having grown up on starships, I still haven't."

I turned to look up at him. "Are we really just foolish kids in over our heads?"

"Oh, Elle, we're definitely in over our heads, but to be *foolish* I think we'd need to not recognize what we're up against. I have no doubts that we each understand what's at stake."

"That's true."

He wrapped his arms around me, and I laid my head against his chest. The embrace had the same familiarity and comfort I'd experienced during our kiss before. If there had been a reset, whatever bond was developing between us seemed to transcend our other memories. I couldn't help wondering where we might have left off with things in the alternative version of our future.

"It feels right, doesn't it?" Kaiden murmured into my hair. "I don't know how, but I feel I know you more than I should."

"For all we know, we could have been together for years before the reset."

"No, there's still something new here." He pulled back slightly to look into my eyes. "I can't explain it, but I somehow sense that we're still figuring things out. It's like we went through something that brought us closer, but the amount of time together hasn't caught up with the closeness of experience."

"You're right, there's comfort to a point and then... the unknown." If that instinct held, we weren't an old married couple. I found myself strangely relieved as I processed the half-memories, realizing that there were still unexplored elements to our relationship. The happiness worried me for a moment as I thought it might stem from second-guessing the romance, but then I realized it was rooted in a desire to have a natural progression uncolored by echoes of another path. There was still a chance for us to have firsts together—proper new experience, not re-creations. I would hate to think that important moments in my life could have been erased without memory. When those moments did happen, I wanted to have it forever as a part of myself.

"You still with me?" Kaiden asked softly.

"Sorry, just thinking." I traced my hand down his chest.

"About what?"

"You. Us. That maybe despite everything going on, there's a sliver of a chance that we can still get to know each other like a normal couple."

He gave me a light kiss. "I'd like that very much."

I kissed him back, longer and deeper. "But I don't want to forget any of it. How can we move forward when all of this could go away again?"

"We've been resetting for our whole lives."

"Always with our memories. This isn't the same."

He studied me. "I think I know what you're hinting at."

"Are you okay taking things slow?"

"Considering we just had our first kiss, I had no expectations."

I looked down. "It's probably way too soon to bring that up, sorry."

"No, never apologize for being honest. We need to be able to be open and trust each other."

"I do feel I can trust you."

"Good. You can." He placed his hands on my shoulders. "And after seeing you take on a dragon single-handed today, I have no doubts about being able to trust you with my life."

"Heh, yeah. Let's hope battles like that aren't an everyday occurrence."

"This, on the other hand," he gave me a kiss, "I'd be happy to have as a regular thing."

"I was just thinking that." I closed my eyes and shut out the world around me, happy to be there with him.

When we eventually parted, I linked my arm through his and we watched the sun rise over Crystallis. There was so much light... I was filled with a sense of hope that we still had a chance of defeating the Darkness.

"We saved this world, and there will be others," Kaiden said, holding me close.

"I believe that, even if everyone isn't on our side."

"Those people in the mess hall didn't know what they were talking about. They don't know us or what we can do."

"As petty as it is, that makes me want to try even harder to prove them wrong."

Kaiden laughed. "I appreciate that about you."

"I suspect you're much the same way." I leaned against him,

He kissed the top of my head. "Having a little fighting spirit comes in handy."

As we stared down at the light-bathed planet, my mind drifted to the Darkness I'd seen consume other worlds. It took this kind of vantage—being in orbit—to appreciate the scale of what we were up against. Entire planets, systems, a civilization… Images of the Darkness tore through planets in my mind's eye, twisting tranquil landscapes into corrupted, savage environments and morphing native creatures into vicious killers. But as I thought about Erusan, Wantu, and the horrors of the Valor artifact world, new visions began to surface of a place I'd never seen before. I saw myself in the environment. Felt it. It was like I had experienced it myself and the memory was only now surfacing.

"No." I pulled away from Kaiden, heart pounding in my ears.

"What's wrong?"

I massaged my temples. "It can't be."

Kaiden stood silently and waited for me to collect myself.

I took several deep breaths, trying to relax my racing heart. "I think I just remembered something that hasn't happened yet."

17

KAIDEN PROCESSED MY words. "That's good, though, right? Weren't we hoping to remember what might have happened before the reset... assuming there was one?"

I wiped my hands down my face. "Yes. Except, now I wish I didn't know."

"What did you see, Elle?" He took a step toward me, his eyes fill with worry.

"We were on a world—completely consumed by the Darkness. But it wasn't the Valor world. This one has been infected long ago, and all of the terrible creatures we've seen were mature." I described the tentacle monster and the fields of tendrils. The visceral element of the memories had me on edge. Only Kaiden's presence kept me centered.

"Do you have a sense of where this planet was?" he asked me when I finished going over the scattered recollections.

"No idea. I got the impression that it was our first time there, wherever it was."

"If the corrupted environment was mature, then it has to be one of the first Hegemony worlds to be infected by the Darkness."

I frowned. "Assuming my memories were recent. What if we make that visit two months from now?"

He smiled coyly. "I don't think so."

"Why?"

"Well, we already established that we have a good thing going between us, but it hasn't advanced too far, near as we can tell. Based on what we're feeling now, I doubt it wouldn't have advanced by two months from now."

I couldn't argue that logic. I was already craving to be closer to him; I couldn't fathom delaying those explorations. I'd been waiting for years to find someone I could trust, and I was eager to make up for lost time. Plus, having the looming cloud of potential death being around every turn, I could really use another outlet to help me decompress.

"Okay, so we're maybe dealing with a timeline of a few weeks?" I said.

He nodded, a smirk playing on his lips. "Assuming you can resist me for that long."

I rolled my eyes, hating that he had a valid point. "All right, so, a week or two," I amended.

Kaiden looked pleased with the adjustment but said nothing.

"Anyway," I continued, "if I've correctly interpreted the nonsense going on in my head, at some time in the next two weeks we're going to find ourselves on an apocalyptically terrible world to attempt to access a crystal. Then, it would seem something soon afterward makes us resort to a universal reset, which results in… this."

"Lots of hypotheticals in that explanation."

"Do you have anything better to offer?"

He shook his head. "Having not had a new vision—or memory burst, whatever you want to call it—of my own, I can't comment. But I do believe something along those lines is happening. I still can't explain it, but I feel it."

"Why haven't Maris or Toran been as affected by it?" I wondered.

"Maybe they haven't had the right stimulus to jog their memories. You didn't start to remember until we... you know."

I took several paces, thinking. "Okay, so we might be able to spark other memories with the right experience. In that case, should we do as many things as possible to see what's familiar, or just forget that other timeline and do our own thing now?"

He smiled. "Well, I suppose that depends on what 'experiences' you have in mind."

I rolled my eyes and groaned. "Not with *us*. I mean, going around the ship, or—"

"I know, I'm just teasing." Kaiden turned more serious. "I keep going back and forth about whether I really *want* to know what happened before."

"And what are you thinking now?"

"That we should go to bed and worry about it in the morning. Maybe a path will present itself."

"That's a classic non-answer if I've ever heard one."

"I've heard it's a necessary survival skill in any relationship."

I smiled. "Like when I ask you what you want for dinner but I've already made up my mind?"

"Exactly."

I laughed. "With that kind of wisdom, I can't believe you were single."

"Mostly by choice, but I'm ready to not be."

"Good. In that case, I'm inviting myself over for the night."

His eyed widened with surprise. "Not that I mind, but why?"

"Do I really have to explain?"

"Of course not." He placed an arm around my shoulders, and we headed for the door. "Honestly, I didn't want to be alone staring at the ceiling of my cabin tonight, either."

I stopped by my cabin to brush my teeth and then slinked over to Kaiden's cabin next door. Despite the vastly different circumstances, I was reminded of going to sleepovers at Adrianne's house as a kid. I wasn't sure if my former self from before the reset would have opted for a sleepover in this moment, but it's what *I* wanted.

Kaiden's eyes lit up when he opened his cabin door. "Welcome. It's exactly like yours, so I don't think you'll have any trouble finding your way around." Even if the space was unfamiliar, the compact design with a bed, wardrobe, and wash room at the back didn't leave much opportunity for getting lost.

I stepped inside. "Thank you for humoring me."

"I didn't want to be alone, either, to be honest. It feels like everything could fall apart at any moment."

"I can't shake that feeling, either."

He glanced between the bed and me, then began taking off his outer clothing like we did before every jump. The white base layers made for comfy pajamas, I'd found, so I'd brought nothing else over to wear.

When we'd finished stripping down, we sat down on the bed next to each other.

"Forget everything that's going on out there," Kaiden said. "Right now, we're here together." He reclined on the bed, gently pulling me with him. With our heads sharing the pillow, he wrapped one arm around me.

For the first time in days, I felt truly secure. I'd expected dark thoughts to keep me awake all night, but Kaiden's warmth at my back and his arm around me really did help me forget the outside world.

Pounding on the door snapped me to attention. "Wha…?"

The clock indicated two hours had passed. I hadn't even realized I'd fallen asleep.

Kaiden bolted upright next to me. "Who *knocks* rather than paging on the comm?"

"Not thinking clearly?" I speculated, shaking off the grogginess of sleep.

He slipped off the bed then stepped over to the door and cracked it open. His posture relaxed. "Maris, what—"

"You have to come!" she exclaimed. "It's Toran. He keeps muttering about 'ships'—" She cut off when she saw me sitting on the bed through the cracked door. "You…?"

Kaiden started to close the door. "Where is he?"

"Mess Hall," she replied.

"We'll be right there." He latched the door, letting out a long sigh.

I started hastily dressing in my outerwear. "What are they even doing up at this hour?"

"No idea." He started dressing, as well.

"That was nice, by the way," I said as I slipped on my overcoat. "Even though I didn't mean for anyone to see me over here. Not that I mind, just…"

"Yes, it was, and I know what you mean. I didn't want them to make this into a big deal, either."

"Maybe this thing with Toran will be enough of a distraction."

"For Maris? No way. Relationship gossip is her lifeblood." Kaiden finished slipping on his shoes.

"I had to dream."

Once dressed enough to look presentable, we hurried to

the Mess. Maris was nowhere to be seen, but two women and a man stood outside the Mess entrance, looking concerned.

"Do you know what's going on?" I asked them.

"We were unwinding after late shift when he came in—sleepwalking, maybe. She came in right after him," the first woman said.

"He started talking about 'dark ships' and how they were coming," the second added. "Freaked us out."

"Then the brunette came in and told us to leave," the man said.

"Thanks. We'll get Toran calmed down," Kaiden replied.

I approached the entry door with him. "Talk about a setback on our reputation campaign with the non-believers," I whispered.

"We have bigger issues to worry about than our social standing."

The door slid to the side, revealing the mostly empty Mess. Toran was standing in front of the wide viewports, trembling, and Maris was patting one of his broad, bare shoulders in what appeared to be an attempt to comfort him. With his back to us, I couldn't see his face or get a sense of his disposition.

"Hi, Toran, what's wrong?" I said in my friendliest tone.

Maris glanced toward us for a moment before returning her attention to Toran. "You were right earlier," she said. "We're starting to remember now."

My heart skipped a beat. "What have you seen?"

"A world. Death. I don't know where it was, but it's dangerous," Maris replied.

"Sounds an awful lot like what I saw." I approached the viewport. "We should compare notes and see if we can put together a narrative for what happened—or might happen, however you want to put it."

"Nothing we can do to stop it," Toran murmured.

I was finally close enough to see his face, and to my shock there were tears welling in his reddened eyes and his flushed cheeks were damp. I wasn't sure how to react; comforting had never been my specialty, let alone tending to the person who'd always been the rock on our team.

"Toran, hey, what's wrong?" Kaiden asked, visibly shaken by Toran's state.

The huge man sniffled. "I don't know. It hit me all at once—almost like I stepped outside of myself."

"The crew thought maybe you were dreaming," I said.

"No, this wasn't a dream." He dried his eyes with the backs of his hands.

"Tell us what you saw. We've been having flashes, too. Maybe we can make something of it," Kaiden urged.

Toran took a steadying breath. "I'm not so sure there's anything we can do this time."

"The last week has taught me that there's always a way," I told him. "Now, what is it about these ships?"

"We don't stand a chance against them," he said, his voice cracking again.

I swallowed hard. Alien ships... something about that was so familiar. I could envision them in my mind even though I only had a vague description from the Archive visions to go on.

Kaiden and I exchanged glances. "Could these have been the ships I saw in my vision inside the Archive?" he asked.

"Probably, but there's one particular ship I keep seeing. I'm terrified of it and I don't know why." The flush in Toran's face was fading and his eyes were more focused.

"Right now, gut feelings are all we have," Kaiden told him. "Trust that impression."

"I do, but..." Toran shook his head. "What if this *is* a

memory from before the reset? What if that ship made us desperate enough to try anything?"

"This time, we have a heads up. We can be more on guard and not let it happen again," I said. But what had transpired? I could feel the answer somewhere in the back of my mind, but it was just beyond my grasp.

"How?" Maris threw up her arms. "We don't know anything new! We already knew there are dangerous things out there."

"If some memories have surfaced, the rest are buried in there, too," I insisted. "We just need to figure out a way to access them so we can stay a step ahead of the enemy."

"Unless they also know what's coming," Maris countered.

"Things have already started to change," Toran said. "This is a fresh start for both sides."

"Except, now we've seen some of what they can do. We can have countermeasures in place." I didn't know *what* countermeasures were feasible against giant shuttle-snaring Darkness tentacles, but the Hegemony's military needed to have something that stood a chance against them.

"It'd be helpful if we could shake off this amnesia," Maris said.

"No, I don't think it's like that at all," Toran replied, sounding much more like his usual level-headed self.

"If not amnesia, then what?" I asked.

"An incomplete download resulting from the limitations of the distributed hyperdimensional crystal-link."

I stared at Toran and blinked.

He took a deep breath. "Sorry, I was reading up on it before I got distracted by alien ship visions, and all the techno-babble is still in my head."

Kaiden smiled. "A plain-speak explanation would be great."

Toran was silent while he collected his thoughts. "Okay, so, there are two basic parts to it," he began. "Foremost, the crystals are a link to a higher dimension—we've known that for decades. Based on what's commonly accepted, the hyperdimensional link between the crystals is governed by restrictions similar to the limited bandwidth of a computer network. While hyperdimensional storage is theoretically limitless, only so much information can practically be funneled through the crystalline network at one time. Consequently, it gets hashed and compressed when each reset point is established, with the individual crystals functioning as a sort of 'cache' to aid in the recall."

"Okay," Kaiden began, "so when the cache is full, that's why old information is eventually removed from the hyper-memory, and entire prior resets may disappear from a crystal interface?"

Toran nodded. "Exactly."

"What does that have to do with our memories?" Maris asked.

I cast her a silencing glare. "Let him finish."

"This is where things get more contested," Toran continued. "Some scientists believe that a part of our consciousness suspends outside of spacetime during the resets. Usually, that part of ourselves can come right back to our reconstructed bodies and it feels like we reverted to a prior time, reconciling the previous-future *and* the memories of everything leading up to that moment. I think in the case of the universal reset, though, those previous-future memories didn't download."

Kaiden scowled. "Why?"

"To put it simply, bandwidth issues," Toran went on. "For a local reset, the data requirements are fairly small, allowing a long past span of time to be perfectly recovered. A planet-reset is still possible, but the risks of losing some memory of the previous-future increase; this might be one reason why large-scale resets are so rare. Now, beyond that, a universal-scale reset is a huge undertaking—way more information than the crystalline network can reconcile with its limited 'bandwidth', if you will. The hyperdimensional transfer through the crystal-interfaces is simply insufficient to allow full restoration of anything other than the matter, energy, and memories up to the time of the reset. The fragment of consciousness that exists outside of spacetime didn't have a chance to resync, so the previous-future memories are inaccessible."

I tilted my head. "Then how do the four of us remember?"

He shrugged. "Proximity to the locus of the event. The crystalline network might prioritize re-syncing of memories for people closest to the reset crystal."

"So, the further away from the locus, the less a person would remember of the previous-future?" I asked.

"That does fit with what we observed," Kaiden said. "Those crew members talked about the days running together—which could have been from routine, or maybe there was the slightest hint that we'd looped back."

Maris nodded. "That's true."

"The effects in others are weak, even on the same ship. Lightyears away—in the Capital, for instance—would they sense any déjà vu at all?" Kaiden wondered aloud.

"If it scales like anything else we've observed here, then no," Toran stated. "But the scientific models would suggest that the other memories weren't lost, exactly, just that they couldn't be recalled during the reset. They should still exist in the part of our consciousness that dwells in hyperdimensional space—a theory which is supported by us being imbued with abilities we hadn't learned yet."

Suddenly, I wish I'd paid more attention in physics class. "Okay, where does that leave us?" I asked.

"Aware but still disconnected," Toran murmured.

"We need to access those memories that didn't resync," Kaiden said.

"That not something that can be forced," Toran replied. "Regardless, we still need to figure out what to tell the Hegemony's decision-makers. Nothing in our visions points to a specific time or place."

"You're right." I turned away from the others, wracking my mind for the answers I knew must be somewhere within me. The ships... Toran was onto something there. Why couldn't I remember what?

The feelings of familiarity and fear were coming from somewhere. If I knew to be concerned, there was a reason why. For my own sanity, I needed to believe that I was in control. Maybe Toran was right and the details had been lost during the consciousness reintegration, but I wasn't ready to believe that the memories were beyond my grasp.

I focused on the elements I had remembered so far, trying to put them in order so I could develop a sequence of events for what had happened leading up to the presumed reset. The dark planet must have come before the ships, since those seemed to be the end of that timeline. But what had happened in between?

Hazy recollections of something bright against the dark backdrop of space began to come to me. I was mesmerized at first, and then fear crept into the corners of my mind. "A light," I murmured. "Did the ships come from a light?"

Kaiden gripped his head. "Gah! It's right there, but I can't remember!"

An overwhelming sense of destruction filled me as I thought about the light. It was a point of creation, and yet I somehow knew it would take everything from us.

"That place." My brow knit. "That's where we lose the fleet, I think."

"That place keeps appearing to me, too," Kaiden said. "There's a bright point. Beautiful, but danger surrounds it."

The jumble of images in my mind became sharper: an alien fleet birthed for the sole purpose of our destruction, and a weapon that could level the Hegemony defensive line in an instant. We needed to stop them.

I snapped to attention. "Call Colren. We're about to be invaded."

18

THE COMMANDER LISTENED intently across the conference table as I told him what I had remembered. I kept waiting for him to dismiss the statements and say that my imagination had gotten the better of me, but he kept nodding with understanding as I piled on the outlandish claims.

"I wish we had more to give you," I concluded.

"Any information is good information," Colren replied. "I only wish we knew where this place was."

"We might be able to figure it out with a little help," Kaiden said. "Which worlds were the first taken by the Darkness?"

Colren frowned. "Windau, Azura, Tarden. Why?"

"Maybe seeing some records of those worlds will help jog our memories," I said. "If the creatures on the planet were mature—"

"Then the corruption has to have been from some time ago, I follow." He stood up from the conference table and glanced out the glass door toward the bridge. "Access any records you need. Figuring out the site of these engagements is the first step toward finding a different outcome."

Kaiden stood up and nodded. "We'll do our best, Commander."

Colren took a step toward the door then stopped. "Say, would there be any way to tell if we've had this conversation before?"

"Not that I've been able to figure out," Toran replied. "I believe the hyperdimensional component of our consciousness wasn't able to re-link with our physical selves during the reset. But, our memories and abilities still exist in that part of ourselves outside of spacetime. I think, perhaps, this might explain how we have muscle memory for things we've never done before. Part of our hyperdimensional consciousness— that 'self' imbued with our future abilities—imprinted when we were re-formed in the bioprinter. However, I can't tell you if this may have happened before or if this is the first reset."

"That's the most fitting explanation I've heard." Colren smiled wearily. "Are you sure you were only a crystal interface maintenance tech?"

Toran laughed. "I've always had an interest in the metaphysical. I guess this experience turned out to be a good fit for both skills and experience."

The commander appraised us. "We got very lucky with the four of you."

"You've allowed us to come into our own," Kaiden said. "We have everything to lose in this fight, too."

"Keep at it. Let me know if you identify any locations." Colren left the conference room.

"Do you really think looking at pictures is going to help us remember?" Maris asked when the door had closed behind the commander.

"It's about more than that," I replied. "We need to try to immerse ourselves in those worlds. If we can picture ourselves there, then maybe the memories of actually *being* there might come to the forefront."

Kaiden sat back down at the table and tapped the integrated touchscreen to active it. "I'm willing to try anything."

"All right. Let's look at the files on those worlds Colren mentioned." I turned my attention to the holographic display.

Toran navigated to the onboard database of Hegemony worlds and brought up the details of his investigation into the Darkness. I'd suspected that a compiled file existed, but I'd never wanted to try to find it before. Acknowledging its very existence—and especially reading it—meant admitting the scale of the threat we were up against. I'd done my best to avoid any concrete information about how many worlds had been consumed by the alien infection. Seeing the records now, my worst fears were confirmed: more than two dozen worlds had been affected. Hundreds of millions of people's lives hinged on us finding a way to fight back.

"Stars! I didn't know it was so many," Kaiden murmured.

"I honestly thought it might be more." Toran brought up the timeline of when the known worlds had been infected. "These records might not be complete, since we wouldn't have known about the Valor world unless we'd gone there for the artifact."

"If we have memories, that means we went there, which means we know about the place," Kaiden said, looking over the timeline. "That means Windau is the first we know about."

"Logically, that does seem like a place we might investigate," I said.

"It does." Toran selected the planet's file.

In its natural state, Windau was a garden world of forested mountains and deep valleys paired with sophisticated urban developments. Its capital near the equator was a thriving city situated around a central square, with a large crystal at its center.

I recoiled in my chair as the images loaded on the holographic projector. The sight in front of me was a pristine city of sculpted stone and glass, but in my mind the scene was covered in writhing, dark tendrils and a perpetual black haze. "Stars, this is it." I wanted to be excited, but the contrast of the images had my stomach in knots.

"It's familiar to me, too. We went here and something bad happened," Kaiden said.

"We were attacked." Maris' voice was assured, and her gaze was fixed on the projection. "The Darkness didn't want us to leave."

"We should avoid this place," Toran suggested.

"Yeah, I'm all about avoiding places where we almost die," I agreed.

Kaiden pursed his lips. "I wonder why we went down there, though?"

I sifted through the images floating through my mind. "I think it had something to do with that crystal."

"Yes, you're right." Toran let out a long breath. "I believe we were trying to learn about the Darkness and how it transmits through the crystalline network."

"Is there any way to get that information without a direct interface?" Kaiden asked.

"No way that's currently workable. I've been toying with the idea of creating a remote connection using the waveform resonance of your magic pendants, but I haven't been able to make it work yet," the other man replied.

"This might be the time to try again," Maris advised.

"Is there really time to mess around with that?" I asked.

"All of our guts are telling us to avoid this place," Kaiden said. "Weren't you just saying we should listen to those instincts?"

"Yeah, I guess so," I admitted. Still, I couldn't shake the feeling that we'd learned something important there. If we didn't get that information, I had no idea what to expect for our future. But, by that same token, maybe it was that information that led us into the bad situation before, and now we could find another way around it.

"See what you can do, Toran," Kaiden said. "You're welcome to my pendant any time you need it."

"Thank you. If you don't mind, I'll begin work in the morning."

I couldn't believe they were ready to call the matter resolved so easily. "Shouldn't we look at the other worlds, too, to see if anything jumps out at us?"

"Yes, but it can wait a few hours," Toran said. "We'll work better after a night to process, regardless of what Maris' restoration spells can do for our bodies."

Taking a moment to assess my physical state, a wave of tiredness washed over me. Letting myself drop out of work mode, I realized that I was still going on the two hours of sleep we'd snagged before Maris got us up. "You're right. Work always goes better when rested and clear-headed."

"I don't expect my head to be clear any time soon, but sleep, at least, I should be able to manage." Toran ventured a smile.

"Yes, I'm sure you two are eager to get back to whatever it is you were up to," Maris added, eyeing Kaiden and me.

"Did I miss something?" Toran asked.

I rolled my eyes. "I told you she wouldn't let it slide," I muttered under my breath to Kaiden next to me.

"I found Elle in his cabin when I went to get them," Maris revealed.

Toran nodded. "I'm glad something good has come from this situation."

I blushed. "Yeah, it's not all bad."

"We're still a team first and foremost," Kaiden assured them. "What's going on between us will stay between us."

"I trust you," Toran replied.

I detected a twinge of envy from Maris, but she nodded her understanding.

"We'll figure this out." Kaiden rose from his seat. "Meet in our common room in the morning?"

"Sounds good," Toran agreed, and Maris murmured her assent.

We adjourned from the conference room and bid good night to the overnight watch on the bridge, finding that Colren had already returned to his quarters. After taking the lift down to our residential level, Kaiden and I let Toran and Maris go ahead.

"Should I go back to my cabin, or...?" I asked when we were alone.

"I liked having you over, if you're still amenable."

I smiled back at him. "I'd like that very much."

I AWOKE FEELING more refreshed than I had in quite some time. To my relief, Kaiden had proved to be a quiet sleeper, and I looked forward to spending more nights together.

Though the relationship was already out in the open, I sneaked back to my cabin next door to get ready for the day. Once showered and changed into a clean shipsuit, I wandered down the corridor to the lounge.

Toran was already at work on the holographic display above the tabletop, reviewing what appeared to be waveforms like those we'd analyzed during our previous investigates into the crystals. "Good morning," he greeted when he noticed me enter.

"Hey. How was the rest of your night?"

"Took me a while to get to sleep, but I feel better now," he replied. "And you?"

"Things are good." I couldn't help a bashful smile from slipping out.

"I'm happy for you two. You seem good together."

"Yeah, we are. I think he's the kind of complement I've

always needed but didn't know what to look for."

He smiled. "It's funny how those people find us. My wife is an extroverted master of social situations. Before her, I would have been content to remain at the edges, looking in on any event."

"How long have you been together?" I asked.

"Almost thirteen years, though sometimes it feels like we just met. We took our time before having our daughter."

"My parents had me young. My mom hadn't even finished graduate school yet. I got the impression sometimes that they wish they had waited."

"I trust you'll find your own timeline. Don't ever let others tell you what you should do," he advised.

"I won't. When we make it through this, I think I'm going to take some time to focus on myself and what I really want."

He raised an eyebrow. "Having second thoughts about Tactical School?"

"No. Maybe. I don't know." I shrugged. "I kind of like having freedom and being in charge. After being able to call the shots like this, I can't imagine going into boot camp and being a grunt."

"That's very true. Colren has given us amazingly free rein. I wouldn't expect most posts as a Ranger to offer that level of autonomy."

"Yeah. So, I dunno. Maybe there's some way to get that adventure without going down that path. Or, maybe I'll be all adventured out."

"I know you'll accomplish great things no matter what you decide to do, Elle," he told me.

The statement warmed me in the way praise from my parents always did. "Thanks, Toran. I expect to see you on the cover of a major scientific journal after all of this. I don't think you'll remain an anonymous maintenance tech after the ingenuity you've shown to gain understanding of the crystals."

He chuckled. "Perhaps. I guess it's good my wife will be able to help me mingle at all of the fancy awards dinners."

I laughed. "All of the recognition will be well deserved."

"Who's getting recognized for what?" Maris asked, stepping onto the room.

"Just thinking about the good times ahead," I told her.

"Aren't we having good times now?" Kaiden asked from a meter behind. "Or is having things try to kill us not fun?"

"Not ideal, no." I smirked.

"Being showered in fame and fortune for saving known civilization is cool," Maris said. "But, really, I just want my home to be safe."

My heart ached. "Me too."

Kaiden slipped his pendant off his neck. "Here, Toran, you probably need this for the cradle, right?"

"Yes, thank you." The other man took the pendant and placed it on the specialized device he'd connected to the ship's sensor suite. "I don't know why I couldn't get it to work last time, but let's try hitting it with the full spectrum and see if I missed any resonance points before."

While Toran worked, I plopped down in one of the lounge chairs and brought up records about the other worlds consumed by the Darkness. As powerful as the images were, none aside from Windau stood out to me with any clarity.

After half an hour, Toran finally pushed back from the table and groaned. "I don't know what I'm missing."

"You were working on this for days before the reset. I wouldn't expect you to solve it in less than an hour," Kaiden said, who'd settled into a seat next to me with a tablet of his own.

"I know, but I was hoping for an easy solution all the same." Toran sighed. "I wish I understood more about how the network transmits data. I'm not surprised we decided to go down to a planet—a direct link would bypass the need for a remote workaround like this."

"Would it have to be an infected world?" I asked.

"To read the alien signal on the network, yes." He paused. "But, you know, maybe a direct line to a crystal would still yield more insights than analyzing the pendants. We could tap into the network that way and identify the different components of the signals. I could then parse out what's different with the pendant to isolate the elements associated with the remote connection."

I blinked at him. "I'm going to assume you know what you're talking about and I don't have to."

"Yes."

"Okay, so, what do we do?" Maris asked.

"Back to Crystallis?" Kaiden ventured.

"We're already here, and there are more crystals than any other world I know about," Toran replied. "Seems like the best place to be."

Kaiden set down his tablet. "All right. Let's tell Colren and head down."

After relaying our intended plan, we gathered our gear and headed down to the hangar. For once, Tami was nowhere to be seen—finally taking some leave after the grind of the past several days—but her crew got us situated on our shuttle and sent us on our way.

Being our third trip down to Crystallis' surface, Kaiden had figured out the best way to minimize turbulence from the planet's tumultuous atmosphere and adjust for the inertial compensators malfunctioning due to the planet's unique properties. We followed our prior path to the valley containing the Archive, since it held the largest number of crystals we were likely to find anywhere in existence.

Despite seeing the valley before, it still took my breath away as we entered. The towering crystals gleamed in the purple light of the planet, majestic and timeless.

"I'll set us down on the other side of the valley away from the Archive entrance," Kaiden said as he looped the shuttle around. "That should hopefully minimize interactions from the Master Crystals, if that's even an issue."

"Good thinking," Toran agreed.

Kaiden located an open area with minimal slope near the canyon's northeastern edge and landed the shuttle.

I unstrapped from my usual co-pilot's seat. "What's the plan?"

"I brought a standard crystal interface kit from the *Evangiel*, but it'll take some time to hook up before I can start gathering readings," Toran replied.

"Need any help?" Maris asked.

"Not right now." Toran gathered his equipment. "This shouldn't take too long."

"You know where to find me." Maris wandered back toward the sleeping cabins at the aft of the shuttle.

Kaiden and I followed Toran outside into the alien landscape.

"Want to get in some combat practice while we wait?" Kaiden asked me.

"Sure. Is that okay, Toran?"

"Sounds good. I'll call you when I'm ready," he acknowledged.

I followed Kaiden toward the canyon wall. "Are you *really* planning to lob fireballs in a delicate crystal valley?" I asked when we were beyond Toran's earshot.

"Maybe a couple for good measure, but I figured a romantic nature walk might be a nicer way to spend the morning than listening to Maris whine on the shuttle."

We strolled through the crystals until we found a collection of rock boulders that shielded us from the surrounding crystals. It seemed as safe as place as any to unleash a few attack spells without fear of harming the surroundings.

"Actually, I had an ulterior motive for bringing you out here," he revealed.

"We *just* spent the night together."

He smiled. "Not related to that. I indicated I was going to be practicing magic so that you could give it a shot."

"Kaiden…"

"I know you've been reluctant to admit you have casting abilities, but you do, Elle. Maybe you should try tapping into that."

"Maybe," I realized. We'd glimpsed the enemy we were up against, and it would take every advantage we could get to defeat them. If I had new skills locked inside me, I owed it to my team to prepare myself for the upcoming fight.

"There's good energy in this place. The magic comes freely. Just try it out and see if anything comes to you."

I took a deep breath. "Okay, I'll give it a shot."

Having magical abilities had always sounded fun to me, but as I prepared for my first intentional use of magic, I found myself more terrified than excited. It probably stemmed from having no idea where the magic came from or what it was. The idea of manipulating the world around me with unseen force went against the laws of nature that had been a cornerstone of my life.

Yet, I'd seen the bliss on Kaiden's and Maris' faces when they were casting. I wanted to taste that sweet power for myself.

I turned away from Kaiden to face the collection of boulders that were to serve as the object of my target practice. While Kaiden had initially been drawn to fire, I found myself called in a different direction. Competing forces of light and dark filled my mind—not the Darkness, but something else… Something even more powerful.

I extended my gloved hand toward the boulder, palm open. A white orb formed between my fingers, shining brightly even in the daylight. It swelled in my palm for two seconds and then released. The orb shot toward the boulder and struck it at my chest-level. At the impact site, a fist-sized chunk of stone broke away and hovered in the air, seemingly defying gravity.

My mouth fell open. "How…?"

Kaiden's eyes widened. "Well, that's a new kind of magic."

I lowered my outstretched hand, and the rock dropped to the ground. "What…?"

"Hmm." Kaiden crossed his arms. "I'm not sure what to make of that."

"Is it the glove?"

"No, that's just a channeling tool, like my staff. I *maybe* snuck down to the equipment room this morning after you left to go check out the details about the item," he admitted.

"Hence the invite on this nature walk."

"Yep."

I let out a slow breath. "So, what, I can levitate things?"

"After smashing parts of them to bits, apparently."

"I'm not so sure about this magic thing," I replied with a frown. The kind of magic I'd fanaticized about was filled with colorful light and elemental-themed attacks, not… whatever I'd just done.

Kaiden tilted his head. "Elle, you tried *one* thing. I think it's a little premature to draw conclusions."

I shook my head.

"What's wrong?" he asked.

"I'm scared to see what I can do. And if I'm scared of myself, what will others think?"

He softened. "Hey, you don't have to worry about me going anywhere, at least. And besides, anyone who'd ditch you over you manifesting magical abilities wasn't a very good friend to begin with."

"I don't want to hurt anyone."

"You have to trust yourself, Elle. These abilities can catch you by surprise sometimes, I can attest to that, but it doesn't come out of nowhere. *You're* in control. Be clear in your intentions and the abilities will follow."

"You make it sound easy."

"It's natural… it's a part of you."

I scoffed. "Right. This thing that only three known people in existence have is completely 'natural'."

Kaiden paused. "Okay, I could have phrased that better."

"Uh huh."

"How about…" He thought for a moment. "You now have access to something ancient, and unique, and special, shouldn't you embrace that gift?"

I evaluated him. "All right, that's a sentiment I can get behind."

He smiled. "Besides, I know you secretly want to be a mage."

Excitement welled within me as I heard the word. "Okay, yes!" I burst out. "I really do want to learn about this, even if it does scare me."

"Good, harness that desire," Kaiden said. He nodded his head toward the boulder. "Now, see what else you can do."

I held my palm open toward the rock once more,

concentrating on the place I'd struck on my previous attempt. This time, I tried to picture what I wanted to happen—for the entire boulder to lift from the ground. I figured it was way too big of a spell to take on, if it *ever* would be possible, but I may as well aim high.

Another white sphere formed in my palm. It swelled until it was the size of my head, then launched toward the boulder. The light dispersed on impact, enveloping the top half of the rock monolith in light. Cracks scored the stone, and fist-sized fragments levitated along with dust from the destruction. The boulder broke apart before me, the fragments at my command. If an enemy were in sight, there would be no escape from my assault.

"Stars!" A deep voice drew my attention to the edge of the path we'd taken from the shuttle.

My head snapped around. Rock fragments fell to the ground in a thunderous cascade, echoing through the alcove.

Toran stood between the crystals at the path's edge, his heavy brow raised with surprise. "Elle, you can cast magic?"

MY HANDS DROPPED to my sides. "Toran, we thought you were going to call us."

"I did. Apparently, you didn't hear me, and the comms don't work down here." The large man turned his attention to Kaiden. "Did you know about Elle?"

"What's the big deal?" I interjected. "Kaiden and Maris are both casters."

He held up his hands defensively. "I'm just surprised you didn't say anything."

"I wasn't sure I actually *could* do anything," I said, looking over the destroyed boulder. Its top third was missing. Given more time, I may have ripped apart the entire thing.

"This was an experiment," Kaiden said.

I nodded. "Yeah, like I said, it's not as though I'm the only one with magic casting."

"Yes, but Maris and Kaiden don't also have your physical skills," Toran replied.

"That doesn't mean they couldn't. Is there actually a rule against having skills in multiple disciplines? Just because we picked one when we were extracted doesn't mean we should be limited, does it?" I honestly had no idea. If our skills were based in some sort of ancient lore, I'd never read it as a kid. All I knew was that I felt multiple abilities within myself and I was done ignoring certain parts. Kaiden was right: I *did* always want to be a mage. I had been so close to selecting the Spirit discipline during my extraction, maybe part of that desire had manifested, along with some of Protection due to my defensive attitude.

Toran nodded. "You're right, there's no reason to think we can't have multiple skills. That part doesn't bother me. What I do find concerning is that you felt you needed to come out here and test those skills in secret."

I didn't know why I had been so intent on keeping it to myself. I appreciated that Kaiden had honored my wishes, but in this matter, perhaps he had been too accommodating. My mantra to my team had been that we needed to be open and trust each other, yet I had been trying to hide a huge revelation about myself.

"I'm sorry," I murmured, hanging my head. "It wasn't fair or right for me to not say anything."

"In all fairness, it was only yesterday during the battle in the Archive when those abilities came to light," Kaiden said in my defense.

"Yet, somehow the equipment room scanner on the *Evangiel* knew to make this caster-specific device available to me," I said, flexing the glove on my right hand.

"Maybe there's some common marker it picked up in me and Maris, and then also saw in you," Kaiden suggested.

"Whatever the reason, this is still all new to me." I sighed.

"Please don't hide things in the future, Elle," Toran said. "You can trust us."

I nodded. "I know."

"Anyway, we're keeping you from the important work, Toran," Kaiden interjected. "What did you come find us to say?"

"Right." He looked me over again. "I found something interesting through the crystal interface."

"Show us," Kaiden gestured for Toran to lead the way.

"I still want to hear more about this apparent telekinesis," Toran said while we walked.

"I'm not sure what to say," I said. "Caught me completely by surprise! I was kind of going for a lightning attack—I always like the way those looked."

"This definitely wasn't elemental-themed like my magic, but it seems incredibly powerful," Kaiden said.

"Indeed. Especially for an initial attempt." Toran paused. "I can't help but wonder... if you can lift, can you also crush?"

"I have no idea." It hadn't occurred to me to try; I wasn't sure I *wanted* to try.

"Once we get back to the *Evangiel* and have a better sense of the alien fleet, you should test out your new magic the way you encouraged us to do," Kaiden told me.

I eyed him. "Yeah, well, if you thought fireballs were a bad idea on a spaceship, then a boulder-disintegrating gravity-defying light orb thing seems like an even worse idea."

"Might need to come back to a planet like this," he amended.

"You may get practice time before we leave," Toran stated as we reached the open area near the shuttle. "I have more investigating to do. The unique properties of this crystal canyon have resulted in some interesting interactions with the crystal interface."

"What do you mean?" I questioned.

Toran strode to a crystal with equipment hooked up to its base. He pointed toward the portable readout screen. "The signal seems to be augmented. I'm picking up something strange in the background that I can't explain."

I examined the data. I didn't understand what the components indicated, but it was clear that there were strong waveforms at the forefront and something different at a low level in the background. "Have you ever seen anything like this before?"

Toran shook his head. "Looking at the signals emanating from reset crystals wasn't exactly my job before this madness started. But with that said, I never came across anything anomalous before now, including the scans over the last week."

"Does it have something to do with this place? The connection to the Master Archive?" I suggested.

"Or, could this be interference from the Darkness?" Kaiden asked.

"That's the most likely explanation. It appears to propagate through the crystalline network," Toran replied.

I frowned. "And let me guess... to properly analyze it, you'd need to go right to the source on an infected world?"

Toran nodded. "That would offer the greatest insights, yes."

"No wonder we took the risk." Kaiden sighed.

"There might be another way..." Toran began slowly. "I may be able to enhance the signal using the amplification from this place. I don't think I would have even picked up the signal on another world even if I'd been looking for it."

I frowned. "This is very bad."

"It's a *lead*. That's good!" Kaiden said.

"That part, yes, but not what it means," I said. "We suspected the Darkness infects worlds through the crystals, but if we can pick up a signal here, that means it might be throughout the *entire* crystalline network, not just the worlds where it's already shown up."

Kaiden paled. "Or, at a minimum, this world is next."

"But the Archive isn't actually *here*," I reminded him.

"All the same, this is the only way we know to access it."

Toran took a deep breath. "There are no signs of corruption on this world, so I do suspect the signal I'm picking up is from the broader network rather than something specific to this world. It's faint."

Kaiden's shoulders rounded. "So, it's everywhere? I'd always thought of it as hopping from one world to another."

"Yeah, but…" I bit my lower lip. "What if it's not an infection of the *crystals* like we thought, but rather of the hyperdimensional network itself?"

"In that case, it could appear on any world without notice," Kaiden murmured.

"But we can find it," Toran said. "I believe that further analysis of this signal might tell us where it's coming from."

"And once we find the source, we can go on the offensive," I realized.

"Exactly."

I threw up my hands. "Then why are we still talking? Analyze!"

"There's a problem," Toran said. "I don't know how to decode the signal. I can isolate certain components, sure, but I can't interpret what each segment of code does without having more information."

"I thought you said you could trace the signal to its source?" I asked.

"Yes, if I can cross-reference it with some other readings on the *Evangiel*. But as for the big 'how exactly does the

Darkness work?' question, I'm afraid this might be another dead end."

My heart dropped. "I'll settle for learning where it's coming from so we can stop it." Yet, I found myself more concerned than excited about Toran's plan. The déjà vu that had been haunting me for the last day struck once again in its vague an unhelpful way that danger was up ahead. I almost said something about it, but we already knew full-well that there would be risks. These actions were likely what had led us down the path that culminated in our confrontation with the alien invaders. As scary as it was, we needed to move forward.

"Any new insights are more than we have now," Kaiden agreed. "Can we do anything to help?"

"No, if you're good with this plan, I'll get back to it. You may as well resume your practice," Toran replied.

I hesitated. "This work always seems to fall to you. I wish we could do more."

"Never doubt your own contributions, Elle. We all pull our weight in different ways," he assured me.

"You're quite literally the heavyweight around here," Kaiden said with a smile. "We'd be lost without you."

"I'm happy to play my part. I want us all to get back to our families."

An ache gripped my heart with the reminder that my homeworld of Erusan now only existed in the Master Archive, beyond my present grasp. "We'll leave you to it." I turned back toward the path I'd taken earlier with Kaiden.

He followed me. When we had gone several meters in, he jogged forward so we were walking abreast. "Why do I have a bad feeling about this new investigation of Toran's?"

"You too?" I shook my head. "I was really hoping it was just me."

"No, this situation is way too messed up." He sighed.

"I want to be ready for whatever confrontation is coming."

"You did great in the last one."

"But that wasn't against the core of the Darkness—it was tests the crystalline network's creators *wanted* us to pass," I countered. "The next fight is for real."

Kaiden stopped as we reached the open area serving as the practice grounds. "We'll get through this Elle. I trust that those trials were designed to prepare us for facing whatever danger may come our way, and now we have the skills, fortitude, and bonds to take on whatever those alien bastards may throw at us."

I tilted my head. "I kind of like seeing you all fired up."

"I believe in what we're doing."

"Me too, though it's not like we can say 'no'… We're it— we're the plan."

"I can't think of a better quartet to save the day."

I laughed. "Except maybe a quartet of trained, experienced people who actually know what they're doing."

"For faking it, we're doing a pretty spectacular job."

"I suppose we are. Speaking of which," I sized up the boulder I decapitated earlier, "I should probably get back to pretending I know magic."

"An excellent plan." Kaiden leaned against a nearby rock.

I held out my hand toward the boulder and tried to clear my mind. However hard I tried, thoughts of the oppressive force of the Darkness kept creeping in. I closed my eyes and shook my head in an attempt to clear it. When I re-opened my eyes, I discovered that an energy orb was starting to form in my palm. Unlike the others I'd cast, though, this one was black.

"Um… Kaiden?" I wasn't sure if I should try to dispel the new magic or find out what it could do.

I heard him take a step away behind me. "We came out here to learn new skills." His tone was less than assured, but I was just as wary of the black cloud swirling in my palm that looked suspiciously like the Darkness.

"All right, here goes." I released the orb.

It shot from my palm and enveloped the boulder just like the levitating spell, but this time there was no immediate result. I kept waiting for the rock to be mutated into something else, given what we'd witnessed the Darkness do, but three seconds passed with no apparent effect aside from the black cloud.

Then, my sense of reality warped. The boulder began to compress, like it was dough in a baker's hands being flatted into a biscuit. When the boulder was half of its original height, the sides also began to draw inward. As it condensed, the blackness surrounding it became more intense until there was only a black mass the size of my fist where the three-meter-tall boulder once stood. The perfect, black orb dropped onto the gravel with a thud.

"Whoa," Kaiden murmured behind me.

"Was not expecting that," I whispered. I took a steadying breath. "I think I'm a freak. It's official."

"Jury is still out on all of us, but you're fascinating and talented if nothing else." Gravel crunched underfoot as Kaiden walked past me toward the black orb resting on the ground. When he reached it, he nudged it with his toe. It didn't budge. "What the...?"

I jogged up next to him and crouched down to inspect it. There were no distinguishing features on the smooth, matte black finish. "Is there a whole boulder somehow packed in there?"

Cautiously, Kaiden reached out to touch it. Though his fingers easily wrapped around the form, he couldn't get any purchase on it. He tried with both hands. "Gah! This thing must weigh a ton. Or several, maybe."

We tried to lift it together, but it still didn't budge.

Kaiden shook his head and stood up. "I don't think that's going anywhere."

"This magic doesn't make any sense." Kaiden's and Maris' abilities had clear roots in the ancient magic of lore, but I couldn't imagine where mine stemmed from. If our abilities truly were a manifestation of our hyperdimensional consciousness, then it scared me to think what had transpired to make we want this as a part of myself.

"Strange or not, this is a powerful ability, Elle. Based on how you took out that rock, imagine what you could do to a bunch of those monster things that attacked us on the Valor world."

"That's true." Except, it was one thing to rip apart or crush a rock. I didn't love the idea of doing that to a living creature, but that was my reality.

Kaiden seemed to sense my discomfort. "But hey," he continued, "just because you have these abilities doesn't mean you need to use them. We already have a good team dynamic going with the slashy, punchy, magicy-ness. This can be a... last resort."

"Yeah, having a special bonus offense can't be a bad thing," I realized.

"Rocks made for good target practice. You can stick to that as long as you want."

"I guess I'll need to find another victim." I evaluated the black sphere that used to be a boulder. "Too bad, since this one was perfect."

"Maybe the sphere itself can be a target?" Kaiden suggested.

"Not sure what I'll be able to do with that. I doubt I can condense it further. What else is there?"

"Break it apart like you did with the boulder?"

Breaking apart and crushing the same unfortunate piece of rock sounded like a tedious way to spend the afternoon, but I suppose I didn't know what was possible until I tried. "All right, stand back."

We returned to where we had been standing when I'd compressed the sphere. I held out my hand while I concentrated on the light from my first attempt, committed to push back the dark that wanted to close in around my mind. Slowly, a white orb formed in the palm of my hand. I launched it toward the black sphere.

The sphere was encased in white light. I focused on it, willing the form to expand into the boulder that once stood in its place. But, that creation was lost—crushed out of existence. I could feel it.

However, the black sphere began to tremble on the ground. Kaiden and I together hadn't been able to nudge it. The trembling intensified. My brow furrowed with exertion as I attempted to rend the sphere apart. Instead, it began to levitate.

"Elle, that's amazing!" Kaiden whispered behind me.

"I don't know how…" Excitement rippled through me as I thought about the power literally at my fingertips. This new ability combined with my enhanced physical strength and agility would enable me to do almost anything. If I ever came face-to-face with the aliens, they would be in trouble.

I spent the next half-hour trying variations of the techniques—levitating, splitting, and compressing using various rocks around us. None of it felt natural to me, but by the end, my initial reservations had subsided; I had new powers, and I was ready to use them.

The practicing was eventually interrupted by a call from Toran in the distance. "Elle! Kaiden! Come here."

"Coming!" Kaiden yelled back.

I presently had the black sphere suspended in the air, trying to see how long I could hold it. So far, it'd been three minutes and twenty seconds. "Can he wait a few minutes? I'm on a roll," I said. The sphere dipped a little as my concentration faltered.

"You can try again later, Elle."

I glanced toward him. "But this time—" My attention lapsed as I turned away, and the sphere launched in the direction I was looking: right at Kaiden.

He ducked just in time to miss the super-dense orb hurtling toward him. "Whoa!"

The sphere struck the base of a crystal spire, letting out a piercing ringing as the crystal vibrated. I brought my hands up over my ears to deaden the sound, but it pulsed inside me. That trill… I'd heard it before. It was within the Darkness.

Finally, the intense ringing faded, and I removed my hands from my ears. "Sorry! Are you okay?"

Kaiden took a deep breath. "Yeah, I'm fine."

I was horrified to see that the black sphere had been embedded ten centimeters into the hard ground. If it had hit Kaiden, he would have been killed instantly. "I didn't mean to."

"Accidents happen." Kaiden looked shaken.

"Still, I shouldn't have been playing with—"

"It's fine, Elle," he insisted. "Let's just get back to Toran." He turned to leave.

"Hey, did you… sense anything when that crystal vibrated?" I asked as I started to follow.

He nodded after a few seconds. "Yeah, it's weird. Some

images popped into my mind, but I don't know what to make of them."

Now that he mentioned it, there had been a faint visual component to my reaction to the sound. I'd thought it was a vision blackout, but as I reflected, I detected the signs of a starscape.

We hurried back to the shuttle's landing site. Toran and Maris were standing next to the crystal Toran had been observing.

"What was that sound?" he asked as soon as he saw us.

"I accidentally hit a crystal. It's okay—"

"I saw something," Maris murmured. "Why would that make me see anything?"

I had no idea, but the image kept solidifying in my mind. A memory.

And the place… it was so familiar to me.

Dread closed in at the edges my mind. My chest constricted, and my heart pounded in my chest. I could barely breathe through the panic. The memories flooded back to me—Darkness ripping through the fleet and disintegrating the Hegemony ships before my eyes against the bright backdrop of the spatial anomaly.

That place… that was where we did the last reset, moments before we were about to die.

My breath caught in my throat. "Stars! I remember." I looked around at the horrified expressions of my friends.

Tears filled Maris' eyes. "I do, too. It all happened so fast."

Kaiden took an unsteady breath.

"How is that possible? *One* vessel took out a fleet of Hegemony ships?" It didn't seem real to me even though the memory was as strong as if I'd lived it moments before.

"This explains why we reset," Kaiden said. "What chance

do we stand against an enemy where one of their ships can level dozens of ours in a matter of minutes?"

I didn't know what to say. I wanted to dismiss the concerns, but the truth was I believed the worries were legitimate. We *didn't* stand a chance against an enemy that powerful. At least, not facing them head on.

"Let's talk to the commander," I said. "If we're going to beat these bad guys, we need to set a trap."

21

"THEY'RE GOING TO... manufacture the ships?" Colren gave me a quizzical look from across the conference table in Central Command.

"In all fairness, we don't know for sure if they were being generated in real-time or if it was some kind of gate technology," I admitted. "But the point is, if we wait for one of those ships to finish coming through the anomaly, we're done for."

"But we *do* know where they're going to be," Kaiden emphasized. "And if things play out like they did last time, we have a limited window to get the upper hand."

"How do you know the location?" the commander questioned.

"Well, we don't *exactly*," Toran replied. "But I remember the method we used to determine the point. As soon as I've cleaned up and isolated the signal we recorded on Crystallis, we'll be able to segment it and cross-reference it with the other worlds' signals."

"If we need military aid, then I'll need something more to

bring to my superiors than a hunch," Colren said.

"It's not a hunch, Commander. I remembered that I'd analyzed the signals emanating from each of the worlds consumed by the Darkness," Toran explained. "They're paired in a way to denote a set of coordinates. But it's incredibly complex. We need a master key." He tapped on the tabletop where the signal from Crystallis was displayed. "*This* is that key. The amplification from the crystals allowed us to pick up the full pattern without going directly to one where the signal is strongest—an infected world. The network is all... well, connected. Crystallis gave us a strong enough antenna to listen."

The commander considered the explanation. "Without getting bogged down in the technical details, I think I understand the concept well enough to support the case to the admiralty. Finish documenting where we need to go and I'll make sure we have our fleet meet us there."

"I will," Toran acknowledged.

Colren rapped his fingers on the tabletop. "And the timing?"

"Vague," I admitted. "We had a discussion about that on the flight back from the planet, and we suspect the encounter happened maybe a week from now in the other timeline." Using terminology about timelines bothered me since we hadn't actually time-traveled, but it was the easiest way to characterize what we were experiencing. Resets were supposed to be straightforward—to change the outcome of a specific incident. But when that incident affected the fate of interstellar civilization, I suppose matters were bound to get complicated.

"If a week is the target, then we'll shoot for three days to give some breathing room." Colren rose from the table.

"Is there any way we can help with the preparations?" I

asked, standing to face him.

"Nothing at the moment, but stand by. You've given us a fighting chance, thank you." He departed.

"I need to get to it." Toran pushed back from the table.

Kaiden nodded. "I guess we should get in some practice while we wait."

It took Toran nearly seven hours to complete his isolation of the Darkness transmission signal. Kaiden, Maris, and I divided our time between combat practice in an empty storage room and offering feedback to Toran whenever it was requested of us. When Toran had finished segmenting the signal and used the pairings to determine the coordinates, we passed off the information to Colren. Then, the real waiting began.

I expected us to make a jump soon thereafter, but a check-in with Colren revealed that we wouldn't make our move until the rest of the fleet was ready to mobilize. Given the enemy threat we were expecting, the Hegemony's leadership thought a unified front would be best.

Three days passed while the interstellar preparations were made. Two worlds that had been identified before we sealed the Archive as future targets for the Darkness completed evacuations early so the assigned ships would be available for the alien engagement. As the time for action neared, we were told that a scouting party had been sent ahead, and they'd given the all-clear for the fleet to move in. All we could do was hope that nothing changed in the time between the report and when we dropped out of our jump.

Shortly before the scheduled jump, we were summoned to Central Command to meet with Colren. We joined him around the conference table in our usual fashion. Unlike most meetings, however, he adjusted the glass walls facing the bridge to make them opaque.

The action immediately put me on alert, and I exchanged worried glances with Kaiden as we took our seats.

"Thank you for coming," Colren began. "In half an hour's time, we'll jump to the coordinates where we expect the spatial anomaly to appear. We'll be joined by eighty of the Hegemony's warships. The rest of the fleet has been assigned to the most strategic worlds to provide whatever protection they can should this engagement not end well."

"As long as we prevent the anomaly from completely forming, there won't *be* an engagement," Kaiden replied.

"Right. About that…" Colren folded his hands on the tabletop. "That's why I called you here."

My heart dropped. The commander's sober tone was one of reluctant resignation. I braced for the news.

"After stating the case as clearly and in as many ways as I could, the admiralty drew their own conclusions. Whereas I insisted we needed to strike fast and hard, they'd like to attempt a peaceable resolution."

Kaiden laughed. "No! You can't be serious."

Colren's grim nod said it all. "I believe what you've told me. You've earned my trust. That's why I'm telling you this now. I genuinely believe their ordered course of action is not in the Hegemony's best interest, but I'm obligated to obey. After all, if a peaceable solution *is* viable, we could save countless lives. That's too great a chance for me to ignore."

I shook my head with disbelief. Maybe the reset had somehow messed with their heads.

"But when talking to the aliens doesn't work?" Toran prompted.

"I need you ready to perform a reset so we can get another chance and hopefully get things right," the commander stated.

"How?" Kaiden asked. "I only have a vague recollection of some sort of device."

Colren nodded. "The observation crystal—it's near the bridge. If you performed a reset before, it would have been with that."

"Right, but even if we do…" I faded out. He knew full well that we'd face the same situation with the aliens that we were in now. There was no need to spell it out.

"Which is why you need to figure out a way to remember whatever happens here," he said. "It's imperative we find a way to prevail and end this reset cycle. This is your task."

"No offense, but you're just telling us now?" Kaiden shot back. "We've been sitting around twiddling our thumbs for three days."

"The order just came through—probably so I wouldn't have time to submit a formal protest," Colren revealed. "I hate to ask more of you, but as the sole civilians on this ship, you four are the only people not bound strictly to the admiralty's orders."

I imagined even telling us his misgivings was a violation enough as it was, so I didn't press the issue. "We'll do our best to brainstorm a solution before the jump," I said.

He inclined his head. "Thank you. I hope that solution doesn't become necessary, but we need to be prepared for all contingencies."

"We'll get started right away," Toran told him.

Colren looked us each in the eyes in turn. "I'll show you where to find the observation room and set up your access credentials so you'll be ready. We'll meet again after the jump."

After a short tour of the room near Central Command, my team adjourned to our lounge, processing the news that the prevailing plan was now to attempt contact with the aliens.

"There's, like, zero chance they're going to respond in a friendly way, right?" Maris asked, breaking the silence as we gathered around the table.

"Yeah, I can't imagine any other outcome," I agreed.

"That's so stupid. Why would they try to *talk* to them?" Kaiden shook his head and groaned.

"They know we're overpowered," Toran replied. "The Darkness expanding through the crystals is faceless and vicious. Ships mean there might be intelligent life on board. If we can't beat them with force, the next best hope is to appeal to reason."

"Do you think it's the right call to talk to them, then?" I asked.

"Oh, stars no!" He scoffed. "They're going to get everyone killed."

"So, a reset is almost guaranteed to be necessary. How do we make sure we don't make these same mistakes again?" I looked at my friends' faces around the table. They were scared and concerned. We should be.

"Well, maybe going through this more than once will help us remember faster than we did last time," Maris suggested.

Kaiden shook his head. "This to too important to leave to chance."

It was. Somehow, the vital information had to be part of us—a powerful imprint that would still be at the forefront of our consciousness even after a reset.

"We need intentional touchstones," I said, a plan starting to form in my mind. "Focus on things we know we'll see right away after the reset and tie them in our consciousness to the important information we need to remember."

Kaiden lit up. "You may be onto something with that. Like how we started to remember when we kissed."

"That's touching, but how in the stars are we supposed to build memory associations for complex coordinates and information about fleet movements?" Maris asked.

"We don't need coordinates, only a prompt to seek out the lead to that information," I replied. "And we need to know what hasn't worked, but witnessing the destruction seems to help that come through just fine."

"What kind of alternative plan should we suggest?" Kaiden questioned.

"That's for our alternate selves to figure out," Maris said.

Toran didn't look convinced. "That's a difficult situation to put ourselves in, isn't it?"

I was about to take Toran's side, but then I thought it through. "Maris does have a point. Our new selves will potentially have two sets of memories to pull from as they start to remember. I believe in myself and us. They'll figure it out," I said.

"They won't even have a chance if we can't make the memories stick," Kaiden stated. "How do you propose we go about making these 'touchstones'?"

"Hold clear, distinct memories in our minds that are tied to specific places," I began. "We need to think through what actions we'll likely take right after the reset—preferably with a strong emotional component, so we can tie the memories to those actions. We also need to decide what the vital information to convey is. It can't be anything too complex, but it needs to get the point across."

"Let's start with the information," Kaiden said, bringing up a notetaking interface on the tabletop. "First, we need to know the process for determining the coordinates to the anomaly site."

"Yes," Toran concurred. "Really, just directing us to the surface of Crystallis with interface equipment will set me on the right path."

"Let's try for more—like the signal and planet pairings—but you're right about simplifying it to the bare minimum," I said. "We also need to convey that we have to beat the aliens to the anomaly site. No delays, no talking. If we end up resetting, that didn't work."

"Gather a fleet, get there as fast as possible," Kaiden agreed.

Toran nodded. "Keep the anomaly from forming."

"What else?" Maris asked. "There has to be more than that."

"Is there?" I thought about what we'd encountered on the last go-around and what we had experienced so far this time, but most of it was incidental. All the important moments could be traced back to finding the signal and the initial moments of our encounter with the alien ship.

However, there was one other piece of information I wanted to bring forward: my new telekinetic abilities. That would be on me to remember.

"Yes, that's what's most critical," Kaiden agreed with me. "Anything else is bonus, but that's what we *need*."

"Okay, so the touchpoint part," I went on. "What places did we go after the reset that we could tie memories to?"

"It's the pod room near Central Command for us," Kaiden said.

"My memories triggered in my cabin when I lay down on my bed," Toran said. "That's the place I always think about my family before I go to sleep."

"What about you, Maris?" I prompted.

She shook her head. "I didn't remember much of anything until I heard that tone down on Crystallis. I'd just come out of the shuttle to talk to Toran when I heard it."

"Won't be able to recreate that. But maybe there's another auditory trigger you could use." I thought for a moment. "What about the lift's chime?"

"Too common," Kaiden said. "That's a background sound at this point. It should be distinct."

"What about the entry tone on the bridge?" Maris suggested. "We go to see Colren as soon as we get back from sealing the Archive."

"Yes, good!" I took a deep breath. "We have a little over twenty minutes before we need to get ready for the jump. Go to your places. Think about the signal and the alien fleet as much as you can. Sound, touch, visuals—tie those memories, build the association."

"See you for the jump," Toran acknowledged.

Kaiden, Maris, and I ran back to the lift so we could return to the Central Command level. Upon reaching the deck, Maris continued to the bridge's entrance while Kaiden and I entered the pod room along the corridor.

"Okay, that first kiss is what's important, not so much this place itself," I said.

Kaiden smiled at me. "So, you're saying that kissing you will help save the universe?"

I rolled my eyes. "Get over here."

I pulled him close to me and our lips met. I was tempted to revel in the moment, but I focused on the memories I would need after the reset. I hated building a connection between something so terrible with an act that would normally be happy, but it was the strongest feeling at my disposal. There'd be plenty of time once we got through this to overwrite the bad association.

Crystallis, the alien signal, coordinates, the anomaly, the alien ships—I tried to pair each memory with a specific touch. The images seared into my mind.

We spent fifteen minutes soaking in as many details as we could. At last, a ten-minute warning sounded for the impending jump, signaling that crew members would be flooding into the pod room at any moment.

"I'm sorry to ruin this for us," I murmured as we pulled apart.

Kaiden gave me a final light kiss. "Nothing could. We'll make new memories."

With the alien threat at the forefront of my mind, we made our way to our own pod room. Toran and Maris were already stripping down to their shipsuits when we arrived.

"How'd it go?" I asked.

Toran shrugged. "I did what we discussed. Hopefully it will be enough."

"I think I drove the comm techs crazy by opening and closing that bridge door dozens of times," Maris said. "The sound is still reverberating in my ears."

I wrinkled my nose. "That sounds awful, but in this case, I think that's a good thing."

Maris eyed me. "You two definitely had it best."

I began taking off my outer clothes. "Not as good as you think." I didn't expect her to understand how much it tore me up to taint the memory of a significant, happy moment in my life. Even if she did understand, there wasn't time to get into it. I trusted in the bond I was developing with Kaiden, and we'd free ourselves from the association eventually.

We climbed into our pods and strapped in.

"See you on the other side," I wished my friends.

"Keep the memories fresh," Kaiden advised. "Everything will happen quickly once we arrive."

I did my best to hold thoughts of the aliens and the signal in my mind throughout the disorienting jump. As the synesthesia kicked in, I began feeling the visual elements of the memories, even hearing and tasting what had never been a part of my experience before. It made it all the more salient.

Finally, the pressure pinning me against my couch began to diminish. We had reached the jump coordinates.

I stretched my arms as the translucent pod cover slid down. "All right, time to see how terribly this 'conversation' with the aliens goes!"

"May as well go straight to the observation room to reset," Kaiden replied, sitting upright.

"I choose to hope that there's at least a chance this will—" Maris was cut off by a warning claxon.

"Enemy ships inbound. Battle stations," Colren announced over the comm.

"Shit, what?" Kaiden hurdled out of his pod.

Toran squeezed out of his own pod. "How are they here already?"

I scrambled to my feet. "There's not time to get dressed, come on!" I ran toward the door.

We dashed to the lift and piled inside.

"This can't be happening," I murmured under my breath.

Kaiden shook his head. "We should have had days."

"But we didn't do things the same," Toran pointed out. "We went to Crystallis, not Windau."

My head felt like it was about to explode. There were too many variables. It could have been any number of things that led to this different sequence of events.

The lift door opened on the Central Command level and we raced down the corridor to the bridge's entrance. Maris winced as the door unlocked and slid open.

Inside, Colren leaned forward in his seat at the center of the bridge, his attention fixed on a fleet of two hundred alien ships arranged in a defensive spherical formation around the anomaly.

Hegemony ships dropped out of hyperspace around us. Any that were too close to one of the alien vessels were immediately enveloped in a black cloud that began disintegrating the target vessel within seconds.

"They knew we were coming," I realized. "They were *expecting* us."

Kaiden looked sick as he stepped through the open doorway. "What could have clued them in?"

Toran shook his head. "Maybe they could tell we were reading the signal on the crystalline network and they decided to accelerate their plans."

Maris frowned. "That would imply that they knew how we would react."

"They must remember what happened during the last timeline, too—maybe even better than us," Kaiden said.

That was the last realization I wanted to have, but I couldn't disagree with the conclusion. My heart dropped. "If we reset again, they'll also remember whatever we do here."

We exchanged glances. Our plans hadn't taken into account the possibility that the aliens would have any recall of events after we reset. No matter what we did now, they would still have the upper hand.

"Does that mean the reset plan is off?" Maris asked.

The Hegemony fleet was getting slaughtered outside the viewport. I couldn't face that outcome. "No, we need to try again while we still can."

"What will a reset change if the enemy remembers?" questioned Toran.

"We need to do something completely different and unexpected," I said. Once again, it would come down to us. But, maybe we didn't have to be alone. "Except, we need to hedge our bets."

Without hesitation, I ran up to Colren. "Commander, we need to reset."

Defeat was written on his face as he turned to face me. "Good, you're here." He pulled out the locket containing the crystal shard from under his uniform. "Go. The observation room is—"

"You have to come with us," I stated.

He shook his head. "My place is here."

"Us relaying information to you isn't enough. You need to remember for yourself."

"I haven't prepared like you did before the jump. Watching Maris—"

"No, but you've seen this!" I made a sweeping gesture toward the space battle depicted on the screen. "I can't think of a stronger reminder than sitting down in this chair with this view as your most recent memory."

"My duty demands I don't abandon this post," he protested.

"You're not. This will let you come back and prevent all of those people from dying!"

On screen, four of the alien ships disintegrated a defensive line of Hegemony destroyers standing between the enemy and us. We had maybe a minute to act.

I grabbed Colren's arm. "Commander, we need to go *now*!"

He took one last look at the horror unfolding on screen and gave in. "Next time," he whispered to the bridge crew as I urged him toward the exit. The officers gave resolute nods and salutes as he passed by.

He led the way out of Central Command and down the corridor toward what I presumed was the observation room he'd mentioned.

"They began attacking as soon as we arrived," Colren said while we ran. "We were lucky to be far enough away from them."

"They must remember," I replied. "That's why we need you. We'll need a different approach."

He nodded. "Stars be with us."

At what appeared to be a dead-end to the corridor, Colren used a disguised control panel to open a hidden doorway. He held the crystal shard in his hand. "Do you remember what to do?"

I took the crystal fragment from him. "Enough. Think about where you were while we were down in the Master Archive."

"When, exactly, was that?" Colren asked.

"No, that point won't work with him," Toran stated. "We need a time when all of us were together. Maybe the first meeting after we got back—when we gave him the shard?"

"That's after Kaiden's and my touchpoint," I countered.

"No time to argue. It will be the easiest point for the five of us to picture," Toran insisted.

"All right," I yielded, pressing the crystal shard into my palm and holding it in place with my thumb. I extended my hand over the observation sphere. "Everyone ready?"

My friends put their hands in place, and Colren followed suit.

I started the count down. "One…. two… three!"

On my mark, we all placed our hands on the orb. As I released the crystal shard, I held the memory in my head of when Colren first took it from me during our debrief—the sense of hope that we had a tool to let us fight back. As the feeling flooded through me, the world dissolved to blackness.

REALITY RESOLVED AROUND me.

Relief. Joy. Hope. I couldn't put my happiness into words as I processed what Colren had just told me. We now held the key for a universal reset.

I looked over at the faces of my companions seated around the conference table adjacent to the bridge. They seemed as happy as I was feeling. Yet, something nagged at the back of my mind.

Across from us, Colren continued to admire the crystal shard. "You could use this to control a reset event from anywhere," he said.

"But the Master Archive is sealed," Kaiden said. "I thought it couldn't be accessed for resets?"

"If the lore is correct, then a shard like this would be the *only* way to conduct a reset," Colren replied. "Except, those are only legends. There are too many unknowns to be sure how a universal reset could play out."

"A measure for desperate times," Toran murmured.

Desperate times... Sudden tension gripped my chest. I

should be happy; why did I feel stressed?

"Could there be side effects from a reset like that?" Kaiden asked.

Colren shrugged. "It would be impossible to predict. I can only imagine that with something that complex, there could be complications." He smiled. "But no need to worry about that. Today was a victory."

"Yeah, it was," I agreed, my vanquishing of the black dragon still fresh in my mind.

"Take the rest of the day to celebrate," the commander said. "You've earned it." He rose from his seat.

We stood up.

"Thank you, Commander," Kaiden said.

Colren headed out the door. He stopped a pace outside the conference room and turned back. "Have we…?" he faded out, then shook his head. "Never mind. Enjoy your celebrations." He continued toward his command seat at the center of the bridge.

"All right! A party is in order," Maris cheered.

"Not that we have a lot of exciting options," I mumbled.

"Mess hall?" Kaiden proposed.

"That's pretty much it," Maris replied.

Toran nodded. "I'll need to take some time to unwind before I'm up for any festivities."

"That'll give me time to find out if there's anything worthwhile to drink on this ship," Maris placed a hand on her hip. "The selection thus far has been sorely lacking."

"It's a military ship, not a pleasure yacht," I said. The Darkness was still out there; it hardly seemed like a time for a party.

"People have to unwind all the same!" She waved her hand. "We'll meet at… 17:00?"

"Sounds good. Maybe we'll even be able to round up some people to join in the fun," Kaiden said.

A big celebratory bash still felt like the wrong thing to do, but I wanted my friends to be happy—especially Kaiden. If a party was what they wanted, I'd suck it up.

We exited the conference room. As we walked through the bridge, crew members smiled and bowed their heads in acknowledgement for what we'd done. As invisible as our actions were to most, we'd given our civilization its best chance to rebuild once the threat had passed. Seeing their reactions and putting it in those terms, maybe a celebration *was* in order.

When we passed by Colren in his command seat, however, I was surprised to see a very different expression on his face. He seemed almost horrified.

I was about to ask him what was wrong, but Kaiden brushed my arm. "Do you have a few minutes to talk?" he whispered.

"Yeah, of course," I replied, gesturing toward the Central Command exit. "Back in the pod room."

Kaiden nodded.

The four of us continued through the bridge getting a proper hero's treatment from the crew, receiving acknowledgements ranging from nods and smiles to salutes. At any other time, I would have felt the swell of pride from a job well done, but Colren's expression had shaken me. Something had tainted this apparent victory.

When we reached the doorway leading to the outer corridor, the door automatically slid open with a hiss and soft chime.

"Stars!" Maris exclaimed, placing a hand on her stomach.

"What's wrong?" I asked.

"This…" She shook her head. "This isn't right. We've been

through this before."

Kaiden's brow knit. "What do you mean?"

She stared at the open door. "I know this sound."

"We've been through here several times," I replied. "It's not—"

"No, not just a casual visit," she insisted, her voice raising. "That chime is embedded in me."

Colren looked around from his command seat. "Do you feel it, too?"

Maris' gaze met his. "I don't know what I'm feeling. It's like I'm in a dream."

"Elle." Kaiden's fingers brushed against my left hand. The feeling was so familiar—far more than I expected for someone with whom I'd only minutes before shared a first kiss. And there was something else in the touch I couldn't explain that made me want to pull away, though not from him, exactly.

Our eyes met. "What's happening?"

"I don't know, but we need to go—"

"—to the pod room," I completed for him.

He looped his fingers through mine and led me down the corridor, leaving a confused Maris and Toran in Central Command with Colren.

The moment the pod doors opened, I sensed a shift within me. I knew this place—really *knew* it. A scuff on the side of one of the pods, a scratch in the white paneling next to the door, the placement of rivets along the baseboard. I couldn't bring up the images in my mind on command, but there was the strangest sense of déjà vu as I looked around the space.

"Now I get what Maris was saying. Something weird is happening," I said.

"I couldn't shake the feeling that I needed to come back here with you," Kaiden replied. "I don't know why."

I took his hands. "We'll figure it out."

His touch reassured me, drawing me close. I leaned in for a kiss, but as our faces neared, a deep-seated sense of discomfort washed over me. I pulled back, releasing his hands.

"What was it you wanted to talk about?" I asked, taking a step back.

He cleared his throat. "Just, about what happened earlier. I—"

"Kaiden, Elle!" Maris shouted from the corridor. She burst into the pod room. "Do you remember?"

"Remember what?" I asked.

"The invasion."

Kaiden frowned. "Does this have something to do with our visions in the Archive?"

"Yes, and so much more." She sighed. "This wasn't supposed to be our reset point. You missed your trigger."

My brow knit. "What in the stars are you talking about?"

"We've been through this before—at least two times, maybe more," she said. "We tried to make ourselves remember. I don't think I would have had Colren not been experiencing a similar feeling of familiarity."

"And what does that have to do with our 'trigger'?" Kaiden asked.

"Your touchstone," she replied, though that didn't clarify anything for me. She looked between us. "You really don't remember yet?"

"I have no idea what you're talking about," I confessed.

She groaned. "Recreate that moment when we first came back from sealing the Archive—that's when we were supposed to reset to. Come find us in the conference room when you remember."

"What happened to having the night off?" questioned Kaiden.

"Now we know about the invasion. We don't have a lot of time." Maris waved her hands. "Do your thing. Hurry!" She left the room, the door sliding shut behind her.

"What just…" I sucked in a slow breath.

"Either she's totally lost it, or there's our explanation for the weird feelings," Kaiden said.

I nodded cautiously. "What was that about recreating the moment we came back?"

"Last time in here, we kissed."

"How'd she even know about that?"

"We didn't exactly hide it," he pointed out.

"True. But what does it have to do with anything?"

"We can find out."

I eyed him. "You don't really think…?"

"After the week we've had, I'm willing to believe just about anything."

"All right. No harm, I guess." The aversion I'd felt was still at the forefront of my mind, but it competed with the attraction I'd felt for him since we first met. Only a few minutes earlier, we'd shared a first kiss that had been the culmination of those feelings. I didn't understand why I was apprehensive now.

Kaiden approached me. "I think we were standing just about like this." He gently placed his hands on me and leaned in.

Our lips met, sparking a flurry of images in my mind. A fleet of black alien ships, the spreading Darkness, twisted creatures, a bright anomaly standing out against the void surrounded by an unfamiliar starscape. The fleet was coming. They would destroy us.

Kaiden and I parted.

"Did you…?" I asked.

He looked shaken. "Yeah. I think those were memories.

But how could we have memories for something that hasn't happened yet?"

"Not in *this* timeline maybe," I realized. "But if we reset…"

Kaiden opened his mouth like he was about to protest, but instead he nodded. "That's the sensation I couldn't place. We *have* done this before."

The images began to sort in my mind, a narrative forming. "We made ourselves remember. That space battle is the 'make or break' moment for us. We need to find a different strategy."

"We don't have a lot of time. They can get their fleet there faster than we can."

"Where is 'there'?" I rubbed my temples. There was still more I couldn't remember. The memories were so tantalizingly close to my grasp.

"Let's go talk to the others," Kaiden suggested.

I wished I had been able to remember on my own, but I could tell something was off. I needed the rest of my team.

We returned to Central Command. Maris, Toran, and Colren were already back in the conference room. The bridge's crew members no longer had the happy expressions they had displayed minutes earlier, having witnessed the shift in Colren's demeanor.

Kaiden closed the conference room door behind us after we entered. Our three associates were already seated in their customary places around the table.

Colren folded his hands on the tabletop. "Do you remember?"

I glanced at Kaiden then nodded. "Enough."

Toran shook his head. "How can the four of you have these memories when I don't?"

"That's hardly the primary concern at present," the commander cut in. "If my visions are to be believed, we have just been through a universal reset. An alien offensive is preparing to slaughter the Hegemony fleet. If we don't take immediate action, we will be doomed to repeat that fate."

As he spoke, the hazy memories continued to sort in my mind. The aliens had been waiting for us. We hadn't stood a chance. "How can we fight back if they know we're coming?"

"They'll be expecting a fleet," Colren replied. "It's our turn to catch *them* by surprise."

"We should disrupt the anomaly to keep any ships from emerging," Toran stated.

The commander nodded. "Yes, but that alone is a short-term solution; they could always emerge elsewhere. What we really need is a way to fight back."

"What do you have in mind?" Kaiden asked.

"A stealth mission," the commander began. "As soon as the alien ships are fully formed, their weapons can take us out before we even have a chance to fire. But, if we want to learn how to counteract those weapons, we need to gather more information about them. That gives us a very narrow window between when the ship starts to form in the anomaly and before it's operational."

I wasn't sure I liked where this plan was going. From what I could recall, the alien ships appeared to have similar properties to the planets that had been consumed by the Darkness. There were only four people known to have a measure of immunity against the Darkness, and I was one of them. "Let me guess: you want *us* to go investigate?"

Colren nodded. "We need to know the face of our enemy— what's going on beneath the surface."

"It's too risky to allow the anomaly to remain," Kaiden insisted. "There won't be time to destroy it if something goes wrong—we don't even know that we *can* destroy it."

"I have no intention of allowing the ship to emerge completely," the commander continued. "Board, extract information, then destroy the ship and hopefully the anomaly along with it."

Maris raised an eyebrow. "Like, plant a bomb?"

"Not just any bomb, a spatial disrupter," Colren clarified.

Toran breathed out between his teeth. "That could destabilize the whole area."

Colren nodded solemnly. "It's the only thing guaranteed to interact with the anomaly. And we can't deploy it remotely."

"Not even a remote-piloted shuttle?" Toran asked.

"Too many variables for getting it close enough," Colren said. "Placing it by hand on the alien craft is the only way to be sure."

My brow drew together. "Sorry, but what's a spatial disrupter?"

"A weapon I thought was only conceptual," Toran explained. "Theoretically, it can rip the fabric of space through multiple planes, not just affect the matter in this plane we know as 'reality'."

"It's extreme, but since we only have one shot at this and don't know the details about this anomaly, we need to throw everything we have while there's a chance to strike," Colren said.

I frowned. "I'm a little unclear on the part of this plan where all of us *don't die*."

"Yeah, I have to second that sentiment," Kaiden agreed.

"It's simple," Colren said. "You'll board, use your knowledge of the Darkness' signal to tap into the ship's systems, extract any data you can, plant the spatial disrupter, and return to the *Evangiel* for a jump before the disrupter activates."

"Yeah, see, that's still sounds like the kind of insane plan where everyone dies," I said. "There's a slim chance we'd be able to interface with the alien ship's systems, let alone on a time crunch."

"Not to mention, how do we get on the ship? There's no way the environmental controls are the same," Kaiden added.

Maris nodded. "Assuming we can even get close enough to board."

"Insta-death all around," I concluded.

"I'm aware of those factors," Colren insisted. "First, the ship won't be able to attack you if you're already on top of it when it begins to emerge from the anomaly. Furthermore, the ship's environmental controls are irrelevant if you're in an EVA suit. As for timing, yes, interfacing with the ship's systems might be overly aspirational, but you don't know until you try. If nothing else, this mission would enable you to see firsthand what's inside the hull while also planting the spatial disruptor."

"That last part alone makes the risk worthwhile," Kaiden said.

I hated that he was right. We needed to destroy the anomaly, and I had to defer to others who knew far more about these matters than I did about the best way to do it. If they said this was the only way, then we needed to make it happen. "All right. How exactly are we going to do this?"

Maris' eyes widened, and she leaned forward on the table to look over at me. "You aren't actually considering this plan, are you?"

I stared back, resolute. "I'm sick of getting pushed around by these guys. Let's show them what we've got."

EVEN THOUGH I was psyched up to storm the alien ship, there were a lot of preparations to make. For starters, we didn't know *where* the anomaly was, only some vague recollection that we needed to go to Crystallis to get a clue. Even without the reset, it still felt like we were running in circles.

We adjourned from the meeting and prepared to return to the planet's surface. Since we hadn't had any decompression time since our battle in the Master Archive, we agreed to take fifteen minutes to freshen up in our cabins.

I felt much better after a quick shower, and when I stepped into our lounge to reunite with my companions, I was ready to take on any challenge. No sooner had I entered the room than Toran burst in after me.

"I remember!" he declared. "I sat down on my bunk and..." He shook his head. "We're kind of screwed, aren't we?"

"Can't think about it that way," I said. "There's at least a little chance we can pull this off, right?"

Toran pressed the heel of his hand to his temple. "I remember how to find the spatial coordinates we need, but there's no telling if those signals have any bearing on the system interface for the ship."

I shook my head. "Don't worry about that part. Planting that bomb is the important thing."

The large man fixed me in a level gaze. "Since when are we a covert ops team, Elle? Breaching an enemy ship to plant a space-ripping weapon—it's crazy!"

His sudden, raw emotion caught me by surprise. "I know, Toran. We're doing the best we can."

"This plan does not put us on the path of success."

"Then what do you propose we do?" I crossed my arms. "We're the only ones who can get near the Darkness without getting turned to soot, and we have maybe five minutes to act between when the alien ship first appears and when its weapons will be operational. What's a better way to use our time?"

"I don't know," he replied after a pause.

"I don't like this either, but we entered Crazy Town a week ago. Maybe getting up close and personal with the bad guys is exactly the kind of action we need at this stage."

"Don't tell me you're actually excited about this plan?" Kaiden asked from the doorway.

I smiled at him as he stepped into the room. "Only excited that this might be over soon."

"This one engagement won't change the larger circumstances," Toran said solemnly.

"But it's a start," I said. "Right now, we need a win."

Colren had tried to make sealing the Archive sound like a big victory, but I continued to think of it as 'maintaining'—it was a fallback, not a step forward. Taking out an alien ship, though... That was the first step toward reclaiming what had been taken from us. The fact that we might finally be able to put a face to the murderous monsters who'd destroyed our homes was a welcome bonus.

Maris joined us moments later, and we headed to the hangar to board a shuttle back to Crystallis. Tami seemed a little confused about why we were heading back so soon, but the reset loops were far too large of a subject to broach in passing.

We boarded the shuttle and took our typical landing approach through the mountain pass. As we neared the crystal canyon, I was overcome by another intense wave of déjà vu.

"How many loops have we been through?" I asked.

"I seem to have snippets from two floating around," Kaiden said while he looped the shuttle around toward a landing site. "Not to say there weren't more."

"And the enemy remembers," Toran emphasized. "That means they might be preparing to deploy their fleet through the anomaly. We need to beat them there."

"How long will it take to decode the coordinates?" Maris asked.

Toran's flight restraints jangled as he shrugged in the seat behind me. "Hours? Hopefully I remember some shortcuts once I get into it."

Kaiden set down the shuttle on the opposite side of the canyon from the Archive entrance, and Toran immediately got to work.

While Toran connected to the crystals, I wandered through a collection of crystal formations nearby. After a few minutes, I came across a boulder. The rock stood out in my mind, stopping me in my tracks. It'd seen it before, but I also sensed that I'd done something to it.

"What's wrong?" Kaiden asked from a few meters behind me.

I jumped, not realizing he'd followed me away from the landing site. "Nothing."

"You've been acting strange since we've started to remember."

"Isn't it *stranger* that you haven't? This entire thing is nuts," I replied.

He came to stand next to me. "It's affected me plenty. I'm just trying to stay focused."

I shook my head and scoffed. "I don't rightly know what happened when anymore."

"With reality resetting, does it even matter?" he asked. "It's like it didn't happen."

"Except, it *did*. And we can't pretend like it didn't, because our enemy remembers and they're going to use that information against us."

"Then we have to use those memories, too, so we can end this." Kaiden took my left hand. Now, away from the pod room, the touch was reassuring, grounding me.

"What have we been through?" I murmured. "It's all there, right beneath the surface, but none of it's clear."

"Soon we'll know where we have to go, and we'll figure out what we have to do. The rest... maybe it's best we don't know all the details about what happened. After all, it didn't end well."

"What about learning from mistakes?"

He shrugged. "The critical information will come to us as we need it. For now, there are only two things on my mind. First, we need to find that anomaly and stop the bad guys. Beyond that, I know I care about you."

"We barely—"

"Maybe this time around, but there's something between us, Elle. For me, that makes putting up with all the other crap in between worthwhile."

I softened. "Yeah, it does."

He smiled. "As much as I wish we could get to that 'afterward' part, we should probably take a step back for the time being."

I nodded, though I wished circumstances were different.

"Now," he continued, "why were you staring at that rock like you had a vendetta?"

"I think I destroyed it," I replied.

"With your... sword?" Kaiden raised an eyebrow.

His skepticism was well-founded. I couldn't imagine how I'd be able to level a boulder that size with my skills. Even Toran would be hard pressed to smash something on that scale. To further complicate matters, I had a vague recollection of doing something to the rock other than smashing it with physical force.

Kaiden eyed me. "Is this about that other thing you don't want to talk about?" He glanced over his shoulder. "You know, the *magic*," he whispered.

I checked around us and took a step closer to him. "Whatever you think you saw in the Archive, this isn't something I can control. It may have just been some magical version of 'hysterical strength'."

"You don't know if you can control it until you *try*," he urged.

The boulder may as well have had a target painted on it, I had to admit. "Fine," I yielded. "Stand back."

As if on instinct, I raised my hand and a white orb formed in my palm. It launched and enveloped the boulder, breaking it into bits. To my amazement, those rock fragments began to levitate, slowly drifting away from the impact site as if in slow motion. Before I could fully grasp the wonder of it, another orb formed, this one dark. Curious, I released it and a black cloud washed over the remaining boulder and the tiny rock fragments floating above it. The material began to condense, shrinking to a single, black sphere the size of my first.

A sensation of power washed through me. I knew that feeling—it transcended the resets and any time that had passed since those abilities had first become a part of me, even if I didn't know it. "Stars… I know magic!"

Kaiden grinned. "Told ya."

I experimented with the telekinesis for a few more minutes, but Toran soon called us back to the landing site to share the results of the analysis. Reluctantly, I lowered my hands.

"Keep this between us?" I requested.

Kaiden frowned. "Why don't you want to tell anyone about this magic, Elle?"

"I don't want anyone relying on it—it's too new," I insisted.

He held up his hands. "Fine, suit yourself." I could tell he wasn't happy about that arrangement, but I appreciated that he respected my wishes on the matter.

Frankly, I didn't know why I was so reticent, either. The best explanation I had in the moment was that I didn't want anyone to look at me like I was different or special. Right now, we needed to be a unified team. If I was called out as having alignment to multiple disciplines, I'd be set apart. The bonds with my teammates were what would get us through the coming trial, not showing off. I'd use my new abilities to help if the circumstances demanded it, but otherwise, unity was paramount.

And, more than that, the nature of my magic scared me. The ability to crush and rend—that wasn't strength I took lightly, and I vowed that I would only use it when there was no other choice.

Kaiden and I returned to the landing site to find Toran and Maris staring at the portable display screen for the crystal interface equipment.

"Find what you need?" Kaiden asked the other man.

Toran nodded. "I believe so. Once I got over the initial shock, I located the signal a half-memory hinted I should be able to identify." He went on to explain something about segmenting the signal and pairs of fragments across different worlds. I only partially listened, knowing it wasn't relevant to anything I had to do.

He finished what he needed to gather the necessary data, and then we returned to the shuttle.

"This might take hours to analyze," Toran said as we strapped into our seats.

"Don't have that long," I replied. "We need to beat that first alien ship. And, we have no idea how long it takes them to mobilize."

"Wanting things to go faster doesn't change reality," he replied.

I slouched in my seat. "Do what you can."

The ensuing hours were torture while I tried to be patient for Toran to finish the analysis. His initial projection was eight hours, but after two and a half, the pairs were well enough established for us to load the data into a spatial model.

"Should be right... here," Toran said as he made the requisite entries.

The holographic interstellar model above our work table refreshed to show color-coded highlighted worlds with lines linking each pair. The lines intersected to converge on single location outside any known system.

"I guess that's where we need to go," Maris said.

Kaiden nodded. "I'll alert the commander."

Within minutes, we were in our pod room stripping down to prepare for the jump. I still hadn't quite wrapped my head around what we were about to do—taking a shuttle to board an alien vessel that contained tech capable of disintegrating a ship. Even if our bodies were resistant to the Darkness, our suits would be slowly eaten away. Granted, the enemy ship would have formed and the aliens would have taken us out well before the suits failed, but still. I liked living, and the odds weren't in our favor for making it out of this next encounter unscathed.

"Have a good jump," Kaiden said as he climbed into his pod.

"Jumping to our *doom*!" Maris exclaimed with even more melodrama than usual.

Toran sighed. "I choose to believe we'll prevail."

"Of course we will." I dropped onto the ergonomic couch within my pod. "See you soon."

However, as I strapped into the harness, my private worries and doubts continued to multiply in my mind. I did my best to propose counterpoints about the capabilities of my team and my own skills—both those familiar and still being discovered—but the isolation and disorientation of the jump through hyperspace left me running through contrary arguments. One part of me wanted to take what we knew and go back to the Capital to regroup with whatever experts the Hegemony could locate, while the other part of me was convinced we needed to forge ahead with our insane plan. However, the closer we got to our destination, the more I wondered if a more conservative strategy was a better move. Though only a few hours had passed, the alien ships could have already traveled through the anomaly. We very well may be walking into another trap, only this time, alone.

When the *Evangiel* began its transition back into normal space, I tried to refocus on the task at hand. The decision had already been made. We were doing this, last-minute reservations or not.

As soon as our pods opened, we sat up to stretch while our senses normalized.

I smoothed my hair away from my face. "When do—"

The central alarm sounded, and Colren came over the intercom. "Battle stations! Dark Sentinel team to the hangar immediately."

We vaulted out of the pods and started to dress as quickly as possible.

"Shit!" Kaiden exclaimed. "Did they beat us here?"

I shook my head. "Must be."

Toran groaned. "I thought we would be fast enough."

"They didn't need to find the coordinates like us," Maris pointed out unhelpfully.

With my pants and boots donned, I grabbed my coat and sword to carry with me; I'd just have to take them off again when I put on the EVA suit. "Come on, let's get to the hangar."

The others gathered their remaining gear and followed me at a jog out of the pod room. We hurried to the lift and took it down to the hangar level.

Tami was waiting for us next to one of the shuttles—a different craft than the one we'd used on previous missions. "There might still be time," she said by way of greeting. "We loaded the bomb and your other equipment before the jump. I'll explain the activation on your way over."

"Are the alien ships here?" Kaiden asked while we were ushered up the shuttle's entry ramp.

"The anomaly is forming," Tami replied. "Hopefully you can make it to the site before the first ship."

At least we still had a chance. "See you when we get back," I said.

The engineer nodded. "Good luck."

In a flurry of activity, the shuttle's outer door was sealed and we set down our handheld gear in the common area. A black crate and four EVA suits were spread out on the deck.

"Should we get dressed now?" Maris asked.

"Need to get underway first." Kaiden directed us toward the bridge to get situated.

"How long is it going to take to get into position?" I asked while strapping into the co-pilot's seat.

"Should only be a few minutes. Looks like Tami got it warmed up for us," Kaiden said as he looked over the controls. "I guess we're doing this."

I nodded. "Yeah, let's get it over with."

Kaiden activated the auto-pilot to guide our shuttle to pre-programmed coordinates near the anomaly. "I'll take over once we're near the alien ship and know what we're working with."

Maris sighed. "So much for a briefing... or a plan."

"The plan is that we wing it," I replied. The truth, though, was that I hadn't pictured the moments before our mission being anything like this. I thought we'd complete the jump, have an opportunity to scout out the anomaly before it opened, and be able to get into an ideal position to board the enemy ship. Now, we'd be lucky if we made it close enough before the enemy ship's weapons were functional.

The shuttle taxied from the hangar and glided through the electrostatic field. The moment we were clear, a chime sounded in my left ear.

"Sorry for the abrupt departure," Colren said. "We observed an energy spike as soon as we came out of the pods."

"You're right—can't risk it," Kaiden responded.

"I'll be standing by here to reset using the shard if anything goes wrong," Colren said.

The promise of nearby backup should have been reassuring, but I knew better. "We need to treat it like this is a one-shot deal, because it is," I replied. "After this, they'll know this strategy. We can only catch them by surprise this way once."

"That's true," the commander acknowledged.

Toran unstrapped from his seat. "We need instructions about how to deploy the disruptor."

"Yes, Tami will be on in a moment with her technician," Colren stated.

"Let's get dressed in the meantime," I suggested, unbuckling my own harness.

Kaiden glanced between me and the controls. "All right."

The four of us hurried single-file into the common area to claim our EVA suits. The form-fitting suit felt constrictive once I tugged it on, but I suspected that was more in my head than reality. A vague memory tickled the back of my mind about wearing the suit another time and things not ending well. I could only hope this scenario would play out better.

"Placing the disruptor will be the most challenging part," Tami said, joining the comm link. "Brian, one of the weapons techs, is here to explain."

"The disruptor will work best if attached to a large physical mass, ideally the hull of the alien ship," an unfamiliar male voice said over the comm. "The goal is to destroy the anomaly-portal, so you'll want to place it on the ship as close to the spatial event as possible."

"Great, but how are we supposed to accomplish that in… what, two minutes?" I asked.

"That's why I said, 'as possible'," Brian replied. "You can only do so much. Just flip the red switch once you have it in place—that will activate the remote trigger."

"And then you wait for us to get clear?" Kaiden said.

Brian paused for much longer than I would have liked. "Yes," he responded eventually.

"While setting the disruptor, observe anything you can," Colren instructed. "This may be our only chance to get close and learn about these beings… whatever they are. Feeds from your EVA suits will report in real-time. And, Toran, you'll find a device sitting on top of the disruptor that might assist in interfacing with the alien ship's system."

"I see it," Toran acknowledged.

I exchanged glances with my team, now even more concerned than before that this was a suicide run. "We'll do our best, Commander."

A rapid beep sounded from the bridge. "That's our cue!" Kaiden said, running back to the front of the vessel.

I followed close behind him. Out the viewport above the nose, the spatial anomaly had taken on a white glow, and an ethereal sparkle was rippling across the space that had appeared matte black moments before. "Stars, what…?"

"It's beautiful," Maris murmured.

Before I could wonder too much, a dark form began to emerge. My breath caught in my throat. "The ship is coming through."

THE ALIEN VESSEL was more menacing up close. Even with only a few dozen meters exposed at the horizon of the anomaly, it already looked sinister. Inky tendrils intertwined to form the support structure, and a fine mesh with a fibrous appearance spanned the beams. There were no viewports or other openings, just blackness inside and out.

I stared at the ship with distaste. "We're going in... there?"

"Assuming we can find a way in." Kaiden took over manual control of our shuttle and directed it toward the spatial anomaly.

"Don't get too close," Toran cautioned.

Kaiden cracked a wry smile. "Sorry to break this to you, but the entire *point* is to get close."

"Why did I agree to this?" Maris moaned. She waved her hand in the back seat and a shimmering purple wave of light extended outward, encasing all but the shuttle's engines.

I nodded back at her. "Thanks. Good thinking."

Kaiden accelerated toward the outer edge of the spatial disturbance until we were twenty meters from it.

From so close, the sparkling light had the nuance of a cloud, swirling with highlights and shadows. The alien ship really did seem to appear from nothing—dark particles appeared against the white background moments before they joined together in their proper places to form the ship. Of all the amazing things I'd witnessed over the past week, this was one of the most incredible based purely on the scale. The ship rose at least two hundred meters tall, and here it was, apparently being 3D-printed from a glowing cloud.

"Stars, we need to find a place to get inside," Kaiden muttered under his breath, eyes darting across the uneven surface of the ship.

"There's no time to search," Toran said. "We need to *make* an opening."

"Helmets on," I announced.

Maris frowned. "What—"

"Kaiden, bring us around so the side door is facing the ship. Get as close as you can," I instructed.

He nodded and then did as I'd instructed.

We clicked our helmets into place and switched to the suit comms.

"Toran, with me," I said. "Secure the disruptor. We need to open the side hatch."

Fortunately, he didn't protest; seconds might make all the difference.

"Maris, keep that shield active," I continued while I strapped my sword to my waist around the outside of my EVA suit. "I'm going to see what I can do about making us an opening. Everyone hold on to something!"

As soon as Toran had secured the disruptor, I released the emergency seal on the side hatch. The door flew open, and I held on for dear life as the compartment vented. The purple shield around me swelled as I moved away, flickering for a moment during the decompression and then stabilizing again.

"The shield keeps wanting to expand," Maris said with a frown. "Something feels different."

"Might be the anomaly," Kaiden said over the comm. "I remember something about that from another timeline."

"Hold it as steady as you can." I grabbed a length of emergency cord from the supply locker next to the door and hurriedly tied it around my waist. The action was so familiar to me, but I couldn't think of why. I just knew I needed to get outside of the shuttle and make us an opening.

Ninety seconds. We'd barely have any time inside.

Without hesitation, I gripped my sword in my left hand and pushed off from the doorframe, launching myself toward the side of the ship five meters away. As I approached the alien hull, I angled my sword to pierce it.

The blade embedded. I could sense resistance for the first two-thirds of the length of the blade, then an open cavity beyond. With all my strength, I wedged my feet into the uneven covering on the ship to get enough leverage to pull down. I ripped a meter-long gash. It wasn't nearly enough. I'd maybe be able to create a person-sized opening in time, but there was no way we'd be able to get the shuttle inside, and the alien vessel was far too large for us to have a chance to make it anywhere into its depths on foot. But, I'd take getting inside at all over complete failure. Even so, I'd need help.

"Kaiden, fireball now!" I yelled into my comm.

"Maris, get the disrupter," Toran instructed. I could just make out the telltale signs of him running back to the bridge to take the flight controls.

A moment later, Kaiden came onto the comm, "Elle, get clear!"

I shoved off the hull of the alien vessel and swung back toward our shuttle using the tautness of the cord. When I was mid-arc, a bright flash of blue overpowered the white light cast by the anomaly, and in the corner of my vision the largest plume of flames I'd ever seen Kaiden cast erupted from the end of his staff. As I reached the side of our shuttle, the flames were dying back, leaving a charred tunnel into the alien ship. If the anomaly was enhancing our magic, at least we could use that to our advantage.

Kaiden's staff illuminated with a light orb on its tip. "I've got the interface device. Come on!" Gripping his staff in one hand and the equipment pack in the other, he launched himself from the hatch toward the new opening into the alien ship.

"You're all crazy!" With the half-meter-long disruptor box in her hands, Maris followed him in the mad flight across the void.

I needed to get to their position, but my own entry angle was way off. I untied the cord from around my waist and hoped for the best. Steadying myself with a handhold, I squatted against the hull. I leaped toward the opening.

Mid-flight, I realized I was going to overshoot my mark by at least two meters. "I need something to grab!" I shouted. The section of hull was full of the spongy substance that seemed to writhe in interlocking layers, reminding me of tentacles that echoed deep in my memory. I feared if I embedded in it, I might not be able to claw my way out.

Just in time, Kaiden's staff shot out into my flight path. I managed to grab it in my right hand and hang on. He pulled me inside.

"Hurry!" He began scrambling inward as soon as I was safe.

The interior was much like the outside—black structural

fibers that looked more grown than manufactured. The open cavity that I thought I'd detected inside when I jabbed my sword through the hull was actually just a pocket of the moss-type material forming a connective mesh between the structural beams. As far as I could tell, the vessel wouldn't be able to hold an atmosphere, unless there were other containment systems not readily visible. There also didn't appear to be conventional corridors or interior components. Frankly, I wasn't sure how the ship could even operate.

"Let's get in there," Maris said. An orange wave overlaid on the purple, and the subtle pulsing of the ship's walls around me slowed as my own movements and perception accelerated.

The haste spell would get us extra seconds, but not enough to make up for the other delays. We needed to move. Fast.

Kaiden took the lead, shooting occasional bursts of blue flame to clear the path ahead, the apparent influence of the anomaly enhancing the flames.

The gravity inside the ship left us midway between weightlessness and normal. Gentle pushes sent us rocketing forward, and we soon found we could run along the walls and floor through the cylindrical opening left by Kaiden's flames. He angled us backward in the direction of the anomaly while tunneling deeper into the ship.

We'd gone nearly one hundred meters when we entered a chamber that appeared to be a natural structure within the ship rather than simply the tunnel Kaiden had bored. It wasn't large—approximately four meters on each side—but it felt spacious after the tight confines of the flame-forged path. At the center of the space, a bulbous mound protruded approximately two meters from the floor, layered with a tighter weave of fibers than the surroundings. I was inexplicably drawn to it, sensing a power within.

"Do you think this place has any significance?" I asked.

Before anyone could answer, something suddenly grabbed my ankle, stopping me short. I looked down to see black tendrils snaking out from the singed walls to reach for us. Even under the effect of the haste spell, the tendrils were still moving quickly.

"What the...?" I slashed at them with my sword.

"Gah! The ship wants to eat us!" Maris exclaimed, re-upping the protective shell. However, the tendrils pierced right through the barrier, undeterred.

I swiped at the ones reaching out for her legs, and I was able to slice them off at their base along the wall.

"We need to keep moving," Kaiden urged.

Another one gripped me. "Yeah, and these aren't making it easy!"

I cut my sword across the new batch, but before I had completed the swing, another set was already forming. "Try scorching them, Kaiden," I said.

"These walls were already burned. I won't hold them."

"We need to try something!" I insisted.

Kaiden set down his staff and pressed his hands together. When he pulled them apart, the surface of his gloved palms was glowing like molten lava.

My jaw dropped. "That's... new."

He smoothed his hands down the walls around us, leaving a smooth, glass-like finish from which no new tendrils emerged. "You're not the only one learning new skills."

And for that, I was very thankful.

Kaiden quickly dealt with the origin points for the tendrils we had been unable to tame inside the chamber. Finally, the path ahead was clear.

I checked the control display on the wrist readout of my

EVA suit: the ship had appeared almost three minutes prior. We were already over our budgeted entry time. "This location will have to be good enough," I said.

"You're right." Kaiden unslung the interface device from around his shoulder. "Confession: I have no idea how this thing works."

"The interface? Turn it on and start the sync," Toran said over the comm.

I looked over Kaiden's shoulder at it. The controls appeared to be straightforward enough, so I left him to it. "Come on, Maris, let's set this disruptor." I gestured to a place at the base of the tunnel where there was a soft, fibrous bed surrounded by a cluster of the more solid support beams. We wedged the crate into the nook and flipped open the lid.

"Are you in place?" Brian asked over the comm.

I startled, having forgotten that anyone else was listening in on the channel. "Yes, got it."

"You see the red switch in the upper right? Flip that," he instructed.

I hesitated, glancing over my shoulder at Kaiden. "How's it coming with the interface?"

"The system seems to have linked with something, but I don't know what," he reported. "I'm recording, or downloading... I dunno, but it's doing something."

I kept an eye on the strange mound in the center of the chamber. The shadows were jumpy under the lights cast from my EVA suit, but it also seemed like the fibers were unfurling.

"Elle, is the disruptor activated?' Colren asked. "We don't have a link."

I didn't reply at first. Not activating that device was the only thing keeping them from turning it on before we escaped. We'd have to flip the switch before we left, but I had no intention of doing it a nanosecond before we were ready to race back to the shuttle.

My eyes kept darting to the mound. There was no mistaking the movements now. The fibers were pulling back to reveal a pod with interlocking segments forming a seal down its length. The pieces were starting to separate.

"Almost ready," I said over the comm while giving Kaiden a look that told him to wrap it up fast. I nodded toward the thing in the center of the chamber, and he nodded.

After an awkward five-second pause, Kaiden nodded that whatever the interface device had been doing seemed to be complete. He secured it in its case.

"Okay." My hand over the red switch. I flipped it. "It's on."

We propelled ourselves down the corridor as fast as our arms and legs could carry us. Without the cumbersome disruptor or needing to open the path with flames, we made exceptional time on the way back. However, two dozen meters from the exit, the corridor started to close in, brushing against the edges of the protective shields Maris had placed around us. Worse, I sensed a presence stalking us from behind.

"Need those flames!" I told Kaiden while looking behind me. Something red flashed through the darkness of the corridor, and as it passed, the walls vibrated.

He cast a column of flame forward without hesitation. The opening cleared for a moment, but then began rebuilding itself in double-time.

Maris' eyes widened with horror as our escape path closed. "What's it doing?"

"There's something here," I murmured, tightening my grip on my sword.

"Maybe an emergency damage control system finally activated," Kaiden said, casting more flames to keep our path open, but our pace had slowed to a crawl.

"The ship is waking up." Whatever that thing in the chamber was, it might not be the only one. We needed to get out.

"And it must almost be clear from the anomaly," Kaiden added. "We're almost out of time."

The thick silence on the comm didn't set me at ease. I knew Colren was aware of what was at stake with this mission.

Kaiden cast more flames, but each spell did less damage than the last; either the influence of the anomaly was waning, or the ship was adapting. "I can't give it any more," he admitted. His eyes met mine, pleading. None of us wanted to die here.

"Let me try." I repositioned in front of him. I'd never tried to cast magic without my palm device, but I'd had to leave that behind when I put on the gloves of the EVA suit. But, if the magic was truly a part of me, that tool was only a way to focus, not the source of my power.

I held out my hand in front of me, concentrating on the almost-filled path ahead. White light shot from my hand, piercing through the dark tunnel. The black tendrils recoiled, and those that didn't move from its path quickly enough disintegrated.

"Whoa," Maris gasped behind me. "You...?"

"I'll explain later." I dashed ahead, desperate to get back to the shuttle.

"The ship is almost complete," Colren warned.

"We're almost out!" I shouted. The end of the tunnel was in sight.

We bolted through the remaining section of the tunnel. I stopped myself short just before reaching the open gap of space between the ship and the waiting shuttle. It was too far to jump.

"Toran, can you get it any closer?" I asked over the comm.

"I'll try."

The shuttle neared the alien ship, the side door aligning with the crude entryway we'd made. All the same, it would be a four-meter-long leap. I took a few steps back and got a running start. At the last second, I kicked off the alien ship and flew toward the shuttle's hatch. The kick at the end set me on a slight spin, but I was able to track my flight lines and grab one of the handholds around the hatch to keep myself from bouncing off my mark.

I swung inside but stayed next to the hatch to help the others inside.

Maris was next to make the leap. She followed my lead to take a running start, but she miss-timed her final steps and didn't get a good kick off, instead drifting off the alien ship.

"I've got you!" I leaned out the hatch to grab her, but my reach came up short.

Maris flailed. "Get something!"

I popped back inside to look for an object to extend my reach. My scabbard might work.

As I looked down to detach it from the waist belt, two forms spiraled through the opening—Kaiden apparently having made the leap and grabbed Maris along his path. They hit the deck hard with their limbs a jumbled mess.

Maris shook her head down near Kaiden's right knee, climbing off him. "Thanks."

"Close the hatch," Toran ordered from the bridge over our helmet comms.

I quickly pressed the emergency seal, and the door snapped shut. The moment it was closed, a vibration surged in the floor as the shuttle accelerated. I checked the timer on my wrist band again. Our five minutes was almost up. A quick check out the side viewport confirmed that the alien ship was almost fully formed. If the weapons activated, the shuttle and the *Evangiel* would have no means of defense.

With my EVA suit still on, I ran to the bridge. "On our way, Commander."

I took my seat, and Toran moved aside for Kaiden to take over for the landing. With time short, it would almost certainly be a hard, combat-style landing rather than the methodical autopilot control.

"We did it!" Maris cheered from her seat.

"Yeah, we did." However, I couldn't bring myself to celebrate. Though we'd accomplished our objective to plant the disruptor and gather data from the ship, we were far from safe.

The shuttle was accelerating toward the *Evangiel,* but we didn't seem to be closing any distance. They were pulling back from the anomaly, even as we tried to reach them.

We weren't going to make it back in time.

"I'm sorry," Colren murmured.

With a flash and ripple across the surrounding starscape, the *Evangiel* disappeared.

25

"THEY LEFT US?!" Maris exclaimed.

My heart dropped. We were alone in the void within kilometers of where a spatial disruptor was about to detonate. Was this the end?

I shook myself. No, I wasn't going to give up.

"We have to brace!" I shouted. "Hold back the disruptor wave."

"Elle, this weapon—" Toran began.

"It breaks apart matter, I know. But we have magic. If the dragons can make sanctuaries outside of normal reality, maybe we can too."

Maris looked like she was about to object, but she nodded. "It's that or die."

"Fight to the end," Toran agreed.

"Come on." I rose from my seat and motioned everyone toward the center of the bridge.

Kaiden hurriedly set the shuttle's autopilot to full throttle along the escape vector and joined us.

"How do we do this?" Maris asked.

I had absolutely no idea. However, I was certain that if anyone could generate a shield to counteract the disruptor wave, it would be us; we were imbued with ancient powers from a past age, representing the disciplines destined to make us heroes. The answer lay somewhere within ourselves... we just had to find it.

"Maris, you need to create a shield around the shuttle," I instructed. "The rest of us need to feed energy into it. Don't think about it, *feel* it."

"We need a focal point," Toran suggested. "Something we can all concentrate on to help channel the energy."

I glanced around the bridge, not seeing anything that seemed fitting. Instead, I unsheathed my sword and held the glowing blade in front of us. "Grab the hilt and focus on the blade," I said.

Kaiden glanced over with a knowing smile as he wrapped his hands around mine on the hilt, followed by Toran and Maris. We were in a tough spot, but if we didn't make it, at least it would be over quickly and we'd be with each other.

I remained fixated on the sword's blade with my friends, as much as I wanted to watch the alien ship coming through the anomaly. Based on my memories, the ship must almost be clear. I wondered if the creature I glimpsed had somehow removed the disruptor, but maybe the *Evangiel* hadn't set the detonation before they—

A blinding flash forced me to squeeze my eyes shut. When I sensed the brightness diminish through my eyelid, I squinted back toward the viewport.

A black, rippling wave was folding the space around the anomaly. The alien ship disintegrated and twisted against the starscape behind it, its ruined fragments disappearing into the wave. As each fragment struck the wave, it illuminated in a pinpoint flash before being snuffed out. The ship was gone, and so was any sign of the anomaly, but the wave was still rushing outward, and it would reach us in moments.

I squeezed my sword hilt, reaching out with my extrasensory abilities to detect Maris' shield around our shuttle. The barrier didn't stand a chance against the destructive wave. I needed to make it stronger.

As I reached within myself, I sensed Kaiden and Toran directing their own magical energy toward the shield. Toran's pure, protective spirit hardened the shell, and Kaiden augmented it with an electrical charge to help deflect the approaching wave. However, even with those enhancements, I knew in my gut it wouldn't be enough. We needed a different kind of magic, something to manipulate the very underlying forces in our universe.

The disruptor wave ripped apart, but I had the ability to bind.

I tied my sense of self to the shell around the shuttle. I could feel the change in my surroundings as the disruptor wave approached—rending the bonds across spatial planes. My skin tingled with anticipation.

The leading edge of the wave struck the shell, rocking our shuttle to the side. The distance from the epicenter and our forward momentum diminished the blow, but my tether to the shell still made me feel like I was being ripped apart. I struggled to remain on my feet and not lose my concentration.

I focused on the outer shell and holding it together. The bonds threatened to rip apart, but every time they started to fray I pulled them back together. Everything important to me that I had left in the universe was inside that shuttle. I'd do anything to hold onto my friends and keep them safe, even if it meant burning myself up in the process.

The disruptor wave continued to rip into my extended self as the leading edge of the wave passed by our location and we were left in the center of the affected zone. But, the shell held— a tiny sanctuary surrounding by nothingness.

I was slipping. I couldn't hold it for any longer.

The disruptor wave began to dissipate, a gravity well formed at the detonation site. The shuttle's engines were ineffective within the shell, and our bubble was yanked toward the black maw that had opened at the epicenter. The shell had proven successful in keeping us safe, but we'd need the ship's engines if we wanted to avoid getting sucked into the black pit.

"Drop the shield!" I ordered while keeping my own magic active.

"We'll—"

"Just do it!" I cut Maris off.

The shell collapsed in its previous form, but I redoubled my efforts to maintain the structural integrity of the shuttle.

The backward pull of the shuttle ceased as the engines were freed from the shell. Slowly, we began accelerating away from the detonation site.

Even as we pulled away, the ruins of the alien ship and everything else in the vicinity were condensing onto a singular point. In a sudden burst, a secondary wave fanned out from the epicenter, this one re-condensing rather than breaking apart. I quickly shifted my spell to counteract its effects and keep us from smooshing.

I wasn't fast enough. The shuttle shook as its frame twisted and cracked. The engines cut out, leaving us traveling forward on inertia at a slow spin.

The remaining disruptor wave collapsed. It was over.

I released the telekinetic shield and dropped to my knees,

panting.

"Elle!" Kaiden couched down next to me and placed a hand on my back.

"I'm okay," I gasped, wishing I could rip off my helmet and get some fresh air. "Just gimme a sec."

"What was that you did?" Toran asked.

"Elle, maybe it's time you said something," Kaiden whispered to me.

"Okay, confession: I have some sort of telekinesis-style magic," I revealed, slipping my sword into its scabbard.

"That's…" Maris faded out.

I nodded. "I don't understand how it works. I just… knew what I had to do."

Toran and Maris stared at me with raised eyebrows.

"Well, thank you," Toran said at last.

I staggered to my feet with Kaiden's help. By the time I was upright, I realized that the artificial gravity was starting to fail, and I was lifting slightly off the deck. "Unfortunately, now we're trapped here with no escape."

"There must be an emergency signal," Toran stated.

"Right, yes." Kaiden glided back to the front control panel. Only a handful of items were illuminated on the backup battery power. He activated the emergency transponder.

"The commander wouldn't have jumped too far away," I said, hoping that wasn't just wishful thinking.

Maris wrapped her arms around herself. "How long do we have?"

"We have backup oxygen and power for the suits," Toran replied. "We'll be able to make it at least sixteen hours, maybe more."

I prayed to the stars we wouldn't have to wait that long.

Despite my best wishes, the hours dragged on. I spent the

first two hours telling myself that the *Evangiel* would be there any second. By the end of the fourth hour, I was beginning to doubt we'd ever be rescued.

"They should have picked up our distress signal by now, right?" Maris asked.

"Yeah, I'd think so," I agreed.

"Maybe they're out of range, or…" Kaiden faded out.

"Or *what*?" I pressed.

"Or they have no intention of returning to this place," Toran completed for him.

I swallowed. "Why wouldn't they, though? I mean, we activated the beacon—that means our ship wasn't destroyed and we made it through."

"That's a straightforward explanation, yes," Toran agreed.

I frowned. "What else would it be?"

"That the enemy found a way to mimic our signals and is trying to lure them back into another trap."

My heart sank. "Oh." I paused. "Can't we have a custom message saying it's us?"

"I don't know enough about these emergency systems to do that," Kaiden said. "They'll need to authenticate once they send a scout vessel back to check the scene."

"So, we have to keep waiting," I concluded.

And so we did. We remained silent for the next half hour, both to conserve oxygen and because we had nothing to say. In the next several hours, we'd either be rescued or suffocate. All things considered, it was one of the bleaker moments in my life.

I stayed closed to Kaiden, hating that our EVA suits prevented us from being able to seek comfort from closer contact. As I stared out the front viewport, I rested my helmet on Kaiden's shoulder. My eyes had glazed over after looking out into the nothingness for so long, but then a point of light caught my attention.

I sat upright. "Hey, what's that?"

The others roused, following my sightline.

Kaiden squinted. "Can't tell from here." He propelled himself across the bridge in the zero-*g* to the front control panel. "Stars, it's a Hegemony ship!" he cheered.

My ear comm crackled. "Shuttle 2, do you copy?" a male voice asked.

"Yes, we're here!" I replied. "All four members of the Dark Sentinel team accounted for."

"Thank the stars!" the man said with an audible smile. "The commander and rest of the crew will be thrilled to hear it. We're on our way to grab you, hang tight."

The rescue shuttle maneuvered to us and extended an umbilical from their airlock to allow us safe passage out our side hatch. I'd never been quite so happy to be back in artificial gravity and to be able to remove my helmet.

As it turned out, the *Evangiel* had jumped back to wait several hundred kilometers away while the rescue craft went searching for us and to look for any evidence of the alien ship or anomaly. The shuttle would have been deployed sooner, but Colren had called for backup in the event the disruptor hadn't destroyed the anomaly. Waiting near the *Evangiel* were two dozen of the Hegemony's warships poised for action.

"Okay, so they came prepared," I said as I looked over the fleet.

"Glad they weren't needed this time," Kaiden replied.

"But this isn't over yet."

Our rescue craft entered the *Evangiel*'s hangar and came to rest in a decontamination tent. True to form, Tami, dressed in her hazsuit, was the first to meet us as we exited.

"I'm so happy to see you're okay!" she greeted.

I smiled. "It'll take more than an interdimensional bomb to get rid of us."

She laughed. "I have no idea how you did it, and I'm sure you have quite a story to tell. The commander is waiting for you; I'll have to get the inside scoop later."

"And you'll have it," I assured her.

"But first," she pointed to booths at the end of a tunnel leading from the tent, "decontamination, sorry."

I looked down at my EVA suit that had been immersed in the innards of the alien ship. "No complaints here."

We endured the uncomfortable chemical scrub and emerged from our respective stalls to find clean, custom-sized shipsuits waiting for us. I always hated walking around the ship in just the base layer, but I'd grown rather attached to my outfit and would rather the garments get cleaned rather than have new ones made; even if the style was identical, it just wasn't the same.

Once we were dressed in the white suits, Kaiden pulled me aside and wrapped me in a tight hug. I gladly hugged him back.

"We did it," he murmured into my hair.

"Yeah, but what in the stars are we up against?" I asked, pulling away. "Did you see that thing in the chamber?"

He paled. "Yeah, I did. Just a flash of red eyes and more limbs than I could count. It didn't look friendly."

I took his hands. "Whatever it was, we'll face it together."

Kaiden leaned in and gave me a kiss. The unpleasant associations that had tainted our intimacy since the reset had now faded into the background. Once again, it was just the two of us sharing a special moment. For that instant, my worries and fears melted away.

Toran cleared his throat. "Anytime…"

We parted. "Right," I said, flashing a happy smile at Kaiden.

Our party left the hangar and took the lift to Central Command. Applause greeted us as soon as the bridge door opened, led by Commander Colren.

He beamed at us from the center of the room. "I don't know how you survived the disruptor, but thank you for seeing the mission through. Welcome back."

Anger rose in me, hearing his casual words. He'd left us to die. An apology didn't cut it.

"What happened to resetting if something went wrong?" Maris snapped. I was happy for her to say it so I didn't have to.

Colren shifted on his feet. "We first had to see if the anomaly was sealed."

He needn't say more. That was the mission: to stop the alien invasion. Losing us would be a setback, but it would have been a worthwhile sacrifice to ensure that the alien fleet didn't make it through the anomaly. If he had reset in an attempt to save us, our efforts may not have been successful on another go around. We needed to take any victory we could, in part or full. Casualties along the way were to be expected.

Kaiden and Toran nodded with understanding, but Maris only scoffed and tossed her head in response.

"Elle has been holding out on us," Toran said. "She has telekinetic magic, apparently."

Colren's eyes widened and he tilted his head questioningly.

I blushed. "I'm still trying to figure out what I can do with it."

"Whatever the methods, you've demonstrated once again that you were exactly the team we've needed," the commander replied. "I can't express enough how difficult it was to give the departure order without you. But, the data you were able to transmit was too valuable. We had to make sure it got to the capital."

Kaiden came to attention. "What did the interface equipment pick up?"

"A series of codes and signals," Colren explained. "When we compared it to the other data we've gathered, we were able to confirm that alien tech uses the crystalline network's reset ability to restructure physical reality within a crystal's zone. There must have been a crystal inside that anomaly. But, we captured the origin point of the signal, and we believe it will lead us to the location of the alien's homeworld."

"That's... wow," I murmured.

"The anomaly—or hidden crystal... was it destroyed?" Kaiden asked.

"The rescue crew picked up none of the usual readings we had detected before. It's gone, or at least dormant," the commander said.

The others grinned.

"That's excellent news," Toran said.

"Elle, come on, this was a big win today," Kaiden said when he saw I wasn't smiling.

"Was it?" I shook my head. "Yeah, we prevented *this* invasion, but they'll try again. I'm certain of it."

"It bought us time," Toran said.

"But how much? We don't know how that spatial anomaly was formed in the first place," I continued. "For all we know, they could have already opened another one somewhere else, only now we have no idea where."

Colren nodded. "That's why we need to end this while we can still get the upper hand. We've confirmed that we have an effective weapon against them."

"That's true." I finally allowed myself to revel in our

temporary victory. "And now we know where to hit them so they'll never come back."

THE STORY CONTINUES IN *MASTERS OF FATE...*

The final fight will change their perception forever...

Everything Elle and her friends thought they knew about the alien menace—and the nature of their universe—is wrong. As they try to access the aliens' homeworld, the Dark Sentinels discover the threat is far greater than they ever imagined.

With evidence pointing to the aliens residing on a hyperdimensional plane above spacetime, it seems impossible to prevent the impending invasion. However, the artifacts wielded by the Dark Sentinels might hold the key to victory if they can understand and master their true abilities.

ALSO BY A.K. DUBOFF

Dark Stars Trilogy
Book 1: Crystalline Space
Book 2: A Light in the Dark
Book 3: Masters of Fate

Cadicle Space Opera Series
Book 1: Rumors of War (Vol. 1-3)
Book 2: Web of Truth (Vol. 4)
Book 3: Crossroads of Fate (Vol. 5)
Book 4: Path of Justice (Vol. 6)
Book 5: Scions of Change (Vol. 7)

Mindspace Series
Book 1: Infiltration
Book 2: Conspiracy
Book 3: Offensive
Book 4: Endgame

Troubled Space
Vol. 1: Brewing Trouble
Vol. 2: Stealing Trouble
Vol. 3: Making Trouble

AUTHOR'S NOTES

Thank you for reading *A Light in the Dark*!

This book was written during a major transition point in my life. After years of talking about it, my husband (Nick) and I finally decided to move abroad. We had been living in Portland, Oregon, together since we met in August 2012, and during that time we'd always shared a love of travel. In late-summer of 2017, we took a six-week trip around Europe, and we ended up falling in love with the culture. We realized that there was nothing tying us to Portland (no kids or pets or family in the area), so we decided to take the plunge. Incidentally, two of our good friends were moving to the Netherlands at the same time we were setting out, so it really felt like it was meant to be.

We arrived at the end of June 2018, and we couldn't be happier so far. However, packing up one's life to move across an ocean is disruptive, as you can imagine, so this book ended up taking far longer to write than I'd planned. In the end, though, I feel that this new environment will offer an amazing infusion of creative energy and allow me to grow.

I want to give a special shout-out to Jim Dean for his in-depth review and editing of this book. He was incredibly generous with his time and sharing his technical knowledge to help "true up" science components within the context of a fiction story. I had some rough concepts in my head, but he was able to help me articulate those in a way that elevated the story and gave it proper scientific grounding amid the fantastic elements. I know it was a huge undertaking to go through so many iterations, but I am so very thankful he stuck with it and helped refine the story universe into something I hope satisfies sci-fi and fantasy fans alike.

My heartfelt thanks also to Kurt, Eric, Pam, Randy, Liz, Diane, John, Troy, Charlie, Nick, and Leo for their tireless efforts with review and proofing to add the final polish to the book. I am honored to have such a fantastic team to work with!

I hope you are looking forward to *Masters of Fate*. The epic showdown with the Darkness is coming soon!

ABOUT THE AUTHOR

A.K. (Amy) DuBoff has always loved science fiction in all its forms—books, movies, shows and games. If it involves outer space, even better!

Now a full-time author, Amy can frequently be found traveling the world. When she's not writing, she enjoys wine tasting, binge-watching TV series, and playing epic strategy board games.

To learn more or connect, visit www.akduboff.com.

CPSIA information can be obtained
at www.ICGtesting.com
Printed in the USA
BVHW031957060120
568730BV00001B/153/P